Table of Contents

Chapter One: Shallow Pools...3
Chapter Two: A Memorable Initiation..................................24
Chapter Three: Looking-Glass..47
Chapter Four: A Tale of Two...66
Chapter Five: Budding Time..92
Chapter Six: Binary Anomaly...105
Chapter Seven: Ever-changing Reality...............................128
Chapter Eight: Cracks in the Asphalt.................................148
Chapter Nine: A Dozen Moons...167
Chapter Ten: Enneadic Parchments....................................188
Chapter Eleven: Voices and Veils.......................................210
Chapter Twelve: Stars in Pentad..232
Chapter Thirteen: Lone Barrier..253
Chapter Fourteen: Ravaged Remedies................................278
Chapter Fifteen: Blind Amygdalas.....................................295
Chapter Sixteen: The Calm..316
Chapter Seventeen: The Storm...336
Chapter Eighteen: Ripples on the Lock..............................356

Chapter One: Shallow Pools

Birds chirped as the late summer sun rolled over the lush green hills, spreading its warmth between the evergreen branches as they elegantly stirred with each morning breeze. Occasional blue jays and robins whisked about, chiming in with their own soft melodies as they landed on each bare branch they found, often coming close enough to the sidewalks and streets that they could watch people pass and hear them chatter about with others. Along with the birds were the worms, wriggling about as they surfaced to bathe in the morning dew, unaware of the threats above, or at least without concern of what those colorful threats intended as they lived in the moment. Asher was jealous of the worms for this and continued to step around them as he made his way towards Bristlewood High School. It wasn't so much that he cared for them as it was he didn't want to have to clean them off his brand new, all white sneakers. The school year had just started and he intended to make them last this time. Keeping his earbuds in and his hood up, he acknowledged each passing familiar face with a nod and a smile. Until his hood was suddenly jerked back, setting his mid-lengthed dark brown hair free and flowing over his azure eyes, which had just been pierced by fresh sunlight before being shaded once more by the hair. He winced and removed his earbuds before turning to face whoever it was that blinded him.

"Think you were going to just ignore me like that?" Kyden exclaimed, grinning as he did and making his way around Asher to walk alongside him.

"Oh, you know, just figured I should start fresh this year, you know?" Kyden placed a hand against his chest and gasped, stopping in place for a moment as he did so before rushing back up to Asher's side.

"Including me?"

"Especially you." Asher grinned back at Kyden as he put his right bud back in, opposite of the side Kyden was walking along. Kyden then punched Asher across his shoulder and wrapped an arm around his neck, proceeding to dig his knuckles into Asher's skull as he did so and running them back and forth quickly, laughing as Asher struggled to break free.

"Um, excuse me." Kyden stopped moving his knuckles and glanced over his shoulder, spotting a petite long haired brunette standing only a foot or so behind them. Asher then wrestled himself free and looked as well. The brunette stood with several books pressed between her chest and her arms as she nervously returned the stare, smiling innocently as she awaited a response or action suggesting he knew what she wanted. Asher didn't recognize the girl, but he could tell that she recognized him.

"S-sorry, my friend can be a little reckless sometimes, are you okay?" She nodded.

"I'm fine, I just need by." The brunette tipped her head to one side, pointing at the school behind Asher with her eyes and meeting his eyes once more.

"Right, yeah, sorry." Asher moved to the edge of the concrete slab and Kyden moved to the opposite side, clearing a path for the brunette to get through.

"Thank you." She shot Asher one more quick smile and lowered her head, keeping her eyes focused on the building. Asher watched as she walked ahead of them before looking back at Kyden, who had a smug look on his face.

"What?"

"Got a thing for the new girl?" Kyden motioned towards her with his head and smirked.

"What? No. I don't even know who she is."

"Her name's Mabel." Asher raised an eyebrow at Kyden as they proceeded to walk towards the entrance doors. Kyden noticed this and shrugged, stuffing both hands in the pockets of his jacket and looking around at all the other students less than eagerly traveling towards the front of the high school. "She's been popping up on your social media lately, figured I'd see what that was all about and got her name out of it."

"Well, what was it all about then?" Kyden chuckled and removed a hand from his jacket, using it to point at something a few yards ahead of them. Asher looked forward once more and noticed the brunette, Mabel, glancing back at him before pushing one of the two swinging glass doors open with her hip and vanishing behind the tinted frames.

"You got yourself a stalker, man." He then thumped the palm of his hand against Asher's chest twice as they made their way through the doors and then took off down the left side of the two-way hall. "See you at lunch!" Kyden nudged his way through the crowd of confused students, all of whom were looking at schedules and discussing them with others, and was out of Asher's line of sight in only a few moments. Asher looked down the right side of the hall and sighed as he removed his own schedule from the pocket of his jeans before heading to homeroom.

"Come on in students, come on in!" As Asher rounded the

corner he could see his new homeroom teacher beckoning students as they were required to do at the beginning of each day. "Let's not be late on our first day, huh? Mr. Coyle, right this way!" The teacher smiled as he caught a glimpse of Asher in the crowd and motioned with an arm for him to enter the room. As Asher returned the smile and made his way inside, he took a seat and looked back towards the door just in time to see Mabel talking with the same teacher outside the room. He tried listening in best he could as he slung his backpack off his shoulder and onto the desk before him. "Well, I'm glad to see a new face here at Bristlewood! You can call me Mr. Benner, Miss Rose. Please, take a seat anywhere you like while I get the rest of the class gathered up." As Mabel entered the room she glanced at Asher, who quickly looked down at the zipper on his bag and opened it to remove the contents, pretending to have not noticed her.

"Do you mind if I sit here?" Asher looked up again to see Mabel standing to the right of the conjoined desks, resting one hand on the empty seat beside him. He then nodded in approval and collected his things, trying to seem preoccupied with organizing his belongings on his desk according to when his schedule said he'd need them. "Thanks." Mabel smiled and sat down next to him. She then noticed what he was doing and proceeded to do the same, as quietly as he was. Noticing the awkward silence that grew as other students entered after them, Asher cleared his throat and sat his schedule on top of his freshly stacked books.

"My name is Asher." Looking across the desks, he watched as she finished up organizing her own belongings. "We didn't really get to introduce ourselves before." Mabel pulled her bottom lip slightly between her teeth and bit it gently as she rested her schedule on top the stack, just as Asher had done. She then turned in her chair to face him and smiled cheerfully, freeing her lip as she did so.

"Mabel, and... I knew your name already." Asher simply smiled back at her and watched as the white lights and bright surroundings in the classroom danced in her honey-filled eyes with each motion she made. Noticing his stare, Mabel inhaled sharply and looked about her desk for a moment. "I-I was trying to see who I might be going to school with and stumbled onto your account, not that I was trying to be creepy or anything, I just-"

"It's fine," Asher assured her. "I already knew your name too." Mabel seemed confused by this acknowledgment and lightly scrunched her eyebrows together, tipping her head as she did so.

"Kyden told me on our way here and I heard Mr. Benner say your last name, too."

"Who's Kyden?" Asher was taken aback now. How could she know him but not his best friend if she found him online?

"He's the other guy in like, half of my photos. That is where you found me, right?"

"Oh! Of course!" Mabel still seemed as if she had been caught doing something she shouldn't and placed both hands over her mouth. "I guess I just didn't make it to his account yet." Asher chuckled and grabbed his schedule.

"Well, if you want to join me during lunch you'll get to meet him in person, again."

"Oh, sorry. A group of girls already invited me to sit with them today, but maybe tomorrow?" Asher agreed and examined the listed classes as Mr. Benner made his way in after the final student was seated and the bell signaling the beginning of class rang out.

"Good morning, seniors! 179 more days like this and then the real fun begins!"

"That counting weekends and holidays?" The class turned to face the sole student in the back of the room who spoke out. He was wearing a black jacket, dark blue jeans, black boots and had his charcoal hair slicked back with sunglasses on. These features stood out as the jacket was far heavier than it needed to be at this time of the year and his legs had been propped up on his desk. Sunglasses were also against school dress code when worn inside. Mr. Benner finished writing his name on the dry-erase board before turning to face where the voice had come from.

"Very funny, Mr. Feeder. Judging by *your* annual attendance, I'd say it can't be far off." The class giggled in unison as the student in the back grinned toothily whilst chewing a piece of gum. "Now, if you don't mind, feet on the floor, gum in the can, and glasses on your head or a pocket. Thank you."

"Do you know that guy?" Mabel whispered, glancing towards Asher and then back at Feeder. Asher seemed confused as to why she would ask this until he finally realized that he had never seen the kid, yet nobody else seemed to question who he was.

"No," Asher replied, contorting his face in a confused manner. "I've never seen him before, why?" Mabel removed a second sheet of paper out from under her schedule. It was about the same size as half a sheet and printed on it was the class roster. Asher thought it was odd enough that she had been carrying around a roster when she hadn't known anyone at the school well enough to search for names that it at first slipped his mind as to why she would be showing him. Glancing over the names, he recognized all of them, which was strange. Going over the room with his eyes, he found that the roster was off by one student. 23 names, 24 students. Deciding it was no big deal, he shrugged it off and let it sit in the back of his mind for a few moments before seemingly forgetting about it entirely as the class went on. Perhaps the kid was an exchange student from another local school or the roster she had with her wasn't the final copy. Mabel, on the other hand, couldn't seem to let it go no matter how hard she tried. The kid spoke with his peers as if they were lifelong friends, but if he weren't new and she hadn't seen him on the school's roster, why wouldn't a fairly popular individual such as Asher know him? Mabel continued to examine Feeder for a few moments but turned back towards the board with haste when he took off his glasses and leaned forward on his desk, glaring at her with vibrant emeralds and winking smoothly with the same crooked smile he carried through the entire duration of his class-wide introduction. His eyes were captivating, yet seemed so hollow as she felt them on the back of her neck.

"Alright, class. Let's work through the attendance and get to know each other a little better in our spare time, shall we?"

As each student was given the chance to stand and announce something about themselves, Asher drifted off into his own thoughts and proceeded to doodle on a sheet of loose-leaf paper, as he normally would most every day of school prior. He also took that time to examine his surroundings. The classroom was relatively small, but he blamed this partially on the countertops that seemed to surround the entire left and back sides of the room and partially on the clutter of backpacks, anatomy statues, and an old two-sided chalkboard that lay unused for several years all resting near the windows on the right side of the room. The center of the room was made up of three rows of the conjoined desks, with each row going back four desks. The center row also had one lone desk sitting at the back of the room, where Feeder sat. This left one seat empty a row ahead of Feeder and on the right. All of the desks were made up of sturdy wood with rounded corners and a black trim that fitted the entire edge of each desk. Looking back at other aspects of the room, Asher noticed that the walls, floor, and ceiling were all white, which was odd, as the standard coloring for each room would have left the walls with a lower half that was painted grey to about head-height of the students. All of the counters were made of wood colored similarly to the desks and the countertops were a lightly greying marble. On the left wall, where the counter ended closest to the entrance at the front of the room, there was a large supply cabinet with a padlock on the door. Asher thought nothing of this as it was common for teachers to keep things locked up to ensure nosey students didn't go rummaging about. Every surface that wasn't taken up seemed to have a poster related to some inspirational quote hanging on it and most were related to kittens and puppies, which made Asher curl his lip as he was amused by it.

Once the entire class finished going through with introducing themselves the bell signaling the beginning of the first-period class rang out. Asher proceeded with the rest of his day as he usually would, only paying enough attention during the lectures to get by and spending the rest of his time staring out the window, drawing, or speaking in whispers with other classmates. As his fourth-period class ended, he made his way out into the hall with the rest of the students, where a hand suddenly plopped over his shoulder.

"How's it been, Coyle?" Standing behind Asher was another, familiar student. With short blonde hair and greyish blue eyes, the boy lifted his nose a little higher in the air than he needed and smiled weakly.

"Dennis?" The boy's smile grew larger as he removed his hand and walked towards the cafeteria with Asher. "I thought you moved over the summer?" The smile started to fade once more as Dennis seemed to be avoiding eye contact.

"We were supposed to, but some... family matters came up." Dennis shifted his eyes to a student who had been leaning against a pillar in the cafeteria, closest to where others were entering the kitchen and receiving their meals. The student he motioned towards was the stranger from Asher's homeroom, Feeder. Given the feeling that he wasn't supposed to notice who Dennis was talking about, Asher fought off the urge to ask what was going on and instead went off to get his meal and be seated near the middle of the cafeteria, along with Dennis and Kyden.

"Another day, another tray of slop." Kyden stuck a plastic fork in a mass of reds and browns, or chili as the school called it. Asher examined the heap from where he sat across the table and glanced back up at Feeder. He couldn't help but notice how different Dennis looked from him, now knowing that they were somehow related and imaginably close, from how Dennis spoke of it. "You think even the cooks could tell us what's in this?"

"I doubt it," Dennis replied as he piled some of the chili onto a piece of buttered bread. "Odds are the FDA couldn't tell you." He then folded the bread in half and took a large bite, being sure to catch any loose bits that tried to escape his mouth. As the group dug into the warm meats and beans another small posse made their way over to the table and sat alongside them. It was a group of three more guys and one girl. All of the guys were dressed similarly, having grey football jackets with white long leathery sleeves on them and either black or blue jeans on. None of them wore the same color shoes, but they all appeared to be the same brand, carrying the same logos. Even the girl wore the same brand of shoes and jeans, but she had been wearing a short sleeve shirt with a large 'B' on the chest and the number 14 on the back in place of the numbers on the jackets the boys had. However, as they took their seats, the boy closest to her removed his jacket and slung it over her shoulders, being sure to sit as close to her as he could in the process. It was odd for them to be wearing their sports jackets so early into the year, as it wasn't really cold and still far too warm for such heavy articles.

"Dennis, Kyden, Asher." The blonde boy sitting closest to the girl spoke their names as he looked over each one individually.

"Jock One, Two, Three,... Girl." Asher and the other two chuckled as the blonde boy watched Kyden proceed to scarf down a few fries after naming them off like so.

"Funny," he said, "who's the new girl?" The blonde boy used his thumb to point over his shoulder at Mabel, who was sitting two tables away with a group of four other girls, all of whom were laughing and seemingly enjoying the conversation at hand.

"Her name's Mabel. She's crushing on Asher here." The blonde raised his eyebrows and nodded his head three times, maintaining a slightly surprised look.

"That so?" He then scanned over her and looked back at Asher. "You got a thing for her?" Asher glared at him briefly and proceeded to look back at his tray, taking in a few fries himself. "Okay, don't say so then. Only makes it true." The boy grinned menacingly as if satisfied that he was getting under Asher's skin. "You know what that means, right?"

"I doubt he does." The jock sitting next to the blonde said as he ran his fingers through the short, black, curly hair on his head. "Dude hasn't dated anyone in like, five years." Asher shifted his gaze from the blonde to the curly-headed jock and then back at his tray.

"Ah, come on, man. You know you got to."

"What is it?" Dennis scanned over the second party as they turned heads towards each other and then back at Dennis, all sharing the same look of amusement.

"We have to give her a proper initiation." Dennis clearly looked more confused than he had previously been. Then, his face turned white.

"Wait, you mean, like you guys did Kyden?"

"Hey, I remember that." Kyden put down his fork slowly and looked over at the blonde, who was now giggling about the whole thing.

"That's kind of the point." The blonde grabbed a fry from Kyden's tray and threw it into the air, catching it in his mouth. "Welcome to the party, by the way."

"Why would we need to do that to her? She wouldn't even understand what was going on." The blonde shrugged once Asher was finished and wrapped his arm around the girl sitting next to him, who was far too invested in her phone to care for what was going on around her. "We didn't even initiate her." Asher pointed at the girl the blonde was now cradling. Noticing Asher's point, the blonde looked at her and then shrugged.

"I guess she can be initiated by helping us initiate Mabel for you, huh?" The girl then glanced up, noticing that the group was talking about her.

"Wh-what's going on?" The blonde and the other two jocks chuckled and they all stood up from the table. The blonde reached over and grabbed a few more fries before urging the girl away from Asher's group.

"I'll explain on the ride back to your place. Come on." The blonde turned his head on a pivot to spot Asher over his shoulder. "Tonight, huh?" Grinning, he slung his arm over the girl's shoulder once again and started towards the doors, followed by the other two jocks.

"Wait, why does he get to leave early?" Kyden had already seemed annoyed, since the jock first took food from his tray, but seeing him walk out the building's side doors without being stopped by a teacher really seemed to tip him off.

"He's already got all the credits he needs. He might be a lunkhead in most cases, but he knows where to set his priorities when he wants something." Dennis only watched the doors for a moment, before scanning over the cafeteria and getting up, looking slightly concerned. "Good catching up guys. I'll see you two tomorrow." He then walked off, dumping the empty containers and partially eaten chili from his tray into a trash can before speed walking out into the halls.

"What was that all about?" Kyden followed Dennis with his eyes up until Dennis walked around a corner. Asher shrugged and got up to throw away what was left on his tray as well. "So, are you going to do it?"

"Do what?" Kyden dumped his tray as well and placed it on top of the trash can, where a small platform was sitting and covered in many other dirty trays from other students who had finished their lunches.

"You know what. The initiation." Asher walked between the table they had sat at and the table that separated their's from Mabel's, studying her for a moment as they passed. She was oblivious to him at the time, which gave him a few seconds to admire her from afar without being embarrassed. He then sighed and proceeded towards the doors as well, just as the bell had rung, signaling the sixth period of the day. "Well?"

"Do I really have a choice? It's either that or I get tormented for the rest of the year, along with her."

"True. You know the first thing they'll do is tell her you have a thing for her, right?"

"I never said I have a thing for her," Asher snapped as he spoke matter-of-factly, "she has a thing for me. I just don't want them to say or do anything stupid to her."

"Yeah, that's what it means when someone looks at someone else like that."

"Like what?" Asher spoke sooner than he had thought, not even realizing that he was still watching her over his shoulder. He quickly faced the hall and made a turn for the corridor his locker was located in. He then stopped to take a moment and think about what he had to do. Nobody was happy after an initiation. They typically felt betrayed or embarrassed, but it was still better than what the jocks would do if you failed to go through with it. "Just, meet me out at the base of Prominent Peak around four o'clock tonight. I'll have her meet me there around four thirty. Let the others know that I'm on board and I'll try getting her to do it too."

"Okay, do you think she knows of the lore though? It might not work if she has no clue what's going on." Asher watched as students flooded out of the cafeteria and began dispersing in every direction. He searched the crowd carefully, being sure he didn't miss Mabel as she made her way out.

"As much as she knows about the kids that go to this school, I'm sure she's done some reading." Asher then spotted her as she walked through the doors, alone. "Just, go. I'll make sure she gets enough information on the topic." Kyden nodded hard and turned on his heel to head to his next class. Asher, on the other hand, turned to face Mabel, pulling himself off the wall he was resting against and rushing through the crowd to catch up to her. He hated the idea of what he had to do that night, but he knew if he didn't go through with it, and quickly, his reputation and hers would both be at risk.

Chapter Two: A Memorable Initiation

Blurs of greens and browns passed by at a steady pace, with some being larger and smaller than others around them. A continuous arched black snake cut through these blurs as the engine hummed across the paved path ahead. Asher watched as the black snake kept itself several feet off the ground, arching upward as it reached one of the brown blurs, only to relax for a brief moment before arching once again. Occasionally, the snake would cross the street overhead and keep a grip on the blurs as they switched sides, zipping by without ever realizing the snake relied on them. The sun was still far from setting, as the clock on his dash read 3:55, only five minutes before he was to meet Kyden at the entrance of Prominent Peak. His relatively new ruby red truck cut through the natural colors of the forest, giving Kyden a few moments to notice it was Asher coming down the street before Asher could even see Kyden waving him down. As he rounded the last turn leading to the path, there Kyden was. With both hands in the air, he swung them back and forth, as if Asher couldn't tell he was standing there in his neon green jacket and beat up white, but filthy looking car sitting only a few feet from where he stood. Asher pulled off the road and into the gravel, parking a couple of yards away from the Prominent Peak hiking trail sign, which was very old and designed like the signs he had seen at lakes, guiding people to the beach or camping grounds. Opening his door and stepping out the gravel crunched beneath his feet. He was now wearing the shoes he had bought last year, which were similar to those he had bought this year, only they had a black base rather than being all white. They were slightly more worn as well, but hardly in disrepair.

"You intend to move that, right?" Asher pointed briefly in the direction of Kyden's car before placing his hand back in the pocket of his jacket, which matched well with his shoes, having a black surface with a white set of strings that tightened his hood and the zipper itself being white as well.

"Obviously. Not like it's the first time I've done this." Kyden looked out over the road and then down at his wristwatch.

"Might as well be." Asher walked around his truck and leaned on the passenger side door. "Last time we were here it was your initiation."

"I think that gives me some pretty good insight into how these things go." Kyden raised his brow and smiled at Asher as he walked to his side, spun on his heel and thumped his back against the truck as well. Both watched out over the road as they spoke, being sure that nobody else was coming earlier than they anticipated. The sun had begun to sink slowly, but still had hours before it would set. Asher examined the rays of light as they crested over the trees across the street, but were cut off before they could meet the trail entrance. "So, what did you tell her?"

"The usual."

"Which is?" Asher glanced over at Kyden and then back at

the trees' summit.

"I wanted a chance to get to know her better and what better way than a walk?" The question was obviously rhetorical.

"Oh... you know, next time we do this, you should come up with something other than that if it's a guy. Honestly, I thought you were hitting on me that day."

"And you still came out here?" Kyden's eyes grew big and he jerked his neck back about an inch. Asher laughed at this and returned his sight to the road. "Good luck giving that one some patchwork." Kyden scratched the back of his head, obviously displeased about not knowing any way to diffuse Asher's words. As they listened, a distant rumbling could be heard coming from the same direction Asher had arrived from. "Looks like it's about time." Asher examined his own watch, which read only 4:15. "Early too." Kyden shuffled about in his pocket for a moment before tossing something towards Asher. Asher freed a hand from one of his own pockets and caught it.

"Use that to signal when you're ready." Kyden then hooted as he ran over to his car and hopped in, starting up the engine and backing out of the lot as quickly as he could to avoid being seen. As he did so, Asher looked at the object in his hand and noticed that it was a small, cheap pager.

"Clever." As Kyden's engine became more distant and headed off to the left the second engine sounded even closer, entering the opening from the right. It was a small silver car that Asher didn't recognize. As the car pulled in next to his truck opposite of the side that he was standing, he stuffed the pager into the pocket of his jacket, being sure it was in a loose enough area so that he could get to it easily without being noticed. He then proceeded to make his way around the truck again and greet Mabel as she cut off the engine and hopped out, seemingly very energetic.

"Hey!" Finishing her simple greeting she smiled cheerfully at Asher, then reached back into her car and gathered up a water bottle and her cell phone, which was charging off a port in the dash. She then took off her jacket and wrapped it around her waist. With that, she closed the door to her car and pressed a button on the fob to lock it.

"You seem ready enough," Asher remarked, making his way to her side of the car, "got everything?"

"I looked up the distance of the trail before coming here, so I wanted to make sure I was ready for it since there are apparently no water fountains." She shook the icy water, seemingly proud of herself for always thinking one step ahead. "Did you bring anything?" Asher shrugged, knowing that he hadn't brought any beverages with him as he normally never did. Mabel unlocked her car, opened the door, pulled out a second filled water bottle and shut and locked the door again. She then tossed it in Asher's direction and smiled even larger than before, exposing a perfect set of porcelain-like teeth. Asher caught the bottle and smiled back as the ice rattled about inside.

"Thanks." He then tipped the bottle toward the trail entrance. "Ladies first." Mabel took the lead as they started up the trail, but after only a few seconds of walking, they were side-by-side. Asher couldn't help but notice the peculiar scent of rosebuds that seemed to trail her as he caught up. They talked about the first day back at school and everyone that Mabel had met. Asher proceeded to give her advice on how to handle some of the people and who she'd be best to avoid, but she seemed very open-minded about everyone, which kind of set Asher at ease, seeing as where he was taking her.

"I think it's best to give everybody a chance, even if they have a poor history."

"Well, what if that person has a terrible history and that history is very recent?" Mabel shrugged and looked up at Asher as they continued to walk.

"All the more reason for them to want to change." Asher was astounded. He had never met such an optimistic person in his life. He thought that maybe it was best that they were initiating her. After all, scaring someone could be the best way to let them see the real world, rather than just the fantasy they lived in. Then again, once she realized it was just a joke, maybe she'd become even more naive. "Oh, I meant to ask earlier, have you-" *Crack!* Mabel stopped in her tracks, seemingly forgetting that she had been talking and examined the wooded area to Asher's right.

"What is it?"

"Didn't you hear that?" Asher looked off in the direction she had been looking and didn't see anything. The woods had started to darken as the sun sank between a few hills, but visibility was still there. Several evergreens were stirring in the light breeze, but there was nothing moving about at ground level.

"Yeah, but there's nothing there. Probably just a dead branch that finally gave way." Asher knew it could have been Kyden, or one of the jocks straying a little too close to the path, so he brushed it off without a problem and his branch theory seemed to set Mabel at ease.

"You're probably right." She let out a small sigh and started walking once more.

"So, what were you saying?"

"Oh, right! The stories." Asher looked forward a moment, examining the millions of small red pine needles that littered the trail ahead, then looked back towards Mabel, who was taking a swig from the partially transparent green bottle with half melted ice cubes still floating at the top. The outside of the bottle had started to sweat as well. Asher had hardly noticed the heat under the canopy of trees and removed his jacket too, tying it around his waist as Mabel had earlier. Once she swallowed her drink she pushed the cap back down, creating a dull popping sound as it sealed and nodded her head. "Local legends." Asher inhaled sharply, realizing that he had forgotten to bring this up entirely himself, but he was relieved to know that she had in fact done some research on the topic.

"What about them?"

"Well, Bristlewood was established in 1805, so the town is only 214 years old."

"Only?" Asher watched as Mabel's facial expression changed from cheery to heavily thoughtful.

"I mean, it's a decent age for a town here, but the weird thing about the legends is that they take place in times prior to when Bristlewood existed." Confused, Asher gave her a look that suggested so and she proceeded to explain. "Well, before Bristlewood, there was an earlier settlement known only as Prosper. It has no official name to this day and the only documentation on it is in the library's archive."

"The school's library?"

"No." Mabel giggled as she spoke and looked over the path thoroughly. "The town library has a section dedicated to Bristlewood's history, that's where I found it. Well, the book that told me everything was in the restricted section, but nobody has to know that." Mabel grinned mischievously in Asher's direction after informing him of this.

"Well, what's significant about Prosper?" Mabel returned to her concentrated, thoughtful look.

"It existed for several years before anyone had set foot here from another land. The documentary remarks on how much amber this long-lost settlement had collected, all stored beneath one home at the far end of the settlement." Asher was confused about how this could be the most interesting part of lore to her and his face must have shown something along that line. "I just thought that was curious."

"Well, what about the vampires and witches the town is said to have had? Don't you find that interesting?" Mabel nodded and smiled, seemingly relieved that Asher had engaged in the topic as well now.

"That's the thing. The house the amber was found under was the home of the so-called witch, who created the vampires, but they weren't your typical night walkers." Confused once more, Asher prodded for her to go on. "Apparently, these beings didn't just drink blood, like your typical sanguine lore. They found a way to stay alive and walk amongst humans without being detected, by feeding off their souls rather than their blood." Asher fell silent as he listened intently to Mabel's findings. How had he not heard of any of this before? "This made it so they could be discrete and not need to feed so often, but they were found out before too long. After several months of feeding off the souls, people in the settlement of Prosper began to fall ill with an unknown disease. They grew cold, clammy, vomited and were often too weak to move. The settlement's leader, who remains unknown, believed that the witch was behind it all, but he couldn't prove it. With a little more than a month's time, the settlers began to die of the illness. The documentary says that at this point, they were losing at least one settler a day." Mabel broke her story off for a moment and examined the edges of the forest once more, seemingly putting herself on edge. "Anyways, this was enough for the settlement to enter a state of panic and they were willing to take any steps they could to avoid losing more innocent lives. With that, they entered the witch's home and found a large stockpile of amber in her cellar. The odd amount of crystal-like stone she collected was enough for the townsmen to condemn her as a witch and she was hanged. However, the deaths didn't stop, even with the witch gone. Panicked even more so than before, they decided that there must have been another witch at work. With almost another month having passed, the settlement had lost over half its population, but there was something else the leader had begun to notice."

"What was it?" Asher asked as Mabel had stopped speaking once more. He assumed she was either still on edge or was so deep in thought that she forgot to speak out loud. Coming back around, she started up again.

"He realized that there were several members of the settlement who weren't sick at all, though some of them seemed to be ill in the beginning. With that knowledge, he planned one of history's largest executions at the time, at least on paper."

"On paper?" Mabel nodded, assuring Asher that she was speaking clearly.

"He never got to go through with it. Once the decree was written and sent out to a higher power for official approval, the settlers began to die off faster. In the time it took the decree to reach their superiors and arrive back at the settlement, the post rider came back to a heap of ash, with very little still standing. The only building that remained was the deceased witch's home. After gathering what remnants they could, including documentations the settlement's leader, had written, they discovered the Amber Cellar, but it contained far more amber than the leader had previously written about." They walked in silence for a moment as Asher processed everything that Mabel had thrown at him, still unsure as to how he had never heard this story before, given all of the lore that surfaced over the years. "None of the bodies came up, that I know of." Asher remained silent for a few more moments before speaking.

"Well, do you know the significance of Prominent Peak?" Mabel nodded her head and looked towards the top of the hill, which they were now no more than a mile away from.

"This is where the vampires are said to meet each year, under every full moon the year offers." Mabel seemed cautious as she continuously examined their surroundings from left to right, before looking up towards the stars. "Much like tonight." Asher looked up at this point, not noticing that the night sky was already protruding through the coats of dull blues. Almost directly overhead, a large white moon, like the entrance of a well being looked up at, beamed down on them.

"That'll add to the effect." Asher thought to himself, grinning as he did so, but only from the right side of his lips as he didn't want Mabel to question it. The forest was now so dark that they couldn't make out anything passed the tree line on either side of them. The forest was nothing more than dark posts with fluffy cores that became more narrow as they towered into the skies above. Asher wanted to turn on his phone's flashlight but was concerned that he may accidentally give away one of his friends hiding somewhere in the trees if they hadn't already made their way to the peak. As he finished this thought, he noticed a beam of light on the ground to his left. Mabel must have been thinking about it at the same time, but

not having any reason not to, she turned hers on. Asher used her light to keep an eye on the trees. Once he was certain they were the only two on the trail he flipped his on as well and kept the beam focused ahead of them. As they came upon the peak, Asher reached into his jacket and pulled out the pager, keeping it clenched in a tight fist to be sure it wasn't exposed enough to be noticed.

"Wow," Mabel exclaimed, approaching the edge of the peak as she looked up at the stars in awe, "there are so many out here." Asher moved his hand behind his back as he walked alongside her, joining her stargazing moment. He then brushed his thumb over the smooth surface of the pager before finding a small, rough button protruding from it. *Beep!*

"What was that?" Mabel looked towards Asher as the small noise was emitted.

"I-I have no idea." He quickly squeezed the corners of the pager, covering the speakers as best he could, but it didn't make the sound again either way. "M-maybe it was a bat." Mabel looked at him, sort of in disbelief, before remembering the stories that were being told earlier. A faint smile then crossed her face as she looked back up at the moon and the stars.

"Vampire bats, here for their meeting, no doubt." They laughed quietly as they looked out over the edge of Prominent before both fell silent. A similar sound came out from the forest behind them. Both noticed this and turned to face the sound. Mabel, without hesitating, flashed her light towards where it had come from and for a brief moment, a larger shadow could be seen, swiftly pushing itself against a nearby tree. "Who's there?" The sound could be heard again, only this time it came from over the cliff and seemed a little less mechanical. Mabel once again whipped her light around, trying to spot the source, but of course, in the direction of the cliff, there was nothing but dark sky and the tops of the trees that rested at the bottom of the cliff. The branches in a nearby shrubbery began rustling about and Mabel squeaked as she continued to reach a state of panic. This time, however, the thing in the woods made itself known. Two glowing eyes protruded from the bushes, unblinking and without any signs of fear or shock for having been noticed. Mabel took a sharp breath and swung a hand back, gripping Asher's wrist tightly. He felt a fair amount of weight remove itself from his pocket because of this and after a light *thump,* water could be heard sloshing about. Mabel was clearly terrified, but the thing in the woods wasn't letting up. It began to growl as it pushed its way out of the hiding place it was in. Mabel took an unsteady step backward, not thinking about her surroundings. As the creature exposed itself, the face caused Mabel to shriek, as it was that of some hellish beast, having dark fur around the features and large yellow eyes. The beast progressively took small steps towards them. Noticing that it walked on two legs ending in talons, Mabel began to tremble and her grip on Asher grew weaker. Even Asher was growing uncomfortable in the presence of the thing, but he couldn't show this to Mabel. Instead, he backed away a foot or so as well. The beast then hastily extended two large bat-like wings in place of its arms and screeched into the night, opening its mouth wide as it did so. Mabel then screamed and tripped over something. She had lost her grip on Asher entirely and the light of her cell phone spiraled about as it fell to the ground. Her screams grew more distant and Asher couldn't hear her footsteps on the forest floor anymore. Concerned, he reached out for her cell phone and held the light up just in time to see the curly-haired jock removing the large bat mask, a look of horror spread across his face as he rushed passed Asher and toward where Mabel stood. Confused, Asher turned the light to face where the jock was heading. His heart sank as the light met... nothing. The cliff was all that there was behind him and the only thing on the ground was a bottle of water covered in dirt as if it were pushed into the ground by something heavy. He knew then that Mabel had tripped over the bottle he dropped and his blood ran cold, instantly making him light-headed and shaky.

"Mabel?! Mabel!" The jock shouted as he scanned over the edge of the cliff, but without a light, he could see nothing. Asher wanted to shine the phone over the edge, to see that Mabel was okay, but he knew better. Suddenly, the light was snatched from his hands and Kyden rushed to the edge as well, shining it into the depths below. From where Asher stood, a few feet away, he could see the tops of trees in the light's glow. The tops of trees, straight ahead of him, at his own height. He knew by the silence that fell over the group that the site was not something he wanted to see. The other two jocks and the girl from the cafeteria all rushed to the edge and looked over. The girl almost immediately screamed and took off back down the trail, followed by the blond jock, who was then followed by the curly-haired jock, who seemed guiltier than everyone else, but couldn't utter a word besides "I-I can't be here. I can't be here."

"Asher... we have to go." Kyden looked back at Asher, who

was still unable to move and kept the light on the base of the cliff. "We need to tell somebody what happened."

"Are you crazy? We'll all get charged with manslaughter!" The third jock was still standing there with them, breathing heavily and obviously panicked as he was thinking of what to do. "We need to clean this up. Come on, we're going down there."

"The hell if we are!" Kyden grabbed the jock up by his collar as he tried taking off for the walkway down. "You, get out of here." He then threw the jock to the side. Moments later the jock got up and took off down the trail after the others. "Asher, what do we do?" Asher, still unsure of how to process what had just happened, slowly edged his way towards the cliff and finally took a look for himself. At the base of Prominent Peak, he could see her. Mabel was laying flat on her back, with her hair thrown about over the ground around her. She didn't appear to be moving, but her eyes were wide open.

"W-we have to get out of here."

"What?" Kyden seemed to be enraged by this. Asher noticed and tried to face him briefly, but he could no longer peel his eyes away from the site below. "That's it? Just go?"

"We go home, we call the police and we sleep if we can." Kyden began to breathe aggressively before forcing Mabel's phone into Asher's hand and trudging down the path quickly, pulling out his own phone as he did so. Asher stayed behind for a moment, taking one last look at the site below. He could now see that there was a single tear rolling down Mabel's face, even from the distance he was at, but there was something else there too. A few yards from where Mabel was laying, Asher could see the lower half of a figure with its hands resting in the pockets of its jeans. He flashed the light on it, doing nothing but solidifying that what he saw was real. A man was standing only a short distance away from her and was unflinching as he stared back up at Asher.

With his heart now thundering in his chest, Asher dropped the phone and sprinted down the trail faster than he had ever done before. Once at the base, he dove into his truck and floored the pedal. The drive seemed to take hours and seconds at the same time as his tires squealed, entering the parking lot to his house. All of the lights were out except the front porch light, which Asher used to reach the house easier, still unable to hear or think over the sound of his heart, seemingly about to burst. He heaved as he made his way inside, up the stairs, and into his room, where he walked back and forth for a few moments, desperately trying to think of what to do next when he heard it. A strange sound he had never heard before. Turning to face his window, he noticed a small shadowy dot come up to the glass, bounce off and disappear. Somebody was outside, throwing pebbles up at the window. Cautiously, Asher moved towards the window, still breathing heavily, but doing his best to remain calm, thinking that maybe Kyden had come over and was trying not to wake Asher's parents while they figured things out. Once he made it to the window, his heart froze up entirely. Standing out in his yard was the man he had seen standing at the base of the cliff.

"How did he follow me home? He couldn't have gotten up the cliff fast enough to have even seen which way I went." Calming his breathing yet again and trying to keep his balance and his stomach, Asher grabbed a baseball bat from the closet next to the window and made his way back downstairs. Opening the front door, he rushed out into the yard, where the man stood in the same posture he was in at the base of the cliff.

"Who are you?" The man didn't respond. He simply held a blank stare in Asher's direction. "I asked you a question." Asher raised the bat as he had now cleared half the distance between the house and the man. He still ignored Asher and watched intently. Asher, unable to think straight, raised the bat above his head and swung with all the strength he could muster, but to his horror, there was no connection and the swing had seemingly stopped itself. Confused, he looked up at the man. The bat was in his grasp and he was unstirred by the attempt. They were now less than a foot apart and Asher could finally breathe properly, but not because he was calm. It was a clash of fear and rage that seemed to soothe him enough to look over the man carefully. He recognized him. It was Feeder. The same strange kid from school was now standing in his yard, effortlessly stopping Asher from bludgeoning him. "What the-" Before Asher could finish his sentence, Feeder grinned menacingly and with the only free hand he had, he plunged it into Asher's chest. The pain was immense as Asher felt Feeder's fingers digging into the very core of his body, but it was over just as soon as it had started. Breathing with a sigh of relief as the pain slowly subsided, Asher stumbled backward and looked down. In Feeder's hand was a small mass of what appeared to be orange glass, glowing a hue of gold and seemingly pulsating. As the blood rushed back to Asher's brain, he took three deep breaths, looked Feeder in the eye for only a moment and then fell back onto the lawn. The world around him grew quiet and darker than it already was. Only the sound of a neighbor's dog barking and the buzzing of the light on his porch could be heard. The last thing he saw was Feeder crouching down next to him, now grinning maliciously and placing the glowing object he had ripped from Asher's chest into a sleeve concealed in his overcoat. Then, shadows of the night moved over him, coating his body in a cold dark blanket and muffling the sounds around the two of them. As the night gripped at Asher, he closed his eyes and let a deep, fear-driven sleep wash over him.

"Sleep well, Cor."

Chapter Three: Looking-Glass

Blurry white lights moved from the horizon of Asher's vision, upwards towards his hairline and out of sight. One by one they flew overhead, disturbed only by the occasional peachy figure leaning over him before vanishing to his left once again. The frame around his vision quivered as his eyelids grew heavier, but a feminine voice insisted he keep them open, so he did. The white fuzzy squares blinded him as they passed by, causing him to wince with each beam that came and resulting in him desperately pulling his eyes open every time the light was bearable again. He could feel a strange mask over his face, which made his breathing sound heavier as it passed through his partially open mouth. Reaching up towards the mask, he found himself to be extremely weak and lacking much control over his movements. His arm fumbled about as he attempted lifting it from his chest and his fingers remained limp, even as he tried desperately to clench a fist or grab at the mask.

"Don't strain yourself," the same voice as before spoke out, "just focus on staying awake." The vocals were soothing to Asher, making it all the more difficult to remain awake, but they were still distant, yet so close. He let his forearm drop back to his chest and attempted to turn his head, sending shooting pains up his spine. He then realized through the fog shrouding his vision that he was in a hospital, being rushed down a corridor by what appeared to be several doctors. Once he had lifted his head enough to see those around him, a cold hand pressed itself against his forehead and the figure once again asked him to relax and focus only on keeping his eyes open. "We're almost there, hang on." His efforts proved useless. As the palm resting against his head relaxed the muscles above his brow and removed the stress he had put on his neck, Asher passed out, exhaling weakly as he did so, seemingly sensing his own defeat against whatever ailment he had been fighting.

The blurred figures continued to make appearances over

some amount of time, but the lights didn't. Every so often Asher could see the outline of the figures and hear some of the things they were saying, but most of it seemed to be gibberish and slowly spoken. Between the periods of dreamless sleep and noticing the visitors in his room, Asher relived the events that he had just experienced in what seemed to be a recurring memory of sorts, yet it was becoming more and more distant with each repetition. As the memory played itself out once more, Asher watched as the light of the phone swung wildly through the air, though seemingly slower in the memory than it was in reality. The memory then sped up and Asher was now holding the phone, watching the other boy as he looked over the cliff. It sped up again and Asher was now peering over it as well, looking down at Mabel's body. As he looked over her, for what felt like the hundredth time, he began to tear up, accepting now that what had happened couldn't be undone and hating himself for going through with the initiation for whatever reasons he did. Rage and hopelessness boiled up inside of him as the memory slowed down, even more, forcing him to look over the ghastly sight longer than ever before. His heart, at least in the memory, skipped a beat. There was something different about Mabel this time, something that hadn't been there before. Asher held his breath and listened carefully. He was now seemingly in control of his body in the memory and took advantage of this, turning his head to one side and facing his ear towards Mabel. He could see Feeder's feet and jeans in the corner of his eye, watching from just outside the phone's beam as he had before, but Asher paid him no mind and continued to adjust his ear's position. He could feel the increasing need to breathe as he listened to the silence of the forest, but refused to, waiting to hear what he thought was there. After what felt like several minutes, he heard it. One slow, painful breath came from Mabel's lifeless body. Asher shot his sight back down at her and then at Feeder, who was also making a noise he hadn't before. It was laughter. Asher raised the light to see Feeder's face and found it in the same state he had seen it in later that night, grinning with dark intent. With patience like nothing else Asher had ever seen, Feeder parted his teeth and took in a small breath, reminding Asher to breathe himself, yet he couldn't. He was becoming more and more fearful of Feeder's image and the strange occurrences that were happening, making it impossible for him to do anything else but stare as Feeder moved his lips to form words.

"The first, in many years." Feeder removed his right hand and from west to east he let it glide through the air at waist height, stopping only when the open palm and slightly curled fingers met in the direction of Mabel's crippled form. Feeder exposed more teeth as his lower jaw was firmly realigned with the upper and then proceeded to bow, his arm still outstretched towards his right side. He then backed into the tree line as frantic footsteps boomed out from behind Asher. He turned to see himself rushing down the path in the dark, no phone in hand and heading towards the base of Prominent Peak. Curious and in shock, he looked at the ground to see a patch of grass with an illuminated rectangular frame. Darkness surrounded the outside of the frame and the underside of it continued to let off a glow. Mabel's phone was on the forest floor, face down, yet a second version of it was still in his hand, pointing towards the ground below. His head began to swim as he looked back at the phone he had been holding, then to where the flashlight was pointing. The open area below was entirely empty. Both Feeder and Mabel were gone and the only evidence of either of them was a patch of disturbed grass laying flat, where the same tall grass around it remained untouched. Asher was losing his balance and growing more and more nauseous as the unseen events played out, but it all came to an abrupt end as he decided he had had enough and turned to walk away, only to trip over the same bottle as Mabel and stumble off the edge. As he descended he clenched his eyes and teeth shut. Just as his back thumped against the ground he woke up, inhaling heavily and trying not to blink as he shot up in bed.

"Asher! You're awake!" Asher clenched the sheets at his sides as the voice rang out, but quickly relaxed when he recognized it. It was his mother, who was now hugging him and sobbing to herself. Asher rubbed his neck as he looked over his shoulder. Beside an empty seat that he had assumed his mother was sitting in, he saw his father, who was gripping the armrests on both sides of himself and watching over the pair with surprise in his eyes. "I'm so glad you're okay!" His mother proceeded to rub her hand across his back as he moved her dark brown hair away from his face, trying to avoid restricting his breathing as he was still catching his breath.

"You'll be alright, it was just a bad dream." Asher looked back at his father as he embraced his mother. "We were all concerned when you started thrashing about the other night, but-"

"The other night?" His mother's grip loosened as he asked this. She then slipped away, sitting with her back turned but still facing him.

"We were going to wait to tell you, so we didn't stress you

out any more than you already were." She said this as if she weren't directing it towards Asher and his father could tell, pushing his glasses up the bridge of his nose and curling his lip apologetically. She then motioned with a free hand for his father to come to the bedside, which he did, sitting closer to the head of the bed and leaving enough room between himself and his wife for Asher to sit between them. Asher did so and looked over the both of them, noticing that they each appeared to be nervous about something.

"Son," his father said as he proceeded to place an arm around Asher's shoulders, brushing where his hand had landed with his thumb and hesitantly looking him over, "when you hit your head you, uh-"

"You went into a coma." Asher turned from his father to his mother as she interrupted and slightly dropped his jaw, just enough to be noticeable. "B-but-"

"It was a very brief period. You've been out for less than a week and now that you're awake I'm sure we can get you home before the day is up." Asher looked back at his father, leaving his mouth hanging as he did so. Then, he looked to the floor and confusion took over. Slightly cocking his head to one side, Asher furrowed his brow and examined the pair again.

"What about Mabel?" The two seemed confused, which Asher found understandable at first. "The girl, who fell off the cliff. What did the police say? Am I in trouble?" His parents looked at one another, seemingly just as confused as he was. Then, his father took on a soft smile and proceeded to rub his shoulder as he was before.

"Oh, that. It was just the nightmares, son." The confusion only increased on Asher's face, yet his mother looked just as relaxed as his father had when he spoke.

"Mabel is fine. Actually, she'll be very excited to know that you're okay." His mother smiled, kissed him on the side of his head and got up from the bed. "I'm going to go let the doctor know that you're awake now." She then proceeded to leave the room, being sure to close the door behind her as Asher watched her look down both ends of the hall before choosing which way to go. He didn't turn from the door even after the knob clicked it shut.

"Excited?" Asher ran through everything that was said, trying

to avoid communicating with his father until he had fully digested all that had already surfaced. He couldn't figure out how they would have even known Mabel, as he was never given the time to even mention her to them in a conversation. *"Did Kyden tell them about her? Did the police?"*

"You know," his father started, trying to break the ever-growing silence in the room, "the night you hit your head was the first time in a while we had any reason to feel concerned about you." Asher looked back at his father and then out the window, where his father had been watching birds flutter about on the branches of a tree pressed against the building. It was the first time Asher noticed that they weren't on the base floor of the hospital. "You've always seemed to be able to handle yourself, even when you were younger. Never looked twice before making your own choices." Asher looked down as his father said this, knowing well that it wasn't true. His father then sighed and returned to his chair, smiling as he looked over his son. A question Asher's grogginess made him overlook finally came to mind.

"Dad," he paused for a moment, keeping certain he had his father's attention before continuing, "where was I when I hit my head?" His father pushed the glasses up to his eyes once again and rubbed his hands together, running his bony fingers between the gaps of those on the opposite hand.

"You'd just gotten home, made a good bit of ruckus, which is what got our attention and then we heard a thump a few minutes later in your room. Your mother went in the hall to check on you, as I was in the middle of a call and she found you laying on the floor of your room with the window open. The closest thing to your head was the corner of your dresser." Asher found this explanation rather strange, as it was far more information than he had asked for. Shrugging it off, he waited for his mother to return with a doctor.

Several minutes later, Asher and his parents were heading home. As the trip went on, Asher couldn't help but think about everything that was said to have happened. How could his parents not know that the police were called nearly a week ago and would have likely shown up at their house, then the hospital when they found out where everyone was? Nothing seemed to match up the way it should have to Asher and if none of it happened at all, why was his window open? He never left it open and was sure that the window was closed that night. Asher thought harder on the subject and found several holes in the story, including a rather large one he knew the answer to. Looking towards the front of the car, he turned to his mother, who was driving and humming as she did so.

"Mom, if what I said happened was just part of a dream, where was I earlier that night?" Asher knew what the answer would have been had he not gone to Prominent Peak and his mother's response would prove the truth to him. His mother fell silent for a moment, seizing her humming and focusing only on the road ahead, which would soon turn into their driveway. "Mom?" Speaking to her again seemed to snap her out of whatever kind of trance she had previously been in. With a sharp breath, she looked back at him and smiled, then returned her eyes to the road as she prepared to turn into their lot.

"You were out with Kyden." Her reply fell short of what it should have been, as he always told her where he was going before he did so and she hadn't been home yet on that day for him to let her know. It was her rule that he says something before leaving and being as early as it was when he left to go to the trail, Asher never made it inside the house. He knew nobody was home that day and with that, he only came home long enough to get his truck and go.

As the car pulled into the lot, Asher hopped out and decided to play off the rest of the day as he usually would. Once night came, he pushed everything that had happened over the last week into the back of his mind the best he could, trying to ensure a decent night's rest before school the following day. However, despite his efforts, morning came slowly and with even more questions. As his alarm rang out, he noticed that it wasn't echoing off the walls quite like it usually did. He listened for a moment, refusing to get out of bed for the time being. It then dawned on him what his father had said about his window. Sitting up, he looked across the sunlit room and noticed that the window was, in fact, open just as his father had said it was. As he sat and stared at the white frame, halfway between being fully open and closed, his mother knocked twice on the door, softly. She then opened it a hair and peaked in, being sure Asher was awake before coming in. The smell of pancakes, grease, and coffee filled his nostrils as his mother carried in a bedside platter with a stack of three large and very fluffy pancakes, a glass of orange juice, what appeared to be a small plate of french toast, and bacon.

"Good morning, sleepy head." Asher rubbed his eyes and turned back and forth a few times, between his mother and her offerings, and the window. She noticed this and sat the platter down on his bed stand, made her way across the room and closed the window with a small *knock* as the white woods met each other. The alarm was still going as well, though now that the window was closed, the echo had returned to its usual state of irritating. His mother proceeded to shut it off as well and sat at the foot of the bed. "How are you feeling?" Asher started pulling apart one of the cakes with a fork, watching as the syrup poured between the new opening he had created.

"I'm alright, just a headache, I guess." His mother reached across the bed and rested her hand on his forehead. She then sighed and stood back up, adjusting the blue scrubs she was wearing to prevent any wrinkles from forming.

"Well, the doctor said your fever should go away in a few days. Hopefully, he's right." She folded her arms and looked around the room for a moment, then back at her son, smiling as she watched him devour the meal she had made. "Are you planning to stay home today?" Asher shook his head.

"I want to get back to school. I don't want this to take a toll on me right now." His mother seemed proud that he was so eager to return to school, but also slightly concerned about his health.

"Well, don't over do it, okay?" His mother gave him a stern "I mean it" look and made her way over to his door. "Let me know how your first day back goes." She then went to close the door behind herself as she made her way into the upstairs hall, but stopped just before the mechanism clicked. "Oh, Mabel called earlier but I didn't want to wake you." Asher nearly choked as he stopped swallowing a bite of bacon he had taken from a larger piece in his hand. "She seemed very excited to see you," his mother continued, seemingly not noticing this, "you should invite her over after school today." She then smiled widely and shut the door, taking her usual light steps towards the stairs and out the front entrance at the base of them. Asher immediately sat the platter back on his bed stand, as he had moved it over himself for easier access. He then jumped out of bed and wiped his forehead, removing a small amount of sweat that had accumulated and made his way over to his dresser. Once he was dressed how he liked he rushed downstairs and went straight for the front door, grabbing his keys and avoiding communication with his father, who had tried to stop him briefly before having the door shut in his face, almost making him lose his grip on a bowl of cereal.

Asher hastily put the key in the lock and hopped in, stopping only to examine his sickly face in the driver side mirror before plunging the key into the ignition and cranking it. As the engine revved up, he put it in reverse and carefully but quickly backed out of the driveway and into the street, heading straight for the school once he was certain the roads were clear. The drive was rather short, which he had expected, as he lived so close to the school that he hadn't even thought to drive there while it was warm out. It seemed unnecessary given the distance. Once he was in the school's parking lot, Asher pulled into an empty spot and shut the truck off, watching the other students as they made their way inside, but not getting out himself. The truck made small occasional cracking sounds as it cooled off in the usual morning breeze, which Asher acknowledged and used to keep himself calm. He knew if he kept acting crazy people would think he really was and that was the last thing he felt he needed at this point. He began pacing his breathing as he watched a few smaller groups of students gather together at the front entrance of the school, none of which actually went inside. He recognized a few of them as the senior football team, which meant there were a few faces he needed to find in the crowd. Using only his eyes, Asher scanned over each face he met and then to the next, but none of them were who he wanted to see.

"Where are they? Where are they?" He proceeded to strum his fingers against the steering wheel as he leaned over it, glaring at the students ahead. One of the girls then turned, noticing Asher watching them. He quickly ducked his head to the side, pretending he hadn't been staring at them. Just as he looked back out over the dash he heard a knuckle tap on the glass. He jumped as he looked to his right side. It was Kyden, motioning with a finger for Asher to unlock the door. Asher did so and Kyden crawled in on the passenger side. Once he was inside he leaned over the gear stick and pulled Asher in, nearly squeezing the life out of him.

"Man, I'm so glad you're okay." Asher hugged Kyden back and they broke off after Kyden thumped Asher's back a few times. "You aren't looking your best though. What's going on?" Deciding it was best to not let the issue at hand completely take him over, Asher threw a reassuring smile towards Kyden and looked back at the students that gathered at the foot of the school.

"Sick. Doc says I should clear up in a few days." Asher held the smile as he scanned the edge of the schoolyard, still not seeing any of the people he was looking for.

"Lose something?" Kyden asked sarcastically, noticing what Asher was doing.

"No, just looking for a couple of people."

"A couple?" Kyden looked out over the dash as well, obviously unaware of who Asher would be looking for. "Like who?" Asher surrendered his visual efforts when it became clear the others wouldn't be there that day. It was typical of them to skip out when they could.

"Some of the football players. Remember the guys that sat at our table last week?" Asher examined Kyden's confused look before asking again. "You know, Dennis's friends? The three guys and that girl?"

"We sat alone on the first day, man." Kyden chuckled to himself and looked over Asher, expressing more concern, which was replacing his look of relief for having seen Asher at all. "Just me, you," Kyden raised a hand out over the dash and pointed while keeping his finger level with someone who was coming up from the road that met with the schoolyard, "and her." Asher squinted as he made out the girl. Her long dark hair was flowing with the morning winds and with each stride she made. She wore a black hoodie with buttons in place of a zipper, as it was a woven hoodie, a white T-shirt with a colorful paint splatter decal on it, which was visible through the opening of the hoodie, tight black jeans with white threads stringing around the knee on the right side and upper middle thigh on the left, and black top shoes with white bases. She was stunning, even from the distance they were at. The other articles she had with her were a gray backpack, a copper-gold chain around her porcelain white neck, and what looked like small obsidian river stones as earrings, which brought out the vibrant red lipstick and fingernail polish she had on that day, as well.

"Who is that?" Asher looked out over the girl in awe. Kyden laughed, interrupting his fascination. He then opened his door once more and slid out onto his feet, which made clopping sounds as the relatively new rubber hit the pavement.

"That's your girlfriend, dude." Kyden then shut the door and shook his head as he looked back at Asher, who was too dumbfounded to move. The girl seemed to notice Kyden from across the lot and smiled at him before turning to face Asher, who was still dazed. Her smile grew even larger as she waved at him, almost jumping in place as her excitement shown through. Asher tightened his grip on the steering wheel.

"Mabel."

Chapter Four: A Tale of Two

"Was it really all just a dream," Asher thought to himself as he made his way towards the excited Mabel, *"or is this the dream my mind created defensively?"* Mabel rushed towards Asher as he came closer to the sidewalk she was on. *"No, only one of these realities has all the pieces."* Asher chuckled as Mabel rushed into his arms, resting her head on his chest and squeezing him tightly. She then turned her chin up and pursed her lips, preparing for a kiss, which Asher gave into quickly. As their lips pressed together, both smiled cheerfully, listening as Kyden made sounds of gagging in the background. *"This one isn't real."* Asher separated his lips from Mabel's and continued to smile down at her before both proceeded to

walk into the building.

"So," Mabel started as she put the arms of her backpack around her chair, "how was it there?" Asher slung his backpack onto the desk and proceeded to organize his belongings as he had on the first day of school, playing along with the world around him as best he could.

"How was it where?" Mabel giggled as she watched him situate his textbooks at the bottom of the pile, followed by notebooks and then a composition journal.

"At the hospital, of course. Not like you've had many places to go the past few days." Mabel rested her chin on her wrist as she looked up at Asher, who was still standing while getting ready for the day. "You seem kind of distant today." Asher noticed this earlier on and was hoping she hadn't.

"Yeah, it's nothing. Still sick I guess." He smiled down at Mabel and finally took his seat next to her.

"Sick?" Mabel's voice became concerned almost

immediately.

"Oh, don't worry," Asher assured her, "the doctor said it should clear up in just a few days." Mabel's smile said she was at ease with the answer, but her eyes still showed concern. Asher ignored this and looked towards the front of the room, just in time to see Feeder walk in. He was wearing the same sunglasses he had worn the first day of school and even though Asher couldn't see his eyes, he could feel them on him. Feeder remained calm and collected as if Asher being in the room had no effect on him, but the feeling wasn't mutual. Even though Asher had no evidence of the events that took place, he could feel in his gut that they were true. He could also feel that Feeder knew this, which made the air around him grow cold as Feeder passed between the desks to get to his own. "Did you ever find out what the deal was with that guy?" Asher thrust a thumb over his shoulder in Feeder's direction once he had Mabel's attention again, which was apparently a very easy thing to accomplish for him.

"No," She chirped, "he just showed up I suppose. Tons of people here know him, even Dennis. I guess the two of them are cousins." Mabel then pulled a notebook from her backpack and began writing the day's lessons down on a sheet of blank paper, as Mr. Benner was also their 7th-period Physics class.

"Oh, that reminds me. Where is Dennis?" Mabel's pen slipped as she was writing, causing her to smear ink across words she had already finished. She then flipped the page and started over. "He's typically early to school, but I was early today too and I haven't seen him yet."

"Maybe he'll show up around lunch?" Mabel looked over at Asher from the corner of her eye, tipping her head back and slightly in his direction. She seemed to smile every time she had any reason to look at him. Asher did the same and looked towards the board as Mr. Benner made his way to the teacher's desk facing the class.

"Maybe."

Once lunch rolled around, Asher kept an eye out for Dennis, but as he expected, Dennis never showed up. Along with Dennis, the football players never showed either. Asher still thought they could have been ditching, but with the girl missing from the cafeteria too, what were the odds?

"Hey, man, everything alright?" Kyden waved his hand in front of Asher's face, which to Asher's surprise, he hadn't noticed at first. "You still seem pretty wonky." Once Kyden had gotten Asher's attention, he turned back to a sloppy joe he had been working on scarfing down.

"I'm alright, just... trying to put things together."

"Sleeping for a week really messes you up, huh?" Kyden managed to say through a mouth full of brownish meats. Asher shrugged and looked over the cafeteria once again, catching Feeder looking in his direction, or so he thought. He was still wearing his sunglasses, but there weren't many people sitting at their portion of the table. Feeder was leaned against the same pillar he had been leaning on during the first day that school was back in session and wasn't moving from the position he was in. Kyden noticed what Asher was looking at and nodded his head at Feeder, but got no reaction. "Kid's weird, isn't he? Sometimes I see him being extremely social, other times he looks like... well, that." Kyden proceeded to rip another hole in his sandwich, dropping some of the contents on the tray beneath where he held it.

"I think he's just misunderstood, you know?" Mabel said, examining him as well, but with far more shy eyes than the other two had been. It was as if she didn't want to get caught looking at him wrong or something, Asher thought. "Some people just need to be given time and effort to really open up."

"That so?" Asher questioned, leaning forward on his folded arms as he proceeded to glare back at Feeder. Mabel noticed his behavior and seemed uncomfortable with it. She then stood from the table and ran a hand across Asher's shoulder.

"Come on, I want to show you something."

"Oh, don't mind me," Kyden stated, doing his best to keep his mouth closed around the gnarly bits and pieces inside, "I'm just going to chill here and finish this... uh, stuff." He then shooed the two away by swinging his dangling hand like a pendulum.

"Thanks, Kyden," Mabel said sarcastically, leaning over Asher's head, "we'll try being back before lunch is up."

"Mhm, no rush." Asher got up from the table as well, breaking eye contact with Feeder when doing so. Once he was standing and walking towards the double door entrance with Mabel, he turned to see that Feeder was gone. The cafeteria only had one entrance, so as to make maintaining the students easier for teachers and Feeder hadn't had enough time to make it to the doors before them, nor had Asher waited long enough for Feeder to hide at a nearby table. Either way, his fashion would have given him away in the crowd.

Once they were out in the hall, with Mabel having gotten permission from Mr. Benner to go to the library, as he was guarding the doors, the two were heading off in the direction opposite of where she had said that they were going. She kept Asher's hand tightly in hers as they walked, but he couldn't tell if it was her grip that was so strong or his body that was so weak due to his illness.

"Are you sure you're alright?" Mabel spoke softly, being sure that Asher could make out the concern in her voice.

"I'll be fine, like I said." Asher smiled at her and wiped his brow when she looked away. He could tell his face was losing color as his arms were too and the sweating had become worse. "Where are we going?"

"The library, like I said." Confused, Asher looked back in the direction they came and pointed at a black directory board on the far wall.

"But, the library is that way." Mabel giggled as she looked over her shoulder.

"Not *that* library," she whispered, "Bristlewood Public Library." She then sped up a little, as if trying to keep her distance from something that was following them, yet Asher saw nothing. "Come on, go, go, go!" She kept her voice low as she opened one of the side doors at the end of the west wing that was meant to be used as an emergency exit. Seeing as the alarm no longer worked, it would also allow students to walk right out of the building undetected. Unsure of what else to do, Asher moved towards Mabel, who was beckoning him over and squeezed through the opening she had made. "Okay, now, run!" She then took off out into the parking lot, heading for Asher's truck. He followed and a small amount of excitement welled up inside of him, as skipping out halfway through a school day wasn't something he usually did. Once they got to his truck both were laughing and cheering, as if their next destination was at the other end of a thousand-mile road trip. They took off down the street, passing the school speed limit signs well over what was appropriate and headed into town, as the school was on the northern outskirts of Bristlewood. Once they were a decent distance away, Mabel turned on the radio and started singing along with whatever country or pop song came on. Asher listened to her and laughed each time she started to dance to the music.

"So, why are we heading to the library?" Asher turned the music down just a couple of notches and kept his eyes on the empty roads. It was only noon, which meant most townsfolk were either at work or at home, leaving Bristlewood's streets as deserted as ever.

"Don't you remember?" Asher shook his head, seeing as nothing he remembered was anything anyone else remembered. It was as if he were an anomaly himself. Asher Coyle from one world was transported into a very similar world that had far better outcomes via a coma portal. "We were supposed to try finding some of the town's lore. We talked about it the first day that school started." Asher's smile began to fade as he recalled the conversation they had on their way up to Prominent Peak, but he quickly plastered a new one over it and tapped the brakes as they came up to a four-way with a red light.

"Oh, right." Asher pulled the sleeves of his jacket over his hands as far as he could, trying to keep the cold air off his skin. Mabel noticed this and stirred uncomfortably.

"So, what do you think we'll find?"

"I don't know," Asher pressed the gas again and made a left turn as the light changed to green, "but if we can get a hold of that book you had last time I'm sure there'll be plenty to come across." Mabel's side of the truck grew eerily silent as Asher pulled up to the front of the library, which was a single story red brick office building converted into the Bristlewood Public Library only three years prior.

"What book?"

"What?" Asher looked over at Mabel, who seemed genuinely confused as to what he was talking about. "Oh, uh, when we talked about it last you mentioned a book in a restricted historical section or something that carried documents and I think journal entries written by the original town's leader." Asher watched as Mabel's expression grew more and more distressed with each word he spoke, as if she truly didn't remember, but knew there was a reason it wasn't ringing any bells.

"Huh... what was the town called?"

"I-I think it was, Prosper?" Asher could tell now that Mabel was picking something up, but still seemed lost in her own thoughts. "Amber Cellar?" Mabel's sight snapped towards the library when Asher said this, as if she could see right through the walls and was looking at something somewhere within. She leaned forward and clutched at the necklace she had been wearing. Asher could tell by the way her hand cupped the object attached that it was a decent sized amulet of sorts. This wasn't where his main focus was, however. The look on her face was the same look he could only imagine he had on his face when what he thought he knew and what others said was true didn't line up. She then came back and let go of the amulet, reaching out for the door.

"Come on, let's go have a look. Maybe we'll find that book while we're in there." The smile had returned to her face and she was quick to be on her way inside, shading her eyes from the sun overhead as she did so. Asher followed close behind and was hit with cool air as the library doors swung open. The smell of newly printed pages filled the room and the silence inside was almost as deafening as a horn. The only sounds audible were the thumps of their feet on the carpeted floor and an occasional page turning from somewhere amongst the ten or so tables lined against the windows, opposite of the numerical aisles. Asher continued to follow Mabel as she was seemingly navigating the library using a mental map, but based on how she was getting around, he could only assume the map was drawn out with pencil and had something spilled over it. After a few minutes of searching and pointing her finger in different directions, the two of them came across a section marked off with a black belt, like those used to form lines in stores and movie theaters. "This is it." Mabel looked to her left and then her right. Then, she crawled beneath the belt and hushed Asher as he went to question her. "Just wait here and let me know if anybody is coming. I'm going to try finding that book." Asher nodded and turned to face the other aisles as a way to keep an eye out. Trying to be smart about it, he grabbed a book off a neighboring shelf and pretended to be reading as he blocked off the black belt.

The library was extremely quiet still and the only footsteps he could hear were those of Mabel as she moved from the furthest left outer shelf on one side of the aisle to the innermost shelves on the same side. A few times Asher had thought someone was coming, but nobody ever showed themselves, which put him on edge and relaxed him at the same time. He wasn't used to breaking rules, yet today it seemed to be the only thing he could do, especially with Mabel around. After a few more minutes of standing around, he felt a tap on his shoulder. Spinning on his heel, he found Mabel standing there with a rather large, much older leather book. She tipped it side to side and raised her eyebrows as she looked out into the aisles.

"It's clear, come on out." Mabel crawled beneath the belt once again and they made their way further into the aisles, trying to steer clear of anyone who might notice them. Once they were in aisles 29 and 30, they leaned against the racks and began sifting through the book's pages. "Do you think this is the same book?"

"I'm pretty sure." Mabel continued to turn pages as she spoke. "I just did a quick visual search for any of the terms you gave me and only came up with this book."

"Well, which one did you find?" Mabel turned the book to face Asher, who was sitting next to her on the library floor.

"Amber Cellar." Asher looked over the page and one of the contents was a clipped in drawing of a room filled with small stones. The image was entirely black and white, but the attention to detail made mentally coloring it a simple task. "According to this report by, B.A. Bristle, a witch's house contained hundreds of these gemstones in an underground cellar, which was especially odd as none of the houses were ever meant to have a cellar.

"Huh." Mabel looked over at Asher, half expecting an explanation for his simple reaction. "I just figured the town was named Bristlewood because of all the pine needles and... uh... trees." Mabel kept a straight face momentarily before bursting into laughter and quickly cupping a hand over her mouth with large eyes. "Shh." Asher insisted, pressing a finger against his lips as he looked around them. Even though he knew something was off with everything, he couldn't help but feel more comfortable with the lie than he had with the truth.

"Wait, look at this." Mabel pointed at another journal clipping, which contained a small sketch of a heart symbol, shaped as if to be a cut gemstone. "Most ambers in the cellar were found to be pieces of lapidary, yet the art was never brought to Prosper, raising many questions as to how the gems were cut so close to perfection, yet the tools to do so did not exist." Mabel moved her forefinger down the page as she read. "This resulted in Prosper's witch hunt, as many of the settlers began to die of an unknown ailment and the number of those who died of the disease could be closely related to the number of gemstones gathered over an extended period of time. At one point, the number of gemstones was an exact match to the number of dead and the accused witch was hanged, but the deaths did not stop. Once the witch was executed people began to die at a faster rate and the Amber Cellar began to fill rapidly. B.A. Bristlewood declared this a state of emergency and requested from his superiors the necessary permissions to perform a mass execution-"

"But the town had been burned down before it could be done." Mabel looked up from the page to see Asher watching a ceiling fan spiral slowly above him.

"How did you know that?" Asher then turned to face Mabel and then the book.

"You already told me about it." Mabel clutched at the amulet once again and turned to the next page. "What does any of this have to do with the vampiric lore surrounding Bristlewood anyways?" Mabel sighed, flipped a few pages ahead of where she had been and once again turned the book to face Asher. His eyes grew wide as he looked down at the contents. The image of a dark figure clutching an illuminating object was shown. At the creature's feet was a man laying on the ground. His entire form was shaded in gray, except for his chest, where a small portion was left untouched in the shape of a heart. Asher then realized that the object in the creature's hand was the exact same shape.

"The Amber Heart." Mabel seemed to become more concerned as she read the document clipping. "Those who've had their soul removed through The Amber Heart would perish at the hands of the disease without mercy. This action was that of creatures known as Cor Sagina, who must feed on the souls of the living to better preserve themselves." Asher continued to look over the drawing as images of that night flashed across his eyes. "Drinking the blood of the living would allow this as well, but the effects were short-lived in comparison." He could see himself as the lifeless man in the drawing and Feeder as the creature clutching his soul. "Asher, are you alright?"

"None of this is real." He stood up without hesitating and started towards the front of the library, which was the furthest part of the building from where he was at the time. It was the first he had spoken these words out loud and hearing them as he rattled them off seemed to bring the reality of the sentence to life.

"Asher, where are you going?" Mabel was now yelling across the distance to get his attention, but he pushed on anyway, doing his best to ignore her as he removed his keys from his pocket.

"I have to go home, I have to find a way to stop him." He could now hear Mabel trying to catch up, but he was already at the door by the time her feet knocked against the carpet covered concrete and quickly made his way off the lot and towards his house. By this time, it was rounding 2:00 pm and his mother was home early, as he could see her blue car parked in its usual spot. Taking note on the car, he turned off his truck and shut the door quietly. On his way to the front door, he clutched his keys firmly in his right hand and took each step on his forefoot, trying to create only the smallest of sounds. He couldn't hear any movement as he placed his ear against the door, so without dwelling on it too long, he nudged it open, closed it behind himself and crept up to his room. Once there, he retreated to the desk against the far right wall of the room and started looking up as much information as he could on the subject. To his dismay, there was no information on The Amber Heart or Prosper that he could find. Now knowing that his mother was showering, Asher made his way out into the hall and remained as stealthily as he could. He knew his father was obsessed with the stories that shrouded Bristlewood and was confident that his father's office would have some kind of book on the subject somewhere on the many shelves he never seemed to touch anymore. Keeping an ear focused on the sound coming from the bathroom, Asher listened carefully to the jets of water, being sure that they didn't stop as he moved to the opposite side of the hall that his room was on, and opened the door to his father's office. The light was already on, which was a good sign as he wouldn't have to touch it and accidentally bring attention to himself. As he skimmed the shelves for a few moments, he heard two sounds that made his heart sink.

The water had stopped running in the bathroom and the doorbell downstairs was ringing.

"Who could that be?" He heard his mother say to herself. Quickly and without much thought, he rushed out of the room on his toes and accidentally slammed the door shut on his way out. "What the-" Asher dove into his room and shut the door carefully, just as his mother opened the bathroom door and scanned the hall. The bell chimed again and she sighed, walked back into the bathroom and shut the door, locking it this time. Asher knew she'd see his truck when she went to check the door and moved over to his bed, throwing off his jacket and his jeans as he slung himself beneath the covers, pretending to be asleep. After a few minutes, he heard his mother leave the bathroom for good, flipping the light switch as she did so and heading down the stairs to answer the door. The voice on the other side was muffled, but he could still make out what they were saying.

"Sorry to bother you, I just noticed someone was snooping about your front lawn and I wanted to make sure everything was alright."

"Everything is fine," his mother assured the voice, "it must have been my son coming home early is all. I'll call and let you know that everything is okay in a few minutes once I've checked around, alright?"

"Alright, Mrs. Coyle. Sorry to bother you an- oh, well, hello there." Confused, Asher slowed his breathing and sniffled hard to clear his nostrils so that he had no more distractions from the conversation beneath him.

"Ah, good to see you again, dear!" Asher heard the door close as his mother stepped out onto the porch to talk with whoever else had just shown up. At this point, with the door closed, there were too many walls separating him from the group and he couldn't make out what anyone was saying. After a few moments of laying there, his eyelids started to grow heavy, as if a fine powder were slowly weighing down his jet black lashes, but the front door opening and closing again moments later seemed to shake the powder loose. "I'm sure he's just resting, go on up and I'll make something to drink."

"Thank you, Mrs. Coyle." Asher felt his fingertips and scalp tingle as the feet carrying a familiar voice started to climb up the wooden steps.

"Damn!" Bolting upright, he looked around for where he had thrown his pants, but by the time he spotted them, slung over the handle of his closet door, the shadows of two feet were already being cast into the room. As the knob turned he stuffed his blanket beneath his thighs and was once again face to face with Mabel. She smiled softly as she made her way in the room.

"Hey."

"H-hey." Mabel came towards the bed as she looked around the room, but stiffened her neck for a moment when she noticed the pants. She then looked back at Asher with a single eyebrow raised and he fidgeted his eyes towards the pants himself. A smile spread across her face rapidly but she fought it as best she could, curling both lips inward as she walked over to the closet door and lifted the pants by sliding a finger through one of the belt loops. She then carried them over to Asher and handed them off, taking a seat in the desk chair and spinning it to face the laptop and the wall. Asher took advantage of the moment and pulled the jeans beneath the blankets, fighting with them to get his pants back on as fast as he could with little interference.

"So, did you find anything?" Distractedly, Asher looked over at the screen as he forced the button of his jeans through the small incision on the opposite flap. Once the sound of the zipper rang out, Mabel decided she was in the clear and turned to speak with him, face to face.

"What are you doing here?" The room fell silent for a few moments as Mabel strummed her fingers against the spine of a large worn book. "How did you get that out of the library?" She then looked down at the book and the smile returned to her face.

"I'm pretty good with words." Asher pretended he wasn't amused and returned to his original question. "I know you know something you aren't supposed to."

"'Aren't supposed to?'" Asher slid to the edge of his bed, opposite of Mabel and planted his feet on the ground. "It seems everyone else forgot something they shouldn't have, in my opinion." Mabel was silent as she looked back down at the book, turning it in her hands. "Even you are missing pieces." She stopped fiddling with the item and looked up at Asher, who was now shaking, both with rage and a fever.

"You should sit, you don't look well."

"You know exactly why that is too, don't you?" Once again, Mabel fell silent, the smile she usually carried being the furthest expression from what she currently wore. She rested the book on her knees and ran a finger over a lump at the height of her chest several times, seemingly thinking about what their next move was. Asher grew angrier as she did so, yet a sense of ease was washing over him. "Well, don't you?" Mabel nodded weakly, refusing to make eye contact. Asher huffed and walked towards his closet, opening it and rummaging about the contents in a crate on the floor.

"What are you looking for?"

"Something I can use to get my soul back. Something that will scare Feeder into surrendering it." Asher proceeded to throw the contents all around him, desperately looking for something he knew wouldn't be there.

"That's not how it works, A-"

"Then how does it work, Mabel? If that is who you really are." Asher was now standing and facing her once again, obvious displeasure was strewn about his face and body language. Mabel looked him over and her lip began to quiver as she did so. "Why are you messing with my head? Why are you letting everyone live in this illusion, including yourself?" A tear began to form in her eye as she slowly stood up, placing the book on Asher's bed as she did so. She then turned to face him and ran the sleeve of her hoodie across each rosy cheek as she approached him. Seeing her cry made him sick to his stomach, but he was certain it was part of the illusion that had been cast over all of them, including those he was certain couldn't be real. "People I know are missing from this place. Nothing here is my reality, none of these memories that these people have are real." A couple more tears made their way down her face as she looked up at him. She was clearly torn by his words, yet refused to let anything else show except heartbreak.

"You killed me." Asher's agitated expression relented as these shaky words swam around in his mind, seemingly hitting him for the first time as he became aware of how very few people would ever hear them. "You could at least let me have this place." The bedroom door came open once again, but neither of the two looked away from each other.

"Who wants a glass of tea and some-... oh no. Is everything alright?" Asher's mother took a delicate step into the room as if the entire thing were a sensitive situation. Mabel then wiped her face once again and put on a smile. She then turned to face his mother and made her way towards the hall.

"I'll take one of those cookies, to go." She sniffled and carefully removed one of the cookies from the platter, being sure not to touch others on the dish.

"Oh, honey, you can take more than that. Go ahead." Mabel smiled a little bigger and took a second cookie, thanking Mrs. Coyle weakly as she did so and biting into the first cookie as she started down the stairway. "Asher, what happened?" Asher was standing in the same position, Mabel's words still spiraling in his head. A single tear rolled down his cheek as he moved his eyes towards his mother, who rushed into the room and put the platter on the edge of the bed before embracing him. Tears began to stream down his face as she did so. The house was quiet. All that could be heard was Asher's faint cries and his mother's reassuring whispers, knowing not what he had done. "There, there. You two have been together for a while now. Things like this are bound to happen, but they don't have to be the last thing to happen."

Chapter Five: Budding Times

Colors of most every palette carried themselves at their ends, trying to be noticed and more vibrant than their neighbors as they kept organized and in line, desperate to best their most common peers in silence. Water droplets had formed on them as a metallic lining shimmered above, raining down on each head as it glided on to the next with certainty that it had done well at dampening everything below it. Asher looked over the crowd trying to decide for himself which color or colors would do the best. From the farthest on the left to those on the right, a large rainbow could be made out, taking up most of the black plastic shelving. The metallic arm hummed as it passed by, spraying a fine mist over the leaves and stems through the pedals as it did. He pulled his lip in on one side and examined the lush, lively potential before him. A second individual made their way over to him as he hopelessly continued the same process, scanning from left to right, hoping that something would pop out at him. The other watched him do so for a few moments before looking out at them as well.

"Is there something I can help you with?" Asher glanced over at the other, hardly having noticed them when they showed up. She smiled as she maintained eye contact. Asher started to speak but got hung up on his words, shaking his head at a sluggish rate and sighing. The young lady, a similar age to himself, examined his expression before acting. She then moved her long blond ponytail over her shoulder and brushed off the front of her apron. Asher glanced over again as he saw her pull free two large dark green rubber gloves from the front sleeve of the apron and sliding into them once they were free. "Here," she spoke as she made her way around to the opposite side of the table, "let me help you." Asher watched as the girl pulled free four roses, being sure to not shake off the moisture it had accumulated from the mister. She then moved towards the right end of the bowed table, plucking the same number of white tulips from a pot, which they had still been planted in, roots and all. "The red rose is a sign of apology and the white tulip, a sign of forgiveness." The girl looked back up at Asher with the same large smile across her brightly lit face, which made the low hanging lights beam back at him through her ocean blue eyes. She then returned to the work she had at hand and spun to face a smaller table on the far end of the building, which had a large glossy piece of a plastic banner hanging above it reading: The Florist's Greenhouse. Asher moved his head to one side, trying to see over her shoulder or around her, watching without moving as she removed several purple flowers from another pot. She carefully removed them from their roots with some sort of cutting tool similar to scissors. She then returned the tool to her belt and spun back in Asher's direction, exposing the curled petals as they sprang about in her hands. She proceeded to move them about the roses and tulips, encircling the others in a curly purple reef. She then came back around to Asher's side of the rainbow table, passing him as she did so and making her way over to a waist-high wooden post, which had several white plastic wrappings hanging from it. Freeing one, she took the bundle of flowers and carefully navigated them into the wrapping, pressing the stems through the bottom and using a rubber band to keep the wrapping and stems tightly bound together. "There you are."

"Thanks," Asher said, grateful for having a girl do the work he couldn't have done himself, "what are the purple ones called?"

"Oh," she exclaimed, realizing she failed to inform him of the final flower, "Hyacinths, a flower of sincere apology. I know the red rose means essentially the same thing, but whoever she is I'm sure she'll appreciate both." The girl raised herself on her toes and then planted her heels firmly on the ground once more, having both hands bundled together behind her back, obviously proud of her ability to help and her knowledge on her work. She then glanced back at the table they had previously both been at and inhaled sharply. As she made her way back over, Asher followed with the bouquet in hand. "How about a few of these?" She pressed the tips of her fingers beneath the brim of a white rose.

"What do they represent?" Asher questioned, more intrigued than he had ever thought he'd be at the meanings behind colorful weeds.

"Well, they have several meanings. Chastity and silence are a couple of them, but the most important is truth, at least in my opinion." Asher looked at the flower she had been examining and curled his lips.

"I think I'll settle with what I have for now." The girl looked back at him and acknowledged his expression.

"Okay, let's go get you rung up then."

Asher proceeded to leave the shop and made his way back across town trying to think of things to say but was clueless on the subject as he approached Mabel's home. He pulled into the driveway slowly, trying to give himself a few extra moments to think of something and a few extra moments to brace himself for whatever was to come. He then parked and exhaled soothingly through his nostrils, looking over at the flowers in the passenger seat before gathering them and making his way towards the front door of the single story home. Knocking on the door he found it hard to stop himself from smiling, never expecting this to be his next move, considering his current situation. He then ran his sleeve across his forehead and fanned himself with the bouquet, which was still cool from the roses, which were the only flowers he had gotten from the cooling display. He then sniffled and cleared his throat, trying to appear as healthy and lively as he could. Knocking once more, he heard footsteps approaching the door and straightened up his back. The door then cracked open a little less than a foot. Looking in, he could see Mabel peaking out. Once she recognized him, the one eye she exposed grew wide and she slammed the door. Asher was stunned yet not surprised. He began to turn as he heard a metal mechanism rattling about. His brain registered the sound to be that of a chain and he turned back to face the door. Just then, Mabel made her way out onto the front porch, quickly shutting the door behind her.

"W-what are you doing here?" Asher didn't answer her immediately. Instead, he offered her the flowers, which she hesitantly accepted, seemingly shocked to have them in her presence. Asher then pressed forward and embraced her, which was yet again something Mabel did not expect, but she didn't hesitate for quite as long this time and wrapped her arms around him as well. She proceeded to look about the flowers over his shoulder as her sense of concern faded away, soon to be replaced by a comforting warmth.

Mabel cracked the door open once again and placed the bouquet on an entertainment stand that was hardly visible through the gap, then they both made their way off the porch and into the clearing that was her front yard. She then lifted her hood and the pair of them made their way out towards a wooded area, still entirely made up of pines. The forest life seemed more active than Asher had ever remembered it being before. Birds hummed and chirped from almost every tree and the wind, which was nonexistent earlier that day had picked up, playing about with the green needles above. Asher and Mabel spoke as they walked along a dirt trail, which Asher assumed was something she did quite often, as the path was clear of debris and there was no grass in the center of the trail.

"What made you change your mind?" Mabel wondered as she traced the forest floor with her eyes, watching her feet as they passed in front of her. Asher examined her as she did so before looking up to see the sun's rays passing through the many arms of a large pine that stood directly ahead of them, blocking the sun's light from coming into contact as the trunk worked as a barricade against the majority of it. What strands did make it through were either to the left or the right of the path, hitting other trees and in a few places, the ground itself when it was visible through the canopy.

"You were right," Asher began, "yesterday when you said

that this is the least I could do. You were right." Asher looked to his left and at a slight downward angle, meeting with Mabel's eyes as she looked up at him with a victoriously satisfied expression, still relaxed and seemingly comforted by his words. Asher then brushed her knuckles with his as their hands swung by one another. Once his hand had reached the furthest point towards his back that it had freely swung to, he opened his fingers and on the return to his side he met with her once again, only this time her fingers had been opened in the same manner, making it even easier for him to slip his fingers between the gaps in hers. Once their fingers were locked together, Mabel rested her head on his shoulder and placed her other hand on the front of the same shoulder, stabilizing her head as they proceeded to walk further into the forest. Asher couldn't help but notice how pale her skin had been since the first day they met. The paint on her fingernails was still flawless and almost radiant against her skin as the red spots relaxed on contact with his body. He smiled and let his eyes explore them, feeling that he was finally finding his peace with this new life. Once they had reached the end of the trail and turned back the sun had begun to set, creating an almost tie-dye effect in the sky above.

"So, how long have we been dating, again?" Mabel giggled at

his question but kept her head against him. Asher assumed she was embarrassed by it and didn't want him to see it to be true. "Seems to have slipped my mind." She remained quiet a moment before speaking.

"Two months, since the time I knew I was moving here." Mabel then looked up at Asher, who became certain she'd been embarrassed after spotting the cherry color in her cheeks. "I visited once before moving and we ran into each other outside the grocery store. Been together since." Asher chuckled, accepting this jokingly but also somewhat legitimately. He knew it wasn't true but it *was* to everyone else around them. Mabel then returned her head to his shoulder, letting her hair flow over the front and back of his jacket.

The two continued to talk as they wandered back up the barren soils and into the yard, Asher followed Mabel to the front door and slid his hands in his pockets as she took the last couple of steps towards the entrance to her home before stopping with her palm pressed against the knob. She then turned to face Asher, who had a smile spread across his face the moment her eyes met his. She watched as his lips arched on both sides. Then, she rushed back to him at a speed he had never seen anyone move at before. Without realizing what was going on at first, his eyes grew wide before subconsciously reacting to the event and shutting immediately. Mabel's warm lips pressed themselves against his for a few moments before retracting. Her cheeks were a soft pink when she turned back towards the door, giving Asher one final look with lively eyes before closing herself inside. Asher's smile had left his face in the heat of the moment but returned almost instantaneously once he realized it was gone. He then turned and trotted down the three faded wooden steps which led to the landing and made his way back to his truck.

As he continued back towards town he looked out the passenger window, watching as the last of the red sun crept behind the mountains. He was then surrounded by the gray ambient light that took over every late summer night he had ever known. As he continued on his way, the clouds above began to take on the same shade, signaling the demise of the dark blue afternoon atmosphere. Asher admired it for a few moments before his headlights automatically kicked on, flooding over the road and bordering trees. As the lights clicked on and a blue glow illuminated from the dash, Asher glanced back at the street and swiftly crushed the brake pedal beneath his foot. The tires screeched as the truck swerved to the right having nearly collided with a dark figure, which stood in the center of the asphalt. As the blinding eyes of the truck lost sight of the figure, Asher hit gravel. Noticing the change in audio he spun to face the front of the vehicle, almost forgetting about the figure as his concerns turned to his own safety. His head then jerked forward and back again, the sound of wood forcefully cracking taking over the rumbling of the stones below. The truck had stopped on impact, leaving Asher dazed with small white and black spots blocking his vision. Disoriented by the blow he rubbed his neck and felt about the floor in front of him. A cold plastic surface came in contact with his fingers. Now having his phone in hand, Asher raised it to his face and hit the power button, filling the cockpit with a faint blue light. Just as he was about to call for help he looked out the windshield again, noticing a familiar post which was now only held up on the left side. The beams that had been holding it up were all he could see as the headlights sat too low for the rest of it. Asher flipped on the flashlight his phone offered and aimed it at the sign. He was at the entrance of the Prominent Peak trail. Being aware that he was alright, he opened the driver side door and stepped out, pointing the light at the road he had come from. His tire tracks were obvious, but the figure he nearly hit was not.

"Hello?" Asher used his phone to scan over the entire

opening and down both directions of the road. The night grew eerier as the headlights of his truck began to flicker and the engine sputtered. "No, no, no, no!" Asher stopped walking towards the road and rushed back towards his truck to try keeping it running, but just as he was about to reach the door a large black cloud of smoke whipped through the air and slammed into his chest, knocking him off his feet and further from his truck than he was before. As his back hit asphalt the mass of smoke began swirling overhead rapidly and was soon joined by three others.

"You shouldn't have bothered coming to see her." Asher lifted his head off the ground and turned towards the voice to find that it was Feeder. The smoky creatures above him continued to swirl and laughed at Asher as he struggled to get up. "After what you did to her, you come all this way just to cave into her new life due to your well-deserved guilt?"

"What do you want with me?" Asher managed to roll over and lift himself up on one knee as Feeder sneered in his direction.

"You'll find out in time, or perhaps you won't at all, Cor." The continuous laughing from above began to fade as the smoky figures funneled upward and then dispersed in different directions. By the time Asher turned away from them, Feeder was gone too. The squeaking and chirping of bats were all that remained as Asher got back up and limped to his truck, which was miraculously still running. Without bothering to search for them again, he hopped into the driver's seat and backed away from the sign, doing anything he could to calm his nerves and avoid distractions as he drove the rest of the way home. The squeaking of a single bat continued to ring in his ear during the drive, but never once did he catch a glimpse of the creature.

Chapter Six: Binary Anomaly

Asher heaved into a small trash can as his stomach did flips in the night. He was sure not to get any of the contents on the blankets that held snug against his shivering body. As he wretched again, for the third time that night, a switch in the hall flipped on sending a beam of light through the crack at the bottom of his door. Asher paid little attention to the light as he focused on the can he was holding to his face. He could hear the knob jiggle and the heavy wooden door creak open on the old hinges. He tried to look over the lip of the container but only caught a glimpse of who was there before he convulsed again.

"Oh, poor thing." His mother sighed and quietly made her way over to him, rubbing his back as she carefully sat on the mattress, trying not to cause him any more discomfort than he was already in. She then put her hand against his head with her palm away from him, then turned it to have her palm against him. "I'll call the doctor in the morning. I know he said a few days but it's been a couple now and you're only getting worse."

"No, mom," Asher managed as he swallowed hard and took in a painful breath, "it'll pass." She sighed again as a look of pity crossed her face. Asher hadn't actually seen the expression, having been preoccupied, but he knew it was there. The light from the hall comforted him as his stomach started to settle and his mother remained at his side for a few more minutes, rubbing his back and running a damp rag across his face, which had been sitting in a bowl of water on his bed stand

"Just call me if you need anything. Take the day away from school, too. You shouldn't be going in this condition." Asher knew she was right, but he intended to do better this year and already decided against staying home. His mother then stood and crept back into the hall, which Asher assumed was to avoid waking his father.

After a few moments of being alone, he sat the bucket on the floor next to his bed, disgusted with it. He then pulled a finely beaded metal chain that hung from a lamp resting on the same bed stand as the bowl of water, and a yellow glow illuminated the room. The first thing his eyes met when the light came on was the book still sitting at the foot of his bed.

"Doesn't seem like I'll be getting any more sleep tonight anyhow," Asher thought to himself, *"might as well."* He proceeded to lift the book, which seemed far heavier than before in his weakened state. The pages opened and separated with ease, seemingly from years of neglect and use, which was obvious by the yellowing state they were in. He proceeded to flip through the journal entries and unique clippings that were encased in the leather binding, searching for things that were relative to what he was going through. After a few seconds of searching, he found the image of the dark figure holding The Amber Heart. He ran his finger down the page, examining the same piece of writing Mabel had read to him and then passing his finger beneath it to learn more. *"'Sagina and Vampires'?"* Asher reread the title for a moment and continued thinking to himself, *"How didn't I put those two together already?"* He continued beyond the title and started to read the

segment of text, which was a part of the actual page and not an additional piece that had been stitched or pasted in like many others were. The writing was worn with age and some of it was even undecipherable, but he got the gist of what was being said as he continued to go over the words with his finger guiding the way. *'The Witch of Prosper, hanged on June 06, 1506, without trial is the said cause of supernatural creatures being unleashed in the settlement of Prosper.'* Asher scoffed and sniffled as he read this part, keeping his solo conversation in his head. *"Who else would they blame?"* He continued to read after making this remark. *'During her execution, she begged the other settlers to give her a chance to redeem herself, saying that she would lift the curse that was brought down on them, but she wasn't granted the opportunity out of fear that she may make it worse out of spite and was silenced during her plea.'* Asher skimmed the handwriting over a few lines and begun studying it again. *'The disease spread rampantly after the hanging and settlers started telling stories of creatures in the night, removing the light from the living and proceeding to their next victim without hesitation. This resulted in vivisepulture, as the individuals who had been exposed to the creature would be found outdoors the following morning and were assumed to have been claimed by the disease. Prosper began surface burials to avoid this, keeping coffins above the ground until Death's odor loomed.'* Asher's stomach began to turn again, so he skipped the rest of the section and moved on to another, marked by a sketch of a fanged man with sunken eyes and cheeks, titled *'The First Parasite'*. *'Above is a detailed drawing of the first Sagina to be discovered. Adelram Sagina, who the name Sagina originated from. Adelram referred to his victims as 'Cor', once he claimed the light from them.'* Asher paused and remembered Feeder calling him the same thing, confirming that Feeder was *his* parasite. Slightly relieved with knowing that Feeder couldn't hurt him, he proceeded to read the passage and found his relief to be short-lived. *'Adelram had been cornered by several settlers one night after he successfully claimed the light of a young girl named Elyse Bristle, daughter of B.A. Bristle. In an effort to escape, he fled to the abandoned witch's hut and was staked several times as the settlers followed his shadowy form inside. Many lost their lives prematurely in the altercation, but another, more horrific discovery was made. The light a Sagina took from the living was identical to The Amber Heart. This confirmed their theories on the Amber Cellar's contents and the deaths that shrouded the settlement. Before Adelram had been murdered, he surrendered the names of many others who he claimed to be Sagina, so many in fact, that his claim had panicked the remaining settlers, who burned the settlement down the night before the mass execution could be processed and fled, certain they would enrage any Sagina that survived the burning. Several settlers had been found during the following week in odd locations throughout the bordering forest. Some suspect that the burning caused their illnesses to worsen immediately as their Amber Hearts- souls, perished along with the settlement. No trace of The Amber Hearts could be found after newcomers came across B.A. Bristle's journals, which had been rediscovered after the settlement of Bristlewood was well underway and where the settlement got its name. The assumptions that were written about could not be confirmed due to the missing Hearts and the disease soon disappeared along with them.'* Asher felt he had enough information to process over the next thirty or so minutes before school and closed the book. As he did so, he felt a lump in the backside of the cover. Turning the book over, he noticed a bulge at the base of the leather work, where a seam had been made only a few inches across. Curiosity had gotten the best of him at this point. Getting to his feet he made his way over to his desk and opened the only drawer it had on the left side and pulled free a pair of scissors. He then returned to his bed and began to poke at the binding, trying not to damage the book itself as he opened the old wound. Once the scissors had separated the leather covering from the firm material inside, Asher squeezed the handles together and the rope-like stitches gave way. A thick piece of folded parchment slid out as the seam surrendered and landed on Asher's lap. Asher sat the book down on the stand and jumped as his alarm clock rang out. He slapped the button atop the digital frame and examined the parchment for a moment, acknowledging the amount of effort that had gone into the piece of twine holding it shut. He could tell that someone had put a great amount of work into the contents, but he was holding himself to his own word, that he had enough to process for now, and stuffed it in the pocket of the jeans he had laid out on his dresser for school that day, deciding he would examine the works the first chance he got.

The air outside was crisp that morning and wildlife was abnormally quiet. The occasional chirp made its way through the empty space above Asher's head and he pulled the string of his hood tightly to keep his body heat in. Before long, he could hear the sound of someone else making their way up behind him as he continued to walk towards the school, which was still a fair distance away, not even being in sight yet.

"Hey, wait up!" The voice was that of Kyden, who Asher

hadn't given much thought too over the weekend, having been preoccupied with seemingly everything else around him. "Wait." Kyden was huffing as he jogged the rest of the distance that separated them before stopping to rest his hands on his knees and catch his breath. "There you are."

"Are you alright?" Asher was growing more and more concerned the longer it took Kyden to answer and stopped to face him, looking in the direction he had come, just in case he had been running from something.

"Yeah," he panted, "was just trying to catch up." He then stood back up and huffed, motioning with a hand to tell Asher he could keep walking, sort of pushing away the air in front of him with it a few times. "I thought you would be at home, taking your truck or something. I was going to hitch a ride but your mom said you already left."

"I just needed to get some fresh air. Not ready to waste the gas every day, sorry." Kyden shrugged as he proceeded to breathe like a dog under a hot sun.

"It's fine, but what made you decide to go today?" Asher returned the shrug and didn't answer. "Come on, what's up?" Kyden nudged Asher with his shoulder and looked around to see if anyone else was near, seemingly to try keeping the conversation private.

"It's nothing, just got a lot on my mind is all."

"Ah, something with Mabel, huh?" Kyden lifted his brow a few times in a quick motion as he glanced over at Asher from the corner of his eye. Asher smiled and shook his head.

"It's nothing like that, but yeah, it's got something to do with her."

"Uh-hu." Kyden chuckled and turned his head forward, cocking it and letting the smile somewhat slip away over a short period. He then narrowed his eyes and nudged Asher again. "Hey, who's that?" Asher looked towards Kyden, slightly annoyed that he had elbowed him again and then turned to where his eyes were locked. On the far end of the street and heading towards the school just as they were was another individual who stood about the same height as them, being about six feet tall. He had been wearing all black, from his jeans to his heavy jacket and the black cloth that covered the lower half of his face. The figure seemed to be looking for or avoiding something that neither of them could see before darting off the sidewalk and into a neighboring yard. "You think he's up to no good?" Kyden seemed slightly startled by the man but tried playing it off as if he were only curious. Asher ignored his question and shook his head, pressing on without giving the man a second thought. He had many other things on his mind and didn't want to add to the list. Kyden did the same and only looked behind them occasionally, as if to be sure the guy didn't try anything when they weren't paying attention.

The two made their way to the school and Kyden split off from Asher as he did every morning prior, heading down the left hall and hollering over his shoulder that he'd see Asher at lunch. Asher hollered back and went down the right hall towards Mr. Benner's room, but stopped at his locker to pick up his things. He felt a hand lightly brush his shoulder and could see another student's shadow cast over the white locker doors beside him.

"Hey there." Asher smiled and turned to face Mabel, who had rested her back against the metal doors next to his locker. She was already smiling when he met her eyes, which were filled with the colors that surrounded her, as they always were. He then embraced her and she did the same, but with a hint of pity. "You seem worse today." Asher moved away long enough to put a large history textbook beneath his arm and then got close to her again.

"I'll be alright," he insisted, "I know how to fix it." He kept his warm smile and Mabel took comfort in it. He could tell she was still worried for him and he was too. He knew he couldn't stop Feeder on his own but he wanted to keep her at ease for as long as he could.

"Well, I'll see you in class. Okay? Let me know what you're thinking first chance we get to talk." Asher nodded and pecked her on the cheek. Mabel then started towards homeroom and Asher returned to the contents of his locker.

Just as he had shut the door and looked away from it, clanging it against the silver frame, the hairs on the back of his neck stood up and he froze in place. At the end of the hall was the same man from the street, watching over each student that came through the side entrance of the building as he kept himself tucked against the wall and the left swinging door, just out of sight of anyone who was making their way in. He scanned over each person that appeared, seemingly still searching for whatever it was he clearly hadn't found outside. Asher wasted no time confronting the man, who seemed rather youthful, even from the distance he was at. Nudging through the crowd with his hand guiding the way, Asher made his way stealthily over to the entrance, but just as he had come within ten feet of the man he had been spotted. The man shot his attention in Asher's direction and his sunken grayish eyes grew wide. A small amount of blond hair was visible beneath his hood and Asher became certain he knew who the man was as a sense of familiarity came over him. As the guy sprang out the door, almost knocking over a couple of female students who had been unaware of his presence, Asher shot out after him, brushing passed the girls who had just recollected themselves.

"Hey!" Asher shouted at the man as he proceeded to run around the corner of the building, leading towards the back area of the public grounds. Asher knew that if he let the man out of his sight for too long he would lose track of him, as the backside of the school was made up of several smaller buildings which sat close to the primary building and a football field furthest away, just before the pines took over. With this in mind, he pushed himself to move faster even in his weakened state and listened for the sound of someone running once he rounded the corner himself. When a sound did finally break the silence, it wasn't that of footsteps. He could hear the rattling of a chain link fence. Knowing this meant that the man had made his way to the football field, Asher sprinted between two of the smaller buildings, which created an alleyway with a large dumpster blocking where the alley ended. Behind the dumpster was part of the fence, as the side of the buildings that faced towards the football field were also concession stands during games and events. He listened carefully, being sure that the man was trying to climb the fence before doing so himself. *thump! thump!* The sound of someone dropping all of their weight on the ground was clear and Asher swiftly made his way atop the dumpster. He crouched and remained still as he listened to the hasty footsteps approach his part of the fence. Once they were almost directly ahead of him, Asher dove off the dumpster and over the fence, colliding with the man and sending him barreling across the ground. Asher did the same but was quick to make a move after landing on his stomach. He started to stand and found his arms in a jelly-like state. The man noticed he was struggling and threw his hands to his sides to push himself off his back. Asher thought quickly and kicked off with his feet while still being unable to lift himself.

"Ack!" The man exhaled hard as Asher's weight knocked the wind out of him. Finally having caught him, Asher spun about to face him without getting off. The man cradled his chest and expressed pain across what amount of his face Asher could see before he ripped the mask off and gasped.

"Dennis!?" The man's eyes shot open, seemingly forgetting that he had been struggling to breathe. He then looked at Asher in awe.

"Y-you remember me?" Dennis coughed and inhaled harshly as Asher got off and plopped down next to him, still clutching the black cloth in his hand.

"You're 'awake' too?" Asher couldn't help but notice that Dennis had lost a few pounds and was looking rough in the face. His clothes were dirty, which was very much unlike Dennis, who came from a wealthy family and was one to show that wealth in what he wore. "What happened to you?" Dennis gulped and Asher could tell his throat was dry by the raspy breaths he was taking.

"I can't stay here. You can't tell anyone you saw me." Dennis tried to reach for the makeshift mask but Asher pulled it away. Dennis seemed annoyed and glared at him briefly before his face began to relax. He didn't look away from Asher as this happened.

"He got you, didn't he?" Asher was stunned, not knowing what to say yet knowing exactly who and what Dennis was talking about. "He did." Dennis's eyes filled with rage and fear at the same time and he shook his head as he slowly found his feet. "That means there are more now."

"More what?" Asher tried standing as well, but fell into a coughing fit and went down on his hands and knees. Dennis crouched in front of him and spoke with sympathy in his voice.

"You know what. Come on, we need to talk." Dennis put out a hand but Asher didn't accept it right away, still coughing and wheezing. He began to grow fearful himself after spitting out a small amount of blood. He then reached out for Dennis and balanced himself when he was up, which was difficult in the dizzy state the fit put him in. Dennis sighed and shook his head before bending back down. Asher was using the cloth to wipe off his face when he noticed that Dennis had retrieved the folded piece of parchment.

"That's mine!" Asher snatched the parchment out of Dennis's grasp and kept it in his own as he finished cleaning up.

"Sorry. Listen, we have to get out of here now. You'll be in danger if he sees you with me."

"I'm already in danger." Asher sniffled and tossed the cloth aside, watching over the building as Dennis had been doing. "Where have you been?" Dennis became tense and reluctant to answer.

"I tried to stop him." Dennis grabbed Asher by his arm and directed him towards the field's entrance, never turning away from the school. The bell signaling the beginning of class rang out and Asher remembered telling Mabel he'd be there, but knew Dennis couldn't go back inside with him, so he stuck at Dennis's side as they left the field quickly.

The two then made their way out into the woods behind the school so that Dennis could explain further and after several minutes of rough hiking, Asher noticed a small square structure made of large gray bricks. He studied it as they approached and noticed that the door was the only entrance to the thing, with there being no windows or a chimney poking out elsewhere. Dennis wasn't as hesitant as him and proceeded in the direction of the building. Once they made their way up the remaining hill segment they had been climbing, Dennis opened the door, which creaked eerily and had nothing to show but darkness beyond it.

"Welcome, to my new home." Dennis was clearly displeased with the distraught block but saw no reason to justify it. Asher was now the one who felt pity, as this was far from the life Dennis had known growing up. He made his way inside without a word and squinted upon entering. The room had no light source to be seen, but once Dennis was inside he lifted a small blue tarp covering a milk crate and pulled out a wind-up lantern. He then cranked it several times and hung it from a hook in the low ceiling. The room was fairly clean for what it was and Asher sat down on a wooden rocking chair. Dennis sat opposite of him on a cot, leaving the two separated by a turned over metal tub that was being used as a table. Asher continued to look about for a few moments before Dennis broke the silence. "What do you know?" Asher turned his eyes away from the barren stained walls and nervously looked over Dennis before resting them on the flipped tub.

"I know about The Amber Heart or Amber Hearts, Prosper and their leader B.A. Bristle, the Sagina, the witch that made them-"

"That's plenty, but it isn't what I'm looking for." Asher blinked several times in a single second, being caught off guard by Dennis's strange personality change. He wasn't the same guy he'd known for so many years. This Dennis was cold, paranoid, and now a hermit. "Do you know about Feeder?" Asher nodded slowly, not breaking his gaze from that of his friend's.

"He's the reason I'm ill." Dennis grunted in agreement and scanned over Asher's shivering frame.

"Here, let me make you a drink." Dennis twisted his back to reach behind the cot and pulled free a small yellow box. When he opened it, Asher could make out the contents. "I don't have any sugar, but I can make you a cup of tea to warm you up some. Asher accepted and Dennis stepped out of the room for a moment to fetch a bucket that had been sitting on the low roof above the door. Asher peered into the bucket, inspecting it for anything that wasn't sanitary but saw nothing. Once Dennis was back inside with the pail, he poured it into a metal pot and moved over to the back side of the room, opposite of where the door was. He proceeded to pull a brick loose from the bottom of the wall where Asher could see a small burn pile. The small fire pit was just outside the building and Asher could only assume that this was how Dennis stayed warm during the night. Dennis proceeded to place the filled pot over the hole on a filthy grill top and began striking a metallic rod against another of a different sort. The result was repetitive sparking, which Dennis angled into the base of the small pit. After a few attempts, a small flame made itself known, flicking about as Dennis threw in twigs and leaves he had gathered and brought in sometime before. "You know, I actually have no clue when he came about." Asher had been so distracted by the odd fireplace that he'd completely forgotten they were talking. "Feeder, I mean. I never thought we were truly related, just some guy who must have been a part of the family through marriage or something." A short time passed in silence as the tea brewed, giving the smoke a chance to seep inside. Asher didn't mind this though, as the smoke was warm and not nearly enough to make him uncomfortable. He had been lost in thought as it came through anyway.

"Why did you bring me here?" Dennis was silent. "You must have had a reason, otherwise you'd have just ran off without me." He then huffed and plopped back down on the cot. "I just want to pretend like things are going back to normal and get back to class."

"You know you can't do that." Asher didn't reply, being slightly confused and slightly accepting of the statement. "If you try living your life like nothing is wrong, you'll die. Your illness will take over and in only a brief period, it'll claim you too." Dennis leaned back on the cot and rested his head on a thin yellowish pillow. "Not that that will be a problem. I know you, your curiosity won't allow you to act like everything is okay and I believe that me showing up today gave you all the reason you needed to keep looking for answers."

"Where did the others disappear to?" Dennis stopped mid-breath as Asher broke his own silence.

"Others?"

"Yeah, the three guys that sat with us at the lunch table on the first day and the girl that was with them?" Dennis paused yet again before getting up and pulling the pot inside.

"I thought it was odd that I hadn't seen them at Bristlewood High, but I just assumed I'd overlooked them."

"They never came back as far as I'm aware and nobody else seems to even know they existed." Dennis poured the brown liquid into a clear glass, then extended his arm for Asher to accept it, which he did.

"I'd say Feeder got to them too, but he was a little more merciful. At least he gave you a chance to live."

"How?" Nothing from the book told Asher that he was going to live, so this was a stimulating thing to hear.

"When a Sagina claims The Amber Heart, they typically give it to someone else in an effort to create more like themselves." Dennis poured himself a glass and sat the pot on the makeshift tabletop. "That means they have two choices. One, they give the Heart over to someone who is willing to accept it, likely someone with no other choice. Or two, they keep the Heart for themselves and avoid feeding off the living for an extended period."

"How does that mean I have a chance to live?" Dennis had a puzzled look on his face before shaking his head.

"I said he *gave* you a chance, I didn't say you still have it." Dennis then took a sip from his glass, but Asher had sat his own down, agitated by the remark. "If he'd have given your Amber Heart to another, he would still be feeding on people and you'd have a chance to reclaim your Heart before it was ultimately drained of its light, your soul. You'd just have to kill the Newborn Sagina that had been given your Heart." Asher was amused. Dennis was acting as if it were easy to kill these things. Images of being carried around like a small animal and blurred figures flashing around him at lightning speed crossed his mind.

"What makes you so sure he isn't feeding anymore?" Dennis narrowed his eyes and licked his lips, whisking away what tea had missed them. He then leaned forward, having moved back to the cot to sit, and began rolling up his sleeve. Asher's blood ran cold as he examined several small puncture wounds, each of which had another nearby and at a set distance. There were three sets of the marks moving further up his arm as they went. Each of the wounds had a dark layer of tissue over them and looked as if they were infected, but still healing.

"I'm the one he's been feeding on."

Chapter Seven: Ever-changing Reality

Asher was silent throughout the night and the same few thoughts circled his mind with each creeping hour. *"How are we supposed to stop him? Does he know we're up to something? Why hadn't Dennis warned me about him? He probably thought I'd think he was crazy... and he's right. Is Mabel worried about me?"* Asher removed his cellphone from his pocket and turned on the screen, but as he had expected, there were no messages. He hardly acknowledged that he had the thing, but still kept it around just in case something went wrong like before.

"You know, you didn't have to stay here with me." Asher turned the screen off again and peered through the darkness. Opposite of the tub, Dennis could be heard breathing calmly, as if partially asleep. Asher put his head back down against the filthy pillow Dennis offered him earlier on and adjusted his back against the dirt-covered concrete, being sure to keep the thin blanket tucked beneath him.

"The last thing you need is to be alone again another night." Dennis half laughed and half scoffed briefly before Asher heard him rolling over on the cot, seemingly turning to face the wall.

"Not like it's anything I haven't gotten used to." Asher ignored his reply and simply thanked himself for staying in the woods overnight.

As morning approached, Asher stood and stretched to try softening up the tense muscles in his back. He then gathered up his socks and shoes and creaked open the old door, trying not to wake Dennis in the process. The air outside was weightless, unlike the air in the room and a thin morning fog coated the ground, dispersing with each step he took through it. As per usual, the forest life was very active again and seemingly more so now that Asher was further in the woods than he'd usually be when he'd hear the birds begin their morning melodies at home. Admiring each tree trunk and the branches that spanned out overhead from afar, Asher decided it was the perfect time to explore the area some. Even in his fragile state, he couldn't ignore the calling and ventured around the small block building, taking each step with caution so as to avoid making any unnecessary noise. Once he had made his way to the backside of the building he noticed a plot on the ground which spanned the entire length of the cinder block hut, both in length and in width. Green stems poked out through the fog from the plot, covered entirely in the morning mist. Each stem had several thin but lengthy leaves protruding from them, all angled in an upward position and growing rather close to the center stem. Asher got closer to the plants, being sure he didn't step on any as he moved about but still had no luck identifying them.

"Pretty good, huh?" Asher jumped and spun to face the building. Dennis had made his way outside and was leaning against the corner on the right as he scanned the leafy stems. "Typically wards them off and even comes into use when it doesn't." He finished his sentence and approvingly nodded at the plants.

"What is it?"

"Garlic. All of em." He then pointed at Asher's feet. Asher looked down and noticed that he was pushing the base of one plant to the side. He quickly readjusted his footing and the plant began to straighten out again.

"Where's the top part of them?" Asher looked over the plants once again, now recognizing them in a form he wasn't used to.

"The bulbils, you mean? I cut them off for replanting and powders."

"Powders?" Dennis nodded. Asher then took his gaze away from the plants and Dennis for a moment, noticing something else he hadn't spotted before. A round stone birdbath had been resting nearly a foot away from the back of the hut, seemingly untouched and still filled to the brim with water from the last rainfall. Dennis noticed what Asher had directed his attention towards and shrugged.

"It works well too." Just then, Asher's cellphone began to

buzz as an alarm he had set the night before went off, telling him it was time to get ready for school.

"I've got to go soon. You'll still be here when I get back, right?" Dennis nodded and folded his arms across his chest, seemingly distressed. "Okay, I'll be sure to stop by after school." Asher headed back inside and threw his hoodie on as he pushed his hair down against his head. He could tell it looked rough from sleeping on the floor but he didn't care much at the time. He then made his way back outside and started retracing the steps they took the day before stopping and turning to face Dennis one last time. "Oh, by the way, what is it you were looking for when I spotted you?" A look of defeat crossed his eyes, but Dennis held his lips straight, expressing as little emotion as he could.

"Feeder," he muttered, "but it was a bad time to spot him." Dennis then uncrossed his arms and walked inside, closing the door as he did so and leaving Asher out on his own.

The walk was brief as Asher made his way back to the football field, but he chalked this up as a result of his return being a mostly downhill trip. He then proceeded to make his way across the parking lot just outside of the field entrance and passed the smaller schooling buildings, which all sat empty and silent as it was still far too early for other students to be making their way to class at the time. The thin fog from Dennis's hideout was far thicker in town, as Bristlewood sat in the middle of a hilly valley and was often subject to both muddy and foggy weather. Asher paid the weather little mind as he came to the side of the main building, passing the doors he had caught Dennis behind and reaching the corner just in time to see a few other students making their way through the doors. As he got closer to the other students, he noticed that Kyden was a part of the small crowd. Asher thought it was odd to see Kyden at school so early, as he always waited for Asher in one way or another before bothering to show up. Asher shook it off, as he too was there far earlier than he'd usually be under any other circumstances and assumed it was just some sort of coincidence. *"Must finally be taking this place seriously eh, Kyden?"* Asher smirked at his own thought and shuffled over to the stone stairway leading up to the main hall entrance and sat at the bottom step. By the time he had reached the doors, Kyden was already inside. Asher knew Kyden's homeroom teacher from a previous year and was sure she wouldn't let him hang out there for a few before the school day started, so he didn't bother to head in after him, having assumed that that's where he went.

Before long several other groups of students made their way and began filling up the schoolyard, as many students waited for the first bell to ring before bothering to make their way in and stood outside to talk to friends instead. Asher remained outside as well, but not for the same particular reason. He was waiting on Mabel, who still hadn't replied to his apology for not attending class the day before. After a few more minutes of waiting the first bell rang and students began to fill into the school. None of them greeted Asher or even really acknowledged him, which he found odd as he was commonly spoken to or waved at by others on the way in each morning. He ignored the strange occurrence and stretched his neck to see around and over the crowd, but to no avail. *"Did she already go in? Maybe she isn't here today."* Asher sighed and kicked himself for not returning the day prior to see her as he said he would, but also found it irrational for her to be so upset with him over something so simple. Once he was sure she wasn't in the crowd or heading towards the school still, he made his way through the doors after all the other students had and rushed to his locker to get his things ready for the day. Asher turned the corner and caught a glimpse of something that hadn't been there before. On the handle to his locker was a piece of heavy yellow plastic with a metal bar in the shape of an upside down "U" on top of it. It was a school-issued lock. Asher was puzzled by this, as these locks were only for lockers that were currently not in use. As Asher studied the lock and cursed his luck the final bell rang. He puffed and rushed down the hall to get to homeroom before the door was shut and spotted Mr. Benner closing it just as he made the turn.

"Wait, I'm here!" Mr. Benner seemed confused when he heard Asher's shouts and left the door partially open with himself being the only thing blocking Asher out of the room. He smiled as Asher sped across the tile floor, trying to respect the rules in front of a teacher and not run.

"Good morning, young man."

"Morning, Mr. Benner." Asher stopped at the door and waited for Mr. Benner to let him in, but he didn't move.

"Can I help you with something?" Asher cocked his head back and scruffed up his brow as he studied Mr. Benner's face. He then tipped his head to the left and looked passed him, examining the students inside and being sure he was in the right place.

"Th-this is my homeroom. It has been for weeks now." Asher continued to glance up at Mr. Benner as he looked through the small gap. He quickly noticed that the conjoined desks on his right were both empty. Mabel hadn't made it to school and a sense of sadness began to mix in with his confusion.

"I'm sorry, what's your name?" Asher was dumbstruck and shot Mr. Benner a look of offense.

"Mr. Benner, it's me, Asher. We've known each other for a few years now." Mr. Benner seemed slightly ashamed, but also in disbelief as he lifted a roster up to his face and pulled a pair of reading glasses from the pocket on his shirt. He then studied each name and paused to point at one.

"Ah, Asher Coyle. Huh, you know, you're the fifth student this year to end up on a roster like this?" Asher's heart sank as he began to realize what was happening. He then looked beyond Mr. Benner one last time and saw several faces looking back at him. No one spoke up to oppose what Mr. Benner was saying and everyone seemed just as lost as he had. Asher's eyes then narrowed when he noticed that another seat was empty and becoming more visible as

Mr. Benner let the door open. Feeder wasn't in class either. "The only difference is you actually made it in." Mr. Benner chuckled but the look of confusion and apology remained. The door was now wide open and Mr. Benner was waiting for Asher to step inside, but he didn't.

"I-I'm sorry. I'd like to go speak with the Principle and make sure my schedule is right."

"Oh, that's alright. We can call him using the phone line in the room, that way you aren't wandering the halls.

"No, I'd really rather speak to him in person." Asher took a step back and Mr. Benner took a step out into the hall, almost as if he would be willing to pull Asher in by force if he had to.

"Okay, but I can't let you go before attendance is taken and Principle Lough wouldn't appreciate me letting a student go anywhere right now as it's a safety violation and-" Asher didn't wait to hear what Mr. Benner had left to say and cut him off by darting back the way he came. Mr. Benner shouted for him to come back and briefly followed but was far too slow to keep up. Asher sprinted down the main hall where his locker used to be and burst through the doors. An alarm sounded as he did so but he ignored it and pressed on. His heart felt as if it were on fire and his lungs were the same, but he didn't stop until he was back behind the woodline. The alarm was still ringing and he could hear someone on the intercom insisting for everyone to remain calm, but that was all he caught on his way back to the hut in the woods.

Upon his arrival, the fog had cleared and he could see that several plants were plucked from the ground in a neat fashion. He stopped to catch his breath again, wheezing as he did so. Just as his hands had hit his knees he could hear the wooden door creaking. Moments later, Dennis was rounding the corner and staring at him with the same look of defeat across his face that he had earlier on.

"He did it, didn't he?" Asher nodded and tears began to fill his eyes. Dennis took heavy steps towards him and wrapped his arms around Asher firmly. "Don't worry, we'll get him for this. For you and me both, he'll pay." Dennis let Asher go and led him inside. Tears were still streaming down his face as he thought about all that had been taken from him and all that he still wasn't sure of.

"Do my parents still remember me? Do I still have a home or is this my future, too?" It then hit Asher that this was exactly how Dennis had felt for weeks before finding out that Asher remembered him and several more tears filled his eyes.

"What else happened?" Dennis stopped comforting Asher and began moving around the small room gathering several items from various places, including a plastic jug filled with brownish water, a large duffel bag that clattered about when he lifted it and appeared to have weight to it, and the same backpack he used to take to school, which also appeared to contain something heavy and smelled strongly of garlic.

"He took Mabel." Dennis stopped moving once he was seated again and Asher held his breath for several short periods, trying to avoid the strong odor that now filled the room.

"Are you sure?" Dennis seemed to be in a hurry, which Asher noticed immediately and began speaking as rapidly as he could.

"She wasn't at school and neither was he. She hasn't talked to me since yesterday morning and I can feel it in my gut that something is wrong." Dennis was silent for a few moments as his eyes drifted from focusing on Asher to coasting across the floor. He then nodded his head slowly and let out a long breath before lifting the duffel bag from his side and placing it on the tub.

"That's all I needed to know." Asher watched Dennis unzip the bag and begin sorting through large wooden sticks, seemingly getting a count of them. Asher wiped the rest of his face clean and sniffled, trying to push back the recent events and keep focused on what was happening around him.

"What are those?"

"Stakes." Dennis pulled one out of the bag and tossed it towards Asher, who caught it and began examining the object. One end had a small notch carved out of it with some kind of knife and the other end was sharpened into a point. He could tell that a lot of work had been put into each stake as even the bark was removed. Asher assumed this was to give them all a similar shape and girth down the entire body. "Drench one in this before you use it and they won't stand a chance." Dennis lifted the jug and shook it before putting it on the tub as well.

"What is it?"

"Homemade holy water."

"You can make that?" Dennis glanced up at Asher whilst holding several stakes in each hand and noticed the look of seriousness in his eyes. He then proceeded to take the thin stakes from one hand and add them to the counted stakes in the other.

"It's simple if you know what you're doing." Dennis then held out a hand full of the stakes and Asher accepted them, unsure of what he was supposed to do. "Just keep them until I'm finished counting the rest. We need as many as we can get and even that isn't enough." Asher looked at the bundle of stakes and pushed the one he had been in possession of between the elastic band and the others it was holding together.

"You think we can take him on our own? He's... fast... and VERY strong."

"I know. He had my family fooled from the get-go, but I

never let him trick me. Nobody just shows up out of the blue claiming to be your closest aunt's son. The part that truly got me? He hasn't aged a bit since I met him. The day I got into the legends and the stories of this place, I started eating garlic every day, splashed holy water on myself occasionally as a protective coat, slept with a silver cross above my head, and kept a stake beneath my pillow. Feeder doesn't dare to mess with me personally." Dennis put out an open hand and Asher returned the stakes to him. He then stuffed them back in the bag with two other bundles and three small handmade crossbows that appeared to be cut from the same kind of wood. Asher assumed they were all pine, as their branches were rather flexible and the largest source of such materials around. "Now," Dennis said as he stood from the cot, "let's go get this guy." He then trudged out of the room with the backpack on, the duffel bag slung over one should, and the jug of holy water tied around the handle by a rope and hanging from a knot he made in the same rope around one arm of the backpack. Asher had never seen Dennis look so determined and followed him outside without question.

The two hiked back through the woods in a different direction, with Dennis carrying everything and Asher following, feeling slightly useless with his worsening condition. After about 20 minutes of stepping over branches and kicking around pines and occasionally leaves, the two made their way over to a large hedge on the tree line Asher recognized it as being the backyard of the same house he and Kyden noticed the strange man walking behind. Asher then realized that this was where Dennis had been going in and out of the woods to avoid raising suspicion, but it clearly failed him. Dennis let out a small whistle to get Asher's attention. Once he had it, he pointed at a gap between the hedge and a white stone wall that was being used as a fence for the yard and then balled up his hand, leaving his index finger and middle finger hanging loosely. He then made the two fingers move like legs and Asher nodded to show he understood. Taking the lead, Asher crouched down and moved between the two obstacles, staying low and quiet as he made his way to the front end of the hedge. Once at the end, he poked his head out to be sure that nobody else was around. He then nudged Dennis to follow and they both gradually emerged from the bushes, trying to keep the bushes from stirring too much and making noise.

"So, what's next?"

"We have to get your truck." Asher almost stopped in his tracks but kept his feet moving as he stared at Dennis, who remained emotionless and kept his eyes ahead of them.

"How are we supposed to do that?"

"Go in, get the keys, get out. Don't stay to talk to anybody." Dennis's blank expression unnerved Asher, who swallowed hard and accepted that this was something he had to do. He wasn't going to argue with Dennis about speaking to anyone. As much as he wanted to know that his parents still remembered him, he feared that they wouldn't. It was getting dark again by the time they set out and Asher knew they couldn't have but two hours of daylight left and he still wasn't certain where they were going once they had the truck, but before he could ask they were already standing in front of his house. "Okay, here we are." Dennis placed a hand on Asher's shoulder and patted it twice before sliding the hand to the back of his shoulder blade and nudging him forward. "I'll be right here, waiting." Dennis sat on the curb as Asher moved towards the front door.

He left his hood down to avoid any suspicion like that which he had caused before and walked casually across the lawn. Once he was at the door he paused and took in a deep breath before cracking it open. Nobody was downstairs, which made him partially happy and partially concerned, but he let this slide for the time being and stepped inside. The lights were all off and the house was quiet for the most part, however, when Asher had gotten roughly halfway up the stairs he could hear the audio of a TV. The voices talking on whatever show was being watched were fuzzy and the speakers the sounds were coming from seemed to be going bad by letting out an odd vibration when louder sounds passed through them. He soon recognized it as the small antique TV his father would use in his office when looking for inspiration. He paused once he was at the top step and peaked around the corner. His bedroom door was open, which wasn't a state he would ever leave it in. The door to the office right across the hall was luckily closed. An orange light lit up the base of the office door and no new movement could be heard, so Asher tiptoed across the hall and into his room. Just as his foot hit the soft carpet inside he could hear the creaking of leather. His father had gotten up from his seat. Asher froze as he listened. His father's footsteps thumped against the hardwood in the next room and were headed for the hall. In a panic, Asher stepped behind his bedroom door and pulled it as close to his body as he could, trying to mimic where it already was without crushing himself. Just as he stopped moving the door another could be heard creaking open. His father was now in the hall and the audio from the TV had stopped. Asher listened carefully as the footsteps stopped, as well. Then he heard a soft sniffle and the footsteps continued, passing right by him on the opposite side of the door and into the room. From where he stood, he could hear the springs in his mattress squeak as his father sat on the bed. Silence fell over the house for what felt like minutes to Asher before a voice could be heard.

"I don't know where you went, but you need to know, I'm still here." Asher's heart skipped a beat.

"Did he see me come in?"

"Everyone is acting strange around town. They have been since yesterday evening." Asher could hear faint sobbing coming from the other side of the door just as he was about to expose his hiding place. "If I'd have gotten up only an hour earlier...," his father's voice cracked and the pitch varied incredibly as he tried to hold himself together, "if I never left for work, would they still remember you, or would I have forgotten you, too?" His voice quivered as he finished his question and more sobbing became audible. Then, the bed creaked again and a few footsteps could be heard on the carpet as the cries left the room before closing the door and going back across the hall only to shut that door too.

A single tear welled up and slipped free from Asher's eye, as he stepped away from the wall he'd been pressed against. Wicking it away with his sleeve he continued to search for the keys and found them on his bed stand He then fled the room and the house with what will he could pull together, but left behind, written on a piece of torn notebook paper:

"I'm still here."

Chapter Eight: Cracks in the Asphalt

The nighttime winds whipped through the small openings above each window, passing by quickly and making room for another to do the same. Each gust cooled the interior of the truck a little more and Asher shivered as a breeze licked the back of his neck. Dennis and himself sat in silence for most of the ride, trying to avoid creating any more tension than there already was. The keys that hung from the ignition rattled about as the road became increasingly harsh under the tires. Asher clutched them to seize the clinking and clattering as Dennis readjusted himself in the passenger seat.

"Are you sure you don't want me to drive?"

"I'm fine. Besides, you don't even have your license." Silence fell over the two once more, only being disturbed by the whooshing of wind against the glass. Dennis kept his head turned towards the window, seemingly watching the passing trees with caution. "Do you think she's alright?" Asher gulped as he kept his eyes glued on the yellow dotted line to the left of the truck. From where he sat the only light was coming from the dash, where several orange glowing symbols stared at him. He used their faint illumination to see what Dennis was doing without looking away from the lines, but Dennis never turned to face him.

"I don't think you'll have to worry about her."

"What do you mean?" Dennis stirred in his seat again, still keeping his eyes on the trees.

"She's being used as bait. You're the one he wants." Asher broke his gaze away from the lines and lifted his eyes to see an upcoming stop sign at a four-way intersection. He started easing on the brakes but stopped applying additional pressure when Dennis tapped him on the shoulder with the back of his hand and waved for him to keep going. "Don't stop here, just keep driving." Asher did so carefully, being sure that there were no other headlights on the road before pressing the gas again.

"How do you know they'll be there?"

"What, at Mabel's? Where else would he go to lure you in? It's our best bet at finding him. I just don't know what his plans are yet." Silence poured in again, but Dennis made sure it was short-lived. "You know, when I was forgotten, I made a promise to myself that I would make it worth my time to be invisible."

"What do you mean?"

"Well, I wasn't being searched for when I first 'disappeared', so I spent my time going all of the places Feeder never went. Movies, clubs, even motels for the first few nights. Nobody knew who I was and I've always looked older than I am. So, I stayed away from where I knew the trouble was and enjoyed my time doing it." Asher could see from the corner of his eye that Dennis was now smiling and looking ahead. "Now, I only have one more thing to do before I'm satisfied with myself." Dennis turned towards Asher for a moment then back at the road. "I'm going to get my family back to their normal lives. That maniac has ruined so many opportunities for them, all to preserve the safe haven he created within it. I want them to better themselves and when he's gone, they can." Asher didn't reply verbally, he simply nodded in understanding and started making the final turn on to Mabel's road.

The road ahead was dark as Bristlewood didn't have streetlights so far out of town, so Asher drove carefully up the gravel road, using only his headlights as a guide. Dennis rolled his window down the rest of the way and unzipped the largest pocket on his backpack. Just as the headlights met the front porch of the single floor home, Dennis tossed a strand of garlic out the passenger window but kept a grip on it from inside the truck. Once Asher had stopped driving and parked, Dennis hopped out and tied the strand to the antenna.

"It won't keep him from attacking us, but he won't follow too close if we have to make a run for it."

"Run? He's quicker than either of us. He can honestly outrun my truck." Asher stepped out as well, keeping the flashlight on his phone up high so that he could see most of his surroundings.

"I'm well aware, trust me." Dennis then tossed the duffel bag on the hood with a thud and opened it up. Asher could tell he had no intentions of keeping quiet. Dennis then pulled two of the crossbows free from the contents and chucked one over to Asher, who caught it without paying much attention. He then gathered a few stakes and stuffed them in his back pocket with his shirt tucked beneath them for easy access. "Here, drench the end with this." Dennis moved over to the passenger door and reached in for the rope attached to his backpack. He and Asher both plunged the tips of the stakes they were currently armed with into the jug of holy water and then loaded the crossbows. Dennis sealed the jug and opened another pocket which reeked of garlic. He then put one hand inside and scooped out a small amount of fine white powder. "Close your eyes."

"Wha-" Before Asher could finish a cloud of the powder covered his face and body, causing him to retch when he tried catching his breath before getting hit with it.

"Warned you." Asher slowly opened his eyes, which he subconsciously shut as tight as he could only to see Dennis do the same thing to himself. "Alright," Dennis started, pausing only to blow air out hard through his mouth, which made a small amount of the powder break away from his lips and swirl about in the air, "let's go."

The two raised their crossbows and edged their way towards the front of the home, taking caution with each step and keeping an eye on their surroundings. The stairs beneath their feet creaked as they walked up the landing. Asher feared what he would see inside, but Dennis looked as if he had been ready for this moment a long time. Just as they got to the door, Dennis shot up a balled fist and Asher stood perfectly still. There was no sound around them and even the woodland creatures had seemingly obeyed Dennis's command, as they too produced no sound. The darkness around them grew eerier with each passing moment and Asher's hands began to shake. He couldn't tell if it was a result of fear or his illness making his arms weak, but he did his best to keep the crossbow at the ready and his breathing regulated.

"We have a problem," Dennis spoke in a whisper, "if he's

inside, he was given permission."

"So?"

"So *who* let him in?" Asher stopped breathing as the idea crossed his mind. He hadn't been thinking about the rules these creatures were bound to.

"Who did let him in?" Asher kept the thought to himself and shook his head before aiming the crossbow at their breaching point. Dennis looked back at the door and gripped the knob, which turned with ease. He then took a step back and swung it open. As the door hit the wall both boys kept their weapons raised, expecting anything, but were met with nothing. Beyond the entrance was the same darkness that had fallen outside, however, the air from inside seemed heavier as it rolled onto the porch. Asher could feel that something was wrong and took a step forward.

"Hang on." Dennis pulled a small metallic object from his pocket and Asher could hear something sticky being pulled apart as Dennis messed with the item. He then stuck the object to the side of Asher's crossbow and it made an audible clicking sound before sending a ray of light into the home. Dennis then attached a second flashlight to his own crossbow and jutted his head forward, motioning for Asher to go ahead of him.

Once they were both inside Dennis kept his light shining in the opposite direction of Asher's and walked backward to be sure that neither of their backs were exposed as they explored the house. Every room they came to seemed to be empty, but Asher still had the feeling that something wasn't right. After clearing the right end of the home, the two made their way back to the living room area where the front door was. There, Asher scoped about with his light and came across a familiar piece of plastic that reflected small amounts of light back at him. It was the bouquet he had gotten for Mabel. All of the flowers inside had begun to wilt and it didn't appear to have been moved since the day he gave it to her.

"Psst. Over there." Dennis nudged Asher on the shoulder with his own and directed his flashlight towards a hall on the opposite side of the open kitchen area. A familiar orange glow passed by the furthest end of the hall and through an archway. Asher recognized the light immediately and started towards the area it traveled in without hesitation. "Wait for me, Asher!" Dennis stayed as close as he could without making a sound, but with Asher being smaller than he was in several minor ways, he lost ground on him quick.

Once Asher made his way through the archway he momentarily lost sight of the orange glow but soon spotted it again near the floor in a closet on his left. He didn't wait for Dennis to make his way in with him and rushed to the closet, wrapping the crossbow around the corner before himself. The closet had no door and stood open, which told him the glow was coming from the right side of the small area, but when he looked inside his eyes widened. The floor on that side of the closet had been dug out along with the stone foundation. Asher jumped when a hand grabbed his shoulder.

"It's just me. What did you find?" Dennis continued to whisper as he looked around Asher, noticing the hole in the floor as well. For the first time that day, Dennis seemed to be hesitant on what to do. Asher didn't wait for him to decide against following the light and proceeded to sit on the floor and slide into the opening. "This is getting risky, Asher. Think before you make an irrational decision." Dennis followed closely and slid the six or seven feet underground after him. "Woah." The two examined the large opening, sending beams of light across the compacted dirt that made up the entirety of it. "I think we're in his den." Asher was growing more uncomfortable as he thought about Mabel and what Feeder might have done with her and pushed on in the direction of the glow, which had left the area they were in and moved on through another opening that had been carved from the dirt around them. "Asher, we need to get out of here!" Asher continued to ignore him and made his way through the next opening and into the same area the glow was still faintly filling. With his crossbow now at his side, he could see the source of the glow. A golden aura spewing out from a small crystal, which was seemingly floating in the middle of the carved room.

"A-Asher?" Asher broke out of his trance and faced the crossbow in the direction of the voice. The light came over a form that sat low to the ground and seemed far too pale and weak to move. It was Mabel. She seemed disheveled and as if she was being starved, but there was nothing binding her to her place. Asher didn't hesitate to rush over to her, ignoring the glow in an effort to help Mabel. Once he had cleared the distance between her and himself, Asher dropped to his knees and hugged her, losing his grip on his weapon in the process. Just as he met with her, Dennis's heavy steps grew closer and his light shined in at them.

"Asher, he's here!" Asher raised his head from Mabel's shoulder and turned to see a large figure breaking up the light between himself and Dennis. In an instant, he was airborne and slammed against the ground, rolling away from Mabel.

"Don't you dare lay your hands on her, Cor!" Asher looked up at Feeder as he fought to lift himself from the ground. "You've no right to her."

"Feeder," Mabel beckoned, "don't do this! You have me, you don't need him!"

"Don't you tell me what I do and don't need! You just stay right there and wait for your- GAH!" Asher made it back on his feet just in time to see Dennis send a stake through the back of Feeder's ribcage. Feeder turned to face Dennis and rage filled his eyes. The wound in his back appeared to be smoldering and Asher could hear the holy water hissing against his flesh. "You? Ahh!" Feeder raised one arm over his shoulder and gripped the stake as Dennis loaded another into his crossbow.

"Asher, help me!" Mabel grabbed the crossbow at her feet and yipped in pain as she tried to aim it at Feeder. The crossbow landed hard against the ground and sent a stake off into a dark corner of the room. Asher watched as the flashlight spun to face her and saw that her hands were smoking and hissing as well. "Asher!" Breaking free of his confusion he rushed over and collected the crossbow just as Feeder had pulled the stake from his back and Dennis sent another into the front of his right shoulder.

"You'll pay for that, you pitiful boy! Haven't I done enough damage to you for you to know better?" Asher quickly reloaded his crossbow and raised it to fire, but it was swiftly knocked from his hands and the flashlight broke free from it. Just as he had been disarmed, Dennis flew forward into the room. More hissing and screeches of pain could be heard, but they were neither from Mabel nor Feeder.

"W-what's going on?" Asher stood again, now filled with adrenaline and grabbed the flashlight to hunt for his crossbow, but once the light was in his hand he was motionless. Against the wall, where his crossbow had gone, was a set of feet. He then lifted the light to see a familiar but very different face. The boy had the same blond hair, but a very sunken profile. Asher recognized him immediately as one of the jocks who had gone missing. "James?" The boy grinned and pressed his blistered hand against his side to stop the burning.

"Bet that holy water hurt like hell, didn't it, Marcus?" Dennis made his way back to his feet and was facing another figure that had been standing where he stood in the entrance. It was the curly haired jock. Marcus remained silent and enraged as both of his hands simmered.

"Enough!" Feeder shouted as he removed the second stake from his shoulder. He then picked up the glowing crystal which he had dropped when he was shot and faced Asher with it held up like a trophy. "I should have killed you when I had the chance. I should have made you suffer like I did the rest of these pathetic wastes." He then lowered the crystal and backed himself slowly towards Mabel, who was now staring at the crystal with large dilated pupils. "I gave you a chance to walk away and let this happen and yet, here you are."

"Let Mabel go and we'll forget about all of it." Feeder and the others laughed as Asher spoke these words and Dennis made his way across the room and to Asher's side, never letting his crossbow face anywhere but at Feeder's chest.

"Oh, what are you going to do with that? Eh, Dennis? Look around you." Feeder motioned a hand towards the other two in the room, but Dennis refused to acknowledge either of them. "If you kill me, they'll kill both of you." Feeder then chuckled at himself and let his twisted grin make an appearance before taking one more step towards Mabel and handing off the glowing crystal. "It's been a while since I've seen an Amber Heart, you know?" Feeder watched as Mabel tried desperately to ignore the object in her hands, but she began to tremble as a strange eagerness seemed to be creeping over her. She looked at Asher with apologetic eyes and he looked back with confusion. "Don't tell me you really thought *I* was the one with your Heart." Feeder chuckled again as Mabel fought the urge to raise the Heart to her chest, but her efforts were futile. As she clutched the Heart against herself it began to emit the same light it had the day Feeder took it from Asher and the chain attached to it hummed with energy. Just as Asher recognized the chain as the same necklace Mabel had been wearing the past few days he became incredibly dizzy and nauseated. In that same moment, he fell to his knees and began coughing and heaving at the ground, but Feeder didn't wait to speak. "You see, I could have just given her someone else's Heart in place of yours and killed you myself, but I *knew* it was her right to your death, as it was you who caused hers. She deserves to be the one who ends your miserable life and when she does, she'll be mine! The first host's death signs for a Sagina's eternal life." Feeder then looked over his shoulder at Mabel, who was crying as she finally gained the strength to stop draining energy from Asher's Heart. "I'm all she'll ever need." He then turned back towards Asher, who was still on the ground breathing heavily, but no longer retching or dizzy.

"What did you do to her?" Asher demanded as he forced his head up towards Feeder.

"Didn't I just say?" He took several steps back towards Mabel and kneeled in front of her. "I made her one of us." He then brushed her cheek with his fingertips and smiled as she pulled away from him, but the smile faded quickly when he stood back up and stared spitefully at the others in the room. "These two, on the other hand, are cursed with a thirst they can't quite quench and are damned to walk amongst mankind for the rest of eternity for having left her to rot where she fell. They aren't like us. They have impure souls and walk the path of the vampire to do my bidding." The others refused to show emotion towards what Feeder was saying and he could sense their efforts to remain neutral. He shot them each a victorious toothy grin and brought his eyes back to Asher, who was back on his feet but being held up by Dennis. "What are you trying to achieve by being here? Did you think you could get your Heart back and save the girl? Well, she doesn't need your saving and no matter your efforts, the only way you'll get your Heart is if she surrenders it to you and you accept it." Mabel looked up at Asher with hopeful eyes, as if this sparked an idea in her mind, but to Asher, this was only briefly a choice. "But there is a catch." Feeder stood toe to toe with Asher and Asher could feel Dennis's grip tightening on him as his own anger was taking over. "If it's taken from her, she'll die and I'll be on the hunt for you." Feeder didn't move this time and the color in his eyes was engulfed entirely by his pupils.

"Are we going to just let them go?" Marcus appeared ready to pounce on anyone who moved as if starved beyond comprehension and desperate for anything he could sink his fangs into. Asher hadn't noticed this slight feature until he closely studied the appearances of the jocks and even Feeder and Mabel. All of them had exposed, elongated canines and were almost flaunting them in the direction of himself and Dennis.

"I see no other choice. The real fun has only just begun." Feeder's expression returned to that of pure evil and he motioned for Marcus to step out of the way so that Asher and Dennis could return to the surface. "You'll leave Mabel here with me. I can't trust her with two odorous things like yourselves." Dennis shoved Asher towards the exit, knowing very well that if he didn't force him to leave at this point, he wouldn't. "Oh, and if Mabel hasn't drained what remains of your essence from that rock by the next full moon, we'll all meet again." Dennis didn't wait for Feeder to finish these words as he desperately pushed and pulled Asher up through the hole in the floor and out the door of the house.

"Come on, Asher. We have to go! Feeder won't let her die and I won't let you get yourself killed."

Asher could still hear Feeder's laughter from the passenger seat of the truck as Dennis collected the duffel bag, throwing only his crossbow into it before tossing all of it in the backseat. Asher's crossbow was still in the den, but he knew they wouldn't be able to touch it as the image of Mabel burning herself on contact embedded itself in his mind. Dennis then made his way around the truck and into the driver's seat, turning the key and revving the engine as he backed out of the drive and onto the gravel road. Once the road was at its end, Dennis stopped the truck and looked both ways. Asher knew they had run out of options and places to go, as Dennis's hideout wouldn't save them from a vampire attack. But then the faint clinking of metal on metal caught his attention. In his groggy state, Asher looked across to the driver's side of the truck and noticed a particularly new key hanging on the same link as several older copper keys.

"So, where to next?" Dennis asked, hoping only for a miracle of words to come from Asher's mouth. The engine continued to hum as they remained idle in place. Asher continued to examine the key, which was shaped like a small square house with a triangle shaped roof. Where an embossed door and window were near the center of the upper key, the key's teeth began and formed a ridged surface all the way to the lower end. He then looked out the passenger window and rested his forehead against the cold glass.

"The family cabin. It was my idea to buy it and I was to get it as a gift when I graduated." Dennis examined the keys that were at his disposal and noticed the glossy silver that Asher had been looking at. "Got to keep the key as encouragement." Dennis fumbled the key between his fingers and Asher knew he was reading the address that had been engraved into it. The truck then took off once again, heading down the right lane of the asphalt road they had come from, but heading further from the places they had once called home. The last thing Asher saw before dozing off was a large sign covered in painted pines and curvy white words spelling out:

"Now Leaving Bristlewood"

Chapter Nine: A Dozen Moons

"Asher? Asher." Through the abyss, a distant voice called out to him. Acknowledging the beckoning, he parted his heavy eyelids and found himself to be standing in a vaguely familiar place, but the surroundings were shrouded in moving shadows and all that he could make out was the dirt at his feet. He peered around, trying to spot anything in the area with his feet seemingly glued to the ground itself. The voice continued to call his name as it bounced off the walls he could only assume were accompanying him and it grew louder with each passing moment. He was almost certain he knew who it belonged to and tried desperately to lift his feet from their invisible bindings.

"Mabel?" He grew uncomfortable as his awareness towards being alone and knowing where he was caught up with him.

"Asher!?" The voice seemed worried and eager to reach him. In the direction ahead where he thought he pinpointed the voice coming from, a section of the area poured in white bright light, which tore through the lingering darkness. Asher could hear the shadows shriek as they darted away from the pure illumination. Those that couldn't move out of the way fast enough dissolved and were silenced in the vibrant opening.

"I'm here, Mabel!" He continued to fight against the darkness, now seeing large twisting and swirling clouds of it wrapped tightly around his ankles. His efforts seemed less effective the more he struggled against it and he could no longer lift his heels in the least. He shot his gaze from his feet to the light and caught sight of gray buttons on the front of a black hoodie. He couldn't make out anything about the figure's face, but he knew it was her. He jerked hard against his feet as low echoing laughter swam about in the muggy air around him, circling him and getting louder with each round it made. The light that surrounded Mabel grew dimmer, but she remained as still as he was and the darkness started to flow in and out of the fading light, forming a wavy outline against the beam from above. The laughing had split off from itself, traveling both counter and clockwise. Asher could make out five different voices coming from the blurry forms that cut through the light ahead of him, leaving trails of black fog behind as they moved in closer. Mabel's cries for him had been drowned out by the constant laughter and whooshing of wind throwing around his hair and loose clothing as the things launched themselves through the air. "What do you want from me?" Ashed screamed at the creatures as they passed him and darted his head about in an effort to spot one. They had become clear against his surroundings, as the darkness that made them up was deeper than that which filled the room. "What are you?"

"You know who we are," one of the voices proclaimed, seemingly coming from within his own head rather than the form that said it, *"surrender yourself now and we'll make it go away."* Asher recognized the voice as James and his heart began to race. He had nothing to defend himself with and couldn't escape regardless of if he wanted to or not. Aside from his feet, the foggy entities were rushing about all around him and there was no way he could cut a path through the barricade they had made. The dimming

light was nearly impossible to make out at this point and Mabel had disappeared from his view entirely.

"I won't let you take her from me, Feeder!" The strongest of the voices laughed insanely and the form that created it shot far off into the darkness. The others proceeded with their crazed state for a few moments before greatly increasing their speed and bursting away as well. Asher had caught a few glimpses of James and the others, who were traveling ever so slightly faster than the fog that encased them. Each had their mouth agape and their fangs bared as they glared deep into his core. Then, the first form to break away from the pack came soaring back in his direction at full speed, stopping only inches from his face. The fog had parted and sealed itself around Asher and the entity, blocking out the light entirely and even the others who were there. The laughing had seized and Asher could hear steady breathing in his right ear. His own breathing was escalating as he desperately fought to show no fear, but he knew the entity sensed this and it took in a small but paced breath before speaking again.

"In time, you won't have a say." Feeder pulled back his right arm and Asher watched as he lunged forward with it, keeping his

fingers together in a pointed fashion. Just as it made contact with his chest, Asher shot up in bed.

"Hey, you alright?" Asher looked about, still unsure of where he was but relieved to see the sun was out and pouring through surrounding windows. "Asher?" Dennis waved a hand in front of Asher's face whilst applying a cold soaked rag against his forehead with the other. Asher leaned forward and dry heaved. "Yeah, good luck with that one. You already cleaned out your system yesterday."

"Yesterday?" Asher swallowed hard and rubbed his tongue against the roof of his mouth, finding it to be extremely dry.

"Yeah, you've been out since the drive here. I brought you in and did my best to secure the place while you were recovering." Dennis moved away from the bed and into a personal bathroom that was joined to it. Asher heard him running water and wanted nothing more than to jump from the bed and rest his head in the sink so he could chug it, but his head was already swimming and standing didn't seem to be an option. "Here," Dennis returned from the bathroom with a large, clear glass of water, "drink this." Asher snatched the beverage from his hands and gulped loudly, choking when he tried to breathe between them. "Yeah, sorry about that. I didn't want to risk drowning you trying to keep you hydrated, so I resorted to keeping you partially soaked. Apparently, that doesn't work." Dennis walked over and sat down on another bed that was only separated from the one Asher was laying on by a small wooden bed stand with a single white shaded lamp in the middle of it.

Asher examined the room as he paced his drinking. The interior of the cabin was just as the website said it was when they bought it. He'd never stepped inside and the family as a whole had yet to visit it, so he was just as amazed with it as Dennis seemed to be and both took a moment to be appreciative. Asher then sat his empty glass on the stand and took a soothed breath. As he exhaled, he thought he heard a low thump coming from somewhere beneath them. He glanced over at the windows on his right and noticed that the four panels arched into a point near the middle of the room. This told him they were on the top floor and that he might not have just been hearing things.

"Ignore that." Asher could tell by the guilty expression on Dennis's face that he knew what the source was. "We need to talk before I show you what I brought in." Asher nodded and lifted his glass for Dennis to refill, unsure if he was still too parched to speak. Dennis took the glass and returned to the restroom as he started off the conversation. "We have less than two weeks to prepare for the full moon, as you know, and I'm concerned we don't have enough hands on deck to withstand a fight against a Sagina and two or more vampires." Dennis returned to Asher and offered him the refilled glass, which Asher took almost as quickly as he had the first. Dennis then returned to his self-claimed bed and continued to speak. "Feeder is smart. He's been around a very long time and I'm sure he'll find a way to reach us when the time comes."

"Do you know anyone who'd be willing to help us, let alone believe what we have to say?" Dennis shook his head and let his eyes fall to the floor as he did so.

"Believe us, no, but I know somebody who'd be willing to help a couple of close friends." Asher expressed obvious confusion and concern as another thump sounded beneath them. Dennis shot his eyes back up at him in the same moment. "The main problem we face right now is that our trail is still fresh. If Feeder tries tracking us down now, it'll take him minutes, hours at the most to figure out where we're at."

"What do we do?" Dennis dropped his boot against the planks hard, seemingly annoyed with whatever continued to bang around downstairs. After doing so the thumping stopped and he returned to the conversation at hand.

"No matter what we do he'll find us, but I'd rather us have as much time as possible before he figures this place out." Dennis's eyes expressed great seriousness to ensure that what he said next would be taken to heart. "We can NOT return to Bristlewood for any reason. We can travel to the nearest town in the opposite direction, but we can't take your truck."

"How do you suppose we cover our scent and how are we supposed to get around without the truck?" Dennis returned to expressing guilt and motioned with a hand for Asher to follow him out of the room. He then got up and Asher peeled himself off his own mattress as well, keeping a grip on things as he made his way into the hall and down the wooden stairs, which were very sturdy and only attached to the wall with nothing beneath them. The cabin's entire interior seemed to be crafted from polished red pine and as Asher made his way down the stairs, he realized that they were the first people to ever live there, as none of the surfaces they passed had any type of damage done to them, from scuff marks to small indentations created by objects bumping or scraping them. The coat of polish seemed to be ageless and Asher had almost been too caught up in all of the details he was admiring to notice a third individual tied to a chair made of the same heartwood.

"What the- Kyden!?"

"Mmfmmfh!" Kyden was struggling against several bindings and had been lifting the front of the chair with his feet, thumping it against the ground as he gradually made his way from the kitchen to the living area. Asher spun his head on a swivel to see Dennis pursing his lips with his arms folded as he nervously watched Asher's reaction from the corner of his eye. Asher then rushed over to Kyden and removed a rag Dennis had been using as a gag. "Thank god! Help me out of this!" Asher went to the back of the chair to start working on the binding that held Kyden's arms behind it but stopped once the knot was in his hands. He then looked around the chair to see that Dennis remained motionless. He still seemed to feel guilty about what he had done, but he showed sympathy towards Asher. Recognizing this hidden emotion, Asher made his way back to the front of the chair and kneeled next to Kyden, partially to get a better face to face reaction and partially because of his exhausted state.

"Do you remember me?"

"Wh-what? No, I don't kn-..., y-yeah...." Asher raised his brow and noticed that Dennis was scowling at Kyden. This was something he did regularly when he knew Kyden was lying. "Are you going to help me out of this or what, man?" Kyden pointed back at the binding with his eyes.

"No." Kyden froze, eyes wide and breathing heavily.

"Seriously?" He then darted his eyes between Asher and Dennis as Asher stood and backed a few steps away, still standing a couple of feet closer to him than what Dennis was. "Look, man. I don't know what you guys want with me, but I got money. Just let me go and I'll give you whatever you want, okay? I'll go home and-"

"You don't have any money, Kyden." Kyden moved his lips in a manner that suggested he was still trying to speak, but he was caught off guard at the sound of his own name. Asher crossed his own arms and turned his torso so that he was facing Dennis without moving his feet.

"Was the gag really necessary?" Dennis raised both eyebrows and chuckled.

"At first, no, but it's the only way I could finally shut him up."

"How did you even get him here?"

"I hit him with my car!" Both Asher and Dennis looked back at Kyden. "I got a text telling me Ashley Burley was waiting for me at Manover Bar, which I thought was weird because she doesn't drive, is underage, and-." Kyden looked at the others and gulped. "Anyways, this guy was there and he stepped right in front of my car as I was pulling in. When I got out to check on him he wasn't there. I went to call the police but as soon as I pulled out my phone I had a finger in my mouth." Asher looked back at Dennis disgustedly and Dennis, slightly embarrassed, sniffled before speaking.

"I tried putting my hand over his mouth right when he went to scream. He still got one out, but his gag reflex is stronger than his vocals." Dennis cleared his throat and looked back at Kyden, trying desperately to ignore Asher's stare.

"I didn't scream! Oh, then he stuffed me in the trunk of my own car and brought me here. Wait, right, how do you two know me?" Dennis removed his own phone from his pocket and flipped through a few things before walking towards Kyden with the screen facing away from himself. Kyden studied the screen and his eyes grew wide. "Wait, you're the one who messaged me? How the hell did you get my number?"

"You gave it to me a year ago. We've gone to the same schools together for a while. You and Asher here have been going to the same schools since kindergarten." Asher nodded his head in agreement and Kyden seemed to be taken back.

"Wait, is this some kind of jealousy thing? You guys have a problem with me or?"

"No. We're close friends. All of us. You just don't

remember." Kyden laughed at this and let his teeth show as he smiled at the two of them.

"Oh okay, I see. So, why is it I don't remember?" Asher tried speaking first to avoid stirring things, but Dennis quickly and loudly spoke over him.

"You were brainwashed by a Sagina." Kyden's smile went limp as he studied Dennis.

"You don't think we could have started off a little lighter than-?"

"No," Dennis stated as he turned away from the two of them, "we're going to fix this right now." He then moved over to a coffee table that sat in the middle of the living area and the others watched as he unzipped his backpack and rummaged about the contents.

"Psst!" Asher turned his torso back toward Kyden. "Is this guy serious?" Asher nodded and Dennis raised a small necklace from the backpack.

"Here we are." The necklace was made up of a black chain and a small but heavy blue stone that was held in place by four metal teeth. The stone was shaped to a point on both ends, with the lower end having an extended length in comparison to the top. The largest part of the stone was roughly three-fourths of the way up the stone and the entire thing appeared to have a diamond cut from Asher's perspective.

"What is it?" Kyden studied the necklace from afar as Dennis cradled the stone in his palm. He stretched his neck in an effort to keep it in sight as Dennis approached him.

"Amazonite. It'll help us get your memory back and break the trance." Dennis took his place directly in front of Kyden and kneeled, holding the necklace out with the stone dangling from the lowest point.

"It will?" Asher took a step forward to watch what was happening as Dennis confirmed what he had said to be true.

"It's a very uncommon fact that the hypnosis brought on by vampires and Sagina can be broken using the right type of natural stone." Dennis began to slowly swing the stone in front of Kyden's face, but Kyden appeared to be actively avoiding looking directly at it. "The knowledge goes unnoticed without studying it properly. Do so and you'll find that someone affected by their manipulations can't look at the stone for an extended period. Quite an interesting way for them to avoid having their curse lifted from a victim and an easy way to tell who's still being tricked." Asher's interest had been peaked at this point.

"Could we use that to free the others?" Dennis didn't reply for several moments as he continued to swing the stone at a fixed speed before Kyden's eyes, which continued to look around the area the stone was passing through.

"With the amount of resistance one person has? The chances of clearing the minds of everyone in Bristlewood are slim to none." Dennis didn't allow Asher to dwell on the thought and called him closer. "Hold his head still and his eyes open."

"What?"

"Just do it. When the stone is swinging the full length of his view he won't be able to keep it in his peripheral vision and we can't have him closing his eyes." Asher nodded and moved behind Kyden, resting his palms against his head and using his middle fingers and ring fingers to keep his eyelids open.

"Okay, you guys are freaking me out. I played your games long enough, haven't I? Come on, let me go. Let me go!" Kyden tried jerking his head to one side, but Asher already had his arms locked in place. He could tell that as the stone started swinging right to left at the full length of the chain, Kyden was becoming more distressed than he had been throughout the entire time Asher had seen him. He could feel that Kyden was desperately trying to close his eyes and his arms were twisting hard on the bindings.

"I don't need you to cooperate with us Kyden, but if you do it'll be over sooner than later." Dennis was focusing hard on the motion of the stone, being sure that it didn't sway too far to one side and leave Kyden's view. Asher was focusing hard as well in his effort to not lose his grip on Kyden who was now grunting and straining desperately against him and the white cut up sheets that bound him down. "Remember Mabel? The girl who took a liking to Asher? Remember the night you all brought her into our group?"

Kyden's face was turning red and a large vein on his forehead started to bulge out as he gritted his teeth. Asher could feel his arms growing weak under the constant pressure and wasn't sure how much longer he could hold Kyden still. "Think hard about it, Kyden! Who is your best friend?" Kyden's lips began to curl in and out as he fought the urge to speak. Asher could hear his tongue clicking against the roof of his mouth as he did so. "Come on, Kyden. Fight it! Who do you see every day before heading to school?" Asher felt that he could see the struggle Kyden was going through. Memories of the two of them together, but foggy and abandoned in a far corner of his mind. Asher could see with each command and request that Dennis made, Kyden was trying to find the answers and even if he did, he struggled to say what they were. "Say it, Kyden! Say his name!"

"A-Asher." His teeth refused to part as he spoke, which Asher could only assume was Feeder's charm doing its best to survive the treatment.

"Good, good! Tell me, Kyden. Who's the new girl?" Kyden's eyes moved around the entirety of their sockets and Asher was certain that if they could bite he'd lose his fingers. His arms burned as they begged him to stop with his efforts, but he fought the urge to collapse and maintained the pressure he was applying to Kyden's temples to the best of his ability. "Who is she?"

"M-Mabel!" His voice was becoming as vicious as his motions, but he was now watching the stone dance before him.

"Okay, two more. Who am I?" Kyden didn't respond at first, but the color in his face had started to return and his struggles lessened. "Kyden, who a-"

"Dennis!" Asher could no longer tell if it was his arms shaking, or Kyden shaking beneath his hands, but Dennis waved Asher away with his free hand and Asher obliged, dropping them to his sides and rubbing his biceps with sore fingers. Kyden was no longer trying to look away from the stone and was, in fact, the one shaking. Dennis started to slow the stone's motions but didn't stop the swinging entirely.

"Yes! Now, where is Mabel?" Images of the flashlight spiraling about through the night sky crossed Asher's mind. The people he once called friends rushing over to see if she survived and fleeing before anything could be done were plastered there as well. "Do you remember?" Kyden stopped shaking and his eyes started to fill with tears. Asher couldn't tell if this was because of the memories or the amount of pressure he had put on Kyden's eyes at first, but it soon became clear. Kyden broke down and let his upper body fall forward, only being held up by the fabric he was unable to free himself from.

"She's dead..., we killed her." Kyden sobbed. Dennis sighed with relief and stopped swinging the carved amazonite, which came to rest on Kyden's shoulder as he comforted him. Asher watched the two momentarily before Dennis moved away from Kyden a bit, leaving his hand where it sat.

"It's good to have you back."

Asher and Dennis spent the rest of the day informing Kyden about all that had been going on, filling him in on their discoveries and what it was like to be forgotten. After several hours talking about everything that came to mind, the three of them laid down to sleep that night. Both Asher and Kyden found it difficult to fall asleep, for their own reasons. Asher feared he'd have the same nightmare from the night before and Kyden was still adjusting to the thought of the local tales being true events. Just as Asher had started to doze off, he heard someone hissing at him from the floor.

"Hey, are you still awake?" Asher remained silent for a moment, unsure if he wanted to engage in a conversation so late but understanding that Kyden would need somebody at the time.

"What's up?" He replied in a similar whisper, as Dennis was already asleep and neither wanted to wake him.

"I'm sorry about Mabel. We never should have gone there that night. It was reckless and stupid of us." Asher closed his eyes and brushed the thought out of his mind as best he could. He knew that everything was dwindling down to either her life or his own and was trying to avoid the thought entirely. He could hear Kyden rustling about in his sleeping bag on the floor and took the opportunity to readjust himself in the bed.

"Don't worry about it." Asher paused and stared at the ceiling, following the overhead beams from one end of the room to the other. "Right now everyone's alive and that's all that matters."

Kyden's voice began to drop in pitch as he yawned and presumably got comfortable enough to sleep.

"Well, regardless. Oh, and if in the morning I wake up and all of this was just a dream, I'll find the two of you and be sure you get to meet." Asher smirked at him mentally and let his eyes sink into a deep and warm slumber.

Chapter Ten: Enneadic Parchments

Faint lights fluttered about Asher's vision as they hovered through an empty, still atmosphere. Each source seemed to avoid letting him look directly at it and darted away as he tried. He soon realized he wasn't the one guiding his own eyes. They seemed to be in control of themselves as the speckled beams came into focus. He was having another dream and from what he could see, he was back in the den just as he was last time. He didn't speak or even think to himself as his body began to move forward. He was walking through dirt tunnels towards the surface with a single hanging light bulb in the closet above guiding his way. His eyes trailed towards the ground as he made his way up and he caught a glimpse of his hand against the floorboards as it lifted the rest of him out of the den. It was much smaller than it should have been and was a lighter tone as well. Both of these things were minuscule details once he caught sight of red nail polish on each finger. The polish was chipped around the edge of the nails but brightly colored nonetheless. He knew by this note that he wasn't looking through his own eyes, he was looking through Mabel's. Mabel proceeded to exit the closet and Asher could hear whispers coming from the next room over, just outside the door of the master bedroom that encased the closet. Mabel crept forward quietly and peaked around the door frame. Through the hall and beyond the kitchen, Asher saw one of the three boys sitting on a sofa with a leg stretched over the entirety of it. He was talking low and Asher struggled to make out what was being said, but almost as soon as he thought to himself about this, Mabel's hearing improved drastically. He could now hear nearly every sound that was present, including a fly that had been buzzing about the ceiling light in the living room. It hummed as it shot through the air and made small clicking sounds with its legs when it landed and walked across the glass surface of the bulb. He was fascinated by this but fought his interest in it so that he could hear what the boys were saying.

"Any word from Feeder, yet?" The boy on the sofa readjusted himself as he said this and pulled his leg closer, letting a second sit on the opposite end of him. Asher made this one out to be James and the one who had just walked into view to be Marcus.

"Nothing yet. What's he even trying to prove at this point?"

"Isn't that the question?" James scoffed and shook his head, but quickly pressed on with the conversation, seemingly to avoid tension. "What about you, Blaine? Anything to report?" The third jock was still out of range, but Asher knew who it was by the name and voice that made themselves known.

"Not much. With the girl down there and Feeder off doing whatever it is he's doing, who knows what'll happen."

"What do you mean?" Marcus ran a few fingers through his hair, so as to keep it in place and pressed himself into the sofa.

"It just seems like he's wasting time. If you ask me, we should just attack and get it over with. Maybe then we'll get to go back to how things were."

"We're never going back," James folded his arms and stared across the room, which Asher assumed was him glaring at Blaine, "you know that." The three sat silent for a few moments before any of them spoke up again.

"Do you think he'll really kill him?"

"The guy has been around for generations, Blaine." Marcus was growing impatient with Blaine too and showed it as his voice became gradually louder when he spoke. "He made all of us disappear and you really think he won't? If he gets that book he'll-"

"Shh!" James threw up a hand in their directions and faced the end of the hall towards Mabel's. Mabel moved away from the entrance to hide her face in the darkness.

"What is it?" Marcus stood and took a step towards the kitchen.

"I think the girl's up." Marcus chuckled and started towards the hall as Mabel's vision blurred with unnatural speed. Asher could no longer focus on what was happening around her and the last he saw was the hanging light just before she submerged herself underground.

He opened his groggy eyes and blinked several times. He was almost too weak to move but managed to pull himself up as he thought over everything he had just seen. He concluded that Mabel had used some of the energy stored in the Amber Heart to show him something, but he was still unsure of what it was in his tired state. Just then, he heard his cell phone buzz and looked towards the bed stand He stretched his arms and back before leaning over and grabbing the phone. Once it was in his possession, Asher clicked a button on the device's side and read the contents of a small blue notification box.

"Hello! We here at BPL would like to thank you for returning your books on time. There will be no fee due to this successful transaction and we hope to see you again soon!
-Bristlewood Public Library Staff"

"Huh. So that's it." Asher grunted as he turned the screen off, pulled himself away from the mattress and into the bathroom where he took a long hot shower and washed away all the signs of his illness that he could. The sweat, crusty eyes, stuffy nose, and fever all seemed to fade away as the water ran over the entirety of his body. A newly formed rash that spread across his chest and back was something he hadn't expected though. It showed in patches of red spots and made his skin uncomfortable, but he ignored it as best he could and threw on a shirt. Upon leaving the bathroom he could see Dennis and Kyden through the triangular windows out front. Both had shovels and were digging large holes on either end of the forest clearing that made up the yard. Asher proceeded to make his way downstairs and out the door to greet them.

"Morning, sunshine." Kyden gave Asher a cheery but exhausted grin as he rested his hands on the shovel, having the cutting edge placed a few inches into the softened soil.

"Morning. What's all this?"

"Pitfall." Asher looked over at Dennis, who had many large stains on his shirt and who's trench was nearly twice as large as Kyden's.

"Why would we need a pitfall?"

"Kyden suggested it. It's probably one of the smartest things he's come up with." Dennis proceeded to dig at the ground without looking up at Asher and spoke as he did so. "We're going to line the base of it with stakes and only leave a small trail down the middle for ourselves to get in and out, safely." Kyden pulled himself from his trench and brushed off his jeans, which Asher recognized to be one of his nicer pairs, though none of them were impressive.

"Where are you off to?" Asher studied Kyden's attire and pulled out his phone to check the time. 6:00 am.

"School. I figured it was the best option to avoid Feeder getting suspicious." Kyden finished brushing the dirt from his pant legs and shoes and started towards his car.

"Wait, shouldn't we talk about this first?"

"We already did." Dennis, at this point, stuck his shovel in the dirt and pulled off a pair of gardening gloves he had been wearing before looking up at Asher, squinting as the morning sun gazed between horizon clouds. "You think he'd go on his own without being told?" Kyden shrugged knowing this to be true and continued in the direction of his vehicle. "It's better for him to keep his schedule the same and act like nothing ever happened."

"You'll be back though?" Kyden unlocked the car door and kept it ajar, leaning over it to look back at his friends.

"Yeah, I'll be back." He smiled and looked at a small watch on his wrist. "I can't just pretend nothing happened. I might not trust your stories to be all that true, yet, but I still want to figure this thing out." Asher looked at Dennis and Dennis back at him, but he just shrugged and started picking at the ground once more, slinging large heaps of dirt and rock over his shoulder and into a pile the two had made at ground level.

"Wait, Kyden." Asher walked over to the car with his phone still in hand and surfed through his messages. "You think you can retrieve something for me while you're in town?"

"What is it?" Asher turned his phone towards Kyden,

showing him the message he received from the library and number code that was below the text.

"Write this number down. We're going to need that book." Kyden opened the glove box on the passenger side and pulled out an empty envelope and a pen. He proceeded to write the book number down on the front of the envelope and stuff it in his pocket.

"What's so important about a book?"

"It has all the answers in it, trust me. Don't let anyone but the librarian know which book you're getting either. It's best you don't catch anyone's attention in the process, got it?" Kyden nodded and ducked into his car. Asher stepped away as he shut the door and Kyden headed off down the path and away from the forest. Asher could still hear the engine rumbling for almost a solid minute while he watched Dennis dig away at the hole. He then put out a hand to collect Kyden's shovel.

"Don't bother with that." Dennis was back in his state of not looking up, too focused on the work he had at hand. "You don't need to be doing anything right now except resting. You look rough."

Asher sighed a nonverbal agreement and headed back into the cabin.

The day dragged by as he thought about what had happened that night and wondered if Mabel had been caught. Before long, Dennis trudged back in as well and plopped down on a chair that sat opposite the couch, separated by the coffee stand and the red and brown rug beneath it. Asher had been laying on the couch flipping through basic cable channels that he came across while huddled up in a large white fleece blanket. Crossing a news channel he saw that six hours had passed and was relieved to think that Kyden would be back soon.

"Getting anywhere out there?" Dennis nodded and blankly stared at the screen.

"My trench is finished. Just need to carve out more stakes and plant them. We're going to use a fishing net I found out in that shed back there and cover it with moss, needles, and whatever else we can find to make it look natural." Asher momentarily glanced through the open kitchen and out a high window where he could just barely make out the peak of a small roof he hadn't seen before. "How you feeling?" Asher turned back to Dennis and noticed that he was being studied, hard. He could only imagine that to Dennis, he looked like a pale twig wrapped in a cobweb blanket. The steam from a bowl of noodles he had been eating only intensified his running nose and he assumed this worsened his appearance. Dennis appeared genuinely concerned, but Asher shrugged it off and returned to watching the television. After a few moments of static, fuzzy voices coming from the box, and the clinking of his spoon on the bowl, Asher spoke up again.

"Something happened last night."

"What was it?" Dennis seemed relieved that Asher had said something as if the monotone voice of a shopping channel host was the last thing he wished to listen to.

"Mabel. I think she was trying to communicate with me using my Heart."

"How do you mean?" Asher went on to explain the vision he had that night and Dennis took in each word carefully, being sure that he didn't misunderstand any of what was said.

"Wait, so you're telling me that Feeder is after the same book you sent Kyden to collect?" Asher paused for a moment with the spoon elevated halfway between his mouth and the bowl. "You didn't think that might be a little risky?" Asher sat the utensil back in the soup and slowly rolled his eyes towards Dennis before shooting them back at his bowl.

"I wasn't really thinking about that."

"Ugh." Dennis stood from the chair, which rocked as his weight was lifted from it and ran both hands down his face. As he did so he pulled his lower eyelids downward, exposing the pink glossy tissue beneath them before letting both sling back to their normal locations. "It should be fine. That was some time between 4:00 am and 6:00 am, right? So, if Feeder went to try finding the book then odds are him and Kyden won't even cross paths. Either Feeder found it and Kyden will get there too late, in which case Feeder would be long gone, or Feeder never found it, gave up a few hours ago and Kyden will be on his way with it."

"You think Feeder would have given up by now?" Dennis didn't answer and Asher assumed then that he was just saying this as a way to comfort himself. Both then heard small stones grinding together outside as a large amount of weight rolled over them. The two looked at each other and bolted for the door. Dennis swung it open and they both saw Kyden coming up the path with the radio blaring some kind of rock music, which was muffled through the glass and metal. He then rolled down his window and waved out at them with a smile and small head bang.

"What are you doing back so early?" Dennis hollered out at him as Kyden cut the engine and thumped his feet against the ground.

"Perks of being a senior." Kyden reached across the interior of his car and Asher could see him lift up a large brownish object and a rolled-up poster board. He recognized the leathery object as the book he had requested and was quick to collect it from Kyden's hands as he approached. "Easy there, the thing might be too heavy for you." Kyden tapped Asher with the poster board as he made his way between them and into the cabin.

"You don't think *this* is going to look suspicious?" Kyden shrugged at Dennis's question and planted himself where Asher had been sitting as the others made their way in with him. Asher ignored the conversation and began flipping through pages in the book.

"Relax, man. Feeder wasn't even there today." Asher could hear Kyden slurping on something but continued ignoring them as he searched for answers to his vision. He stopped when another article caught his attention.

"I think I found something." Dennis looked to his right and checked the contents out for himself over Asher's shoulder

"Something to do with the vision?"

"Vision?"

"Not now, Echo." Dennis shook his hand in Kyden's direction and kept his eyes locked on the book.

"Yeah, look." Asher goes on to read from a passage titled *Hearts and Heads*, which explains to them that Sagina can communicate with their hosts by drawing the same life force from the Amber Heart. "It says here that a Sagina's most common use in this ability is to let their host witness their own death through the Sagina's eyes."

"Woah, that's dark." Kyden slurped at something again and Asher sighed as he turned the page to find a similar drawing of the Amber Heart to that of one he'd seen previously in the book separately.

"What's that?" Dennis pointed at the sketch, noticing just as Asher had that the Heart had small differences in details, but several notes attached to it. "The Archaic?" Asher skimmed the text beneath the sketch and spoke only key differences between this Heart and the Amber Heart.

"It's the Heart of a Sagina. Only one of them has ever been found. It's also noted that they work just like the Amber Heart, but they're different in that their Essence, or life force, is eternal. the Archaic also emits a faint white light in place of the fiery light of an Amber Heart."

"You guys mind including me in some of this?" Asher finally looked away from the book to see Kyden eating from his bowl of noodles.

"Uh, what are you doing?" Kyden slurped a mouthful of broth and shrugged.

"It was just sitting there, figured I'd finish it." His mouth was still full of the fluid as the sudden realization of what he was doing hit him. He then turned to face his friends and created a spout with his lips, slowly pouring the broth back into the bowl and setting it down when he was finished. "That's not contagious, is it?" Asher and Dennis looked at each other and then down at the book, flipping through pages to find passages about the disease. Kyden took in a few breaths and calmly walked towards the kitchen, twisting both faucet knobs and spraying the small attached hose into his mouth.

As the night came to a close, Asher continued to study the book's contents but found nothing more of interest. He then stood from his bed and quietly made his way over to the window, where he could see that Kyden and Dennis had finished their pitfall trap. He was amazed to see that it was practically unnoticeable with all the coverage they gave it and returned to his nest. The others had already gone to sleep, but he had trouble doing so himself. He wasn't afraid of having another vision, however. With each creeping minute that passed, he had actually been hoping for one. Moments before falling asleep, he had only one thought left on his mind. *"Let me know that you're alright."*

Morning came and the birds outside began to chirp loudly. Asher awoke to see that the sun was already overhead and made his way downstairs. The smell of meat cooking and tea brewing helped to ease his still overactive mind and he sat at the dining table with Kyden. Dennis was at the stove with large steaks on a pan and corn boiling in a pot opposite of it.

"Where did all of this come from?" Kyden looked over the leather book, which Asher hadn't realized was missing from his bedside when he awoke.

"I picked up the corn at the farmer's market. Dennis got the meat." Kyden then flipped a page and returned to the text. "Funny, this place came with a stocked spice rack but no food."

"I imagine it would have gone bad, sitting here for longer than a year." Kyden shrugged and scrunched his brow as he focused on what was at hand. Asher knew he wasn't much of a reader and didn't fully believe everything they had been telling him, so he let Kyden browse the clippings and sketches as he turned his attention towards Dennis. "So, where are they from?"

"What, the steaks?" Asher nodded as Dennis looked him over before returning to the sizzling cuts. "It's venison. Went out this morning and got two. I put the other on ice for later."

"We're lucky enough your parents haven't noticed all these bills in their names, huh?" Kyden chuckled and Asher's face started to drain of color.

"I hadn't thought about that."

"Don't worry about it," Dennis demanded, "I rigged the power to come from another cabin three miles from here."

"What about the water?" Dennis shrugged and flipped the venison steaks, exposing a juicy brown surface with small seasoning flakes covering the glistening mass.

"Apparently it's coming from a well out back. No bill there." He then turned and clattered a glass plate against the table in front of Asher, who quickly started cutting at the meat. Dennis then gave Kyden his plate and Kyden did the same. "Anything happen last night?" Asher shook his head and sighed.

"I just want to know that she's alright."

"Hey, if what you guys say is true and with what I've read from that thing," Kyden jabbed at the spine of the now closed book with his knife, "it's best she doesn't do that too often." He then threw a piece of the steak into his mouth and chewed it quickly, swallowing hard before continuing to speak. "Besides, I have a plan." Both Asher and Dennis stopped what they were doing and listened intently to what Kyden had to say. "Hey, I might not be the most onboard person with vampires being the cause of mass hypnosis, but I still want to get to the bottom of this."

"We know, you've said this." Dennis leaned against the stove, being sure not to bend back too far as another piece of venison was crackling and steaming behind him. "What's your plan?" Kyden grinned and grabbed the poster he had brought in the day prior, removed a rubber band that kept it closed and laid it flat against the table. Asher scanned over the image.

The photo was made up of a black and white background, which started off black at the top right corner and white at the bottom left. In the center of the poster were two masks designed only to cover the area around someone's eyes and the bridge of their nose. The masks colors were the opposites of the backgrounds they rested on, with the mask higher up being smaller, decorative, and white. The mask that sat lower on the poster was larger, bland in comparison, and black. Beneath the masks was a wavy blue line that ran the length of the poster and had a small black boat sitting at the center of it. *"Bristlewood High School's Senior Masquerade Ball"* was written partially above and below the masks, leaving the boat on the water beneath all else.

"You want us to go to the ball?" Kyden nodded proudly at Asher. "Why?"

"Well, who wouldn't show up to it? It's perfect! Apparently, the gymnasium wasn't good enough for them, so they put the money together and rented a yacht."

"Okay, but what does this have to do with what we're trying to do?" Dennis turned to flip his steak, losing a small amount of faith in Kyden's motives as he did so.

"There's no way Feeder won't go. It'll be away from Bristlewood, so your 'scents' aren't going to linger. If you want to be sure Mabel is alright we need to find Feeder first. We'll just sneak around under masks undetected and track him down."

"And what about our scents while we're there?" Dennis became more interested once Kyden explained all of this and piled his own food on another plate before taking a seat on the elongated part of the table.

"Easy fix." Kyden pulled out a small bottle of cologne and the others groaned, recognizing it as the same cologne Kyden used every time he went out to a party.

"That stuff literally makes you smell like the '80s." Asher pushed his plate away as Kyden sprayed a small amount of the yellow liquid on his wrists and transferred it to his neck.

"Yeah? Name one smell it can't cover." Neither Asher nor Dennis answered, both knowing a corpse could go undetected with the smell produced by that round bottle of venom.

"Well," Dennis sighed, "guess I should get some dress shoes."

Chapter Eleven: Voices and Veils

Several nights passed with Asher watching what progress the others were making out in the yard from the bedroom windows. As dawn approached, his eyes would crack open and the sound of their shovels pulling up soil from the large heaps they had made with their trenches and the rattling of them tugging it away in an old wheelbarrow filled his ears. The uneventful mornings would turn to dusk and he would watch under the light of a single, but very large UV spotlight that hung off the front porch roof, facing out over the yard. He couldn't help but be impressed with how much effort Dennis and Kyden were both putting into what was to come and ashamed that he couldn't do more to help. He continued to watch over their tasks every night from the opposite side of the large glass panels for the four moons that separated them from the date of the ball. The morning of, Asher awoke to the sound of tough rubber clopping against the sturdy floorboards. He took in a slow but heavy breath and yawned exhaustedly before opening his eyes and facing the neighboring bed. He could see through blurry vision, Dennis seated at the edge of the mattress where he was fidgeting with the objects that Asher had heard him drop. He continued to knock them about a little while, but with much less audible bursts. Asher proceeded to listen and let his eyes fall heavy so that he could block out what sunlight was cresting over the cabin from the rear and beginning to fill the front yard. *Clop!* He peeked out again, slightly annoyed with the constant fumbling of the two objects at this point. He could tell there were two because as Dennis would drop one, he could still hear small strands of fabric brushing up against a solid body in the hand Dennis was still using.

"You need some help over there?" Dennis paused briefly before turning to face Asher and raising one of the objects in his hand. Once the object was in the air, he shook it left to right and let the two black strands that hung loosely from it swing about with his motions.

"Sorry, just trying to break them in." Dennis returned the shoe to its spot on the floor and started slipping in a foot. "I'd have bothered to use the restroom or even go downstairs, but I figured it was closing in on time to get you up anyhow." Once his foot was in, he moved on to the right shoe and began doing the same with it. Asher, bored of this action, glanced at the bottom of the bed and noticed small balls of tissue paper strewn about.

"Brand new? Where'd you get them?" Dennis didn't reply for a few moments but continued to fight with the shoe until his heel was in. Once he had both shoes on his feet he started gathering up the individual laces in either hand.

"I had Kyden go into town and get me a pair. Here," Dennis remained hunched over in his spot as he shifted his weight to the right and then to the left, "I got you a set too." Asher could hear the sound of cardboard scratching against wood as Dennis took this action. Once he made his way entirely to his left, Asher could make out a rectangular orange box beneath his fingers.

"Where'd you get the money for them?"

"You didn't think I just left home empty-handed, did you?" Asher sat up in bed and rubbed his eyes as Dennis continued to explain. "Feeder might know a thing or two about manipulation, but he's never been good at cleaning the slate. When he did this to me and you, he basically wiped me off the face of the earth, but he failed to make you forget." Dennis scrunched his brow and looked back at Asher before letting his gaze sink downward. "I'm actually not sure how he managed to mess that up. Anyways, then there was your father for you like you said." Asher didn't speak, not wanting to engage in the topic any further and reached out for the box. "My point is, he leaves gaps and along with those gaps are the things he never thinks to do. As long as he has everyone under his spell, he doesn't need to go to the full extent of canceling all your accounts, getting your citizenship revoked, erasing your social, none of it. Of course, this can leave problems for you later on when officials start to realize things don't line up. Such as the people said to be your birth parents don't know who you are and your attendance at school falling beneath what's legally permitted, yet the district has never seen you." Dennis brought himself to his feet once the laces on both shoes were bound tightly and stomped a few times as he bent them at the toe. "If they start to realize something is wrong then they'll turn to video surveillance and find you there, which they will-"

"Are these the right size?" Asher examined one of the polished leathers from the box he was given and Dennis did the same from afar.

"They should be. I picked them based on the size of the sneakers." Dennis pointed towards the bedroom door where Asher had thrown off his shoes, which to his dismay, were far dirtier than he had wanted them to be so early on in the year.

"Hey, you guys up there?" Dennis continued to move about in his shoes by pacing the room and Asher remained in bed, still too groggy to stand on his own.

"Yeah, we're here." Thumping started filling the hall behind the door as Kyden skipped steps on his way up to the others. The pine coasted open as he walked in and both Dennis and Asher stared at him.

"What do you guys think?" Kyden raised his arms in the air

with his palms facing upward and did a slow turn as he grinned and nodded his head at them. He was wearing a white undershirt with a velvet fitted suit jacket over it. The black tie around his neck was made of a fluffy thick fabric and stuck off his chest roughly a half inch before disappearing beneath the jacket. From the waist down, he wore black regular dress pants- which looked to have been ironed- with black glossy shoes, complemented with white tongues that ended by rounding off at the vamps. From the neck up, he wore a velvet glittery mask that started at his jaw on the left of his face and migrated upward, covering only from the base of his eyes to the height of his eyebrows and dipping in the center to cover the bridge of his nose. Asher and Dennis took a few moments to examine him entirely, also noticing that the jacket was designed with a split near the bottom on the backside, creating two lengthy, pointed ends on either side of the center seam. "So?" The two turned away from him briefly and locked eyes before bellowing with laughter. Kyden, confused, started to lower his arms, but the laughing didn't stop. "What is it? Is it torn?" He then felt about the suit for any obvious damages including checking his fly before looking back at his friends.

"No, it's just, the one time you look half decent will be the one time nobody can know it's you." Dennis walked towards the hall and patted Kyden on the shoulder as he walked passed. Kyden stood with his jaw hanging half open before looking back at Asher, who chuckled as he did so.

"Looks good." Asher joked. Kyden huffed and turned on his heel, whipping the pointed ends of his jacket like a cape as he made his way back down the stairs after Dennis.

Once the others had gotten themselves dressed up for the occasion, with both wearing similar black suits, skinny black ties, and flocked black masks that covered the same area as Kyden's, they set off for the party. Kyden drove and Dennis sat in the passenger, as Asher lay sprawled out across the backseat of Kyden's car to rest his eyes some more. It was already getting dark again, as Asher had been sleeping for more and more extended periods with each passing day and napping throughout them as well. He listened to the constant rumble of the engine and felt every small rock that passed beneath the tires. He thought the car could fall apart at any moment in these conditions but didn't speak to Kyden about it, knowing very well it wasn't something he could take care of himself, for more than one reason. After what seemed like an hour, Kyden informed everyone that they had reached the piers and Asher sat up to check out their surroundings. It was already far too dark for him to see much out over the ocean, but he scanned the horizon anyway and took in what little he could find. The piers were barren, which he assumed was a request of the school for the safety of the students attending the ball, but in the water were several small and distant boats. It was the first time he had ever seen the ocean and unfortunately, the world had grown too dark to truly enjoy it. However, his attention quickly switched from the open waters to the yacht they were approaching as Kyden pulled into a parking lot and was directed by teachers carrying large glow sticks into a single parking space. Just as they were getting ready to get out and lock up a knocking came from Kyden's window. Startled, he kept a grip on the seatbelt he had just unclipped and peered out into the shadows. A green glow was coming from the base of the door and was raised to meet the glass again. Once the glow stick tapped the glass, whoever was holding it waved it in a manner that told Kyden to roll down his window, which he did.

"Evening, lads." The large but very young teacher leaned in towards the boys and smiled politely. "I just wanted to let you and everyone else know that we will be keeping a close eye out on the student body as a whole during the voyage and be sure I get your names and admission tickets." The man's long brown hair covered his eyes as he tipped his head downward and pulled a small notepad and pen from his front pocket. He then clicked the pen and turned to face Kyden again, who'd frozen in place.

"Uh- uh..."

"Blaine Cyott, here." Dennis nudged Kyden in the most nonchalant way that he could manage as he spoke. Kyden turned and faced him wide-eyed, realizing that everyone else was wearing their masks too. Asher could see his confidence being restored when he realized that the teacher wouldn't know who they were in the dark.

"Alright, Blaine Cyott." The teacher moved the glow stick close to the notepad and began searching through what Asher assumed was a list of students who were supposed to attend the ball. "Ah, there you are! Okay and the rest of you?"

"They're here too?" Asher thought to himself. *"All of them?"*

"How about you back there?" Asher shot his head towards

the man who was patiently clicking his pen and smiling into the darkness that filled the rear seats.

"Marcus Elk." The teacher searched his list again and placed a check mark next to a second name.

"James Elwood, *sir*." Kyden spat. The teacher chuckled.

"I'd recognize sass like that anywhere, young man. You three enjoy your night." The teacher placed one hand on the open window and nodded them off before walking on to the next vehicle.

"Let's get out of here before they show up and we end up giving ourselves away." Dennis unbuckled his own seatbelt and reached for the door handle. "Thank God he forgot to get our imaginary tickets."

"Wait, wait!" Kyden fumbled around in his pant pockets for a few moments and Asher could hear the new fabrics brushing together like silk as Kyden's hands moved in and out of the hidden compartments. "Here it is." Kyden pulled free the small bottle of cologne and immediately turned it towards Dennis, squirting it three times. Dennis gagged and tried blocking the mist as it came towards him. "Oh relax, you big baby." Kyden then turned it to himself and sprayed it on his wrists, rubbed them together and applied them to his neck. Asher watched him do so and decided he would do the same, as their clothes were new and likely wouldn't have their scent so strongly stuck to them as their own skin would. Kyden handed off the bottle to him and Asher applied some himself before returning the bottle and getting out of the car.

As they came closer to the yacht, Asher could see just how much effort had gone into planning that night. He could also see how much money had been invested by the wealthier families of Bristlewood. The yacht had three platforms, starting with the loading bay, which had rows of hanging paper lanterns strung up along the edge and hanging just a few inches below the railing of the ship. The second platform had dining tables and a DJ booth on the open balcony with white string lights wrapped around the columns and guards that encased it all. The center of the base platform where everyone was filling on also had a pool, which was sealed off with a large glass cover for the party goers to have a dance floor. The lights in the pool were still on and it gave the entire center scene a blue glow. The highest platform didn't seem to be decorated at all, which to Asher meant that students weren't allowed up there. He examined it as the rest of the crowd made their way onboard.

"Attention, students. Attention!" Asher and the others turned to face the rear end of the yacht. A large building section sat just a little further back than what would be the center of the ship's body and stretched to the far end. In front of it, on their end, stood a man on a small staging area. Asher could tell by the glossy bald head that it was Principle Lough. "There we are. Everyone settle down for a moment. I just have a few things I'd like to go over before we commence our annual Masquerade Ball."

"Hey guys," Dennis placed a hand between Asher and Kyden and knocked it back and forth between their arms, "looks like they showed." To the best of his ability, Asher followed Dennis's line of sight and came across four figures standing tall and at the back of the crowd.

"How did they even get their names on the list?" Asher hissed. "They went *missing* too and we used their names to get in."

"I'm sure Feeder had something to do with it. It's an easy task for him to pull off." The three continued to watch over the other four as Principle Lough finished his speech.

"Alright, I don't want to keep anyone held up any longer than I have to, so without further ado, let's celebrate your last year at Bristlewood High, Seniors!" The students all cheered and arms filled the air as the DJ started playing pop music from the second platform.

"Come on, let's keep an eye on them." Kyden started pushing his way through the crowd towards the front of the dance floor, where Feeder and his posse were watching over the rest of the students. Asher followed but kept a close eye on Feeder, who stood with his hands at his sides and a grin across his face. The other three had their arms folded and carried the same blank expressions. In a sense, their group stood out in the same manner as Asher, Dennis, and Kyden. Feeder was wearing an all-white suit with a white mask that covered the left side of his face entirely but exposed the right. All three of the others wore similar outfits to that of Asher and Dennis, being all black and relatively plain with basic masks. Asher assumed this was Feeder's way of standing out in the crowd and planned.

"Do you think they know we're here?" Dennis glanced in Asher's direction and then back towards Feeder and the others as they broke free from the rest of the mass. He nodded as the jock they all assumed to be James behind the mask looked their way and whispered something to Feeder, who then faced them too.

"Come on, follow me." Dennis turned away from them and started towards the back end of the ship, cutting off Feeder's gaze and limiting who else was around them, as most of the crowd stayed at the front and very few people made their way towards the back so early on in the event.

Once they were out of sight, Dennis pulled a small cloth pouch from his pocket and laid out the contents on a nearby table. The first thing he removed was a small silver shackle that had a strange emblem carved into it. As soon as he placed it, Asher took it in hand. The second thing he removed was a long string of garlic bulbils which he seemed to handle very carefully. The last item was a tiny plastic bottle of what Asher thought to be holy water.

"What's this symbol?" Asher slid his wrist into the shackle and went to close it when Dennis jerked it away from him.

"Careful with that!"

"What is it?"

"It's a bleeder," Dennis studied the trinket and ran his fingers along the interior of the loop, as if to be sure there was no damage, "we're going to use it to naturalize one of them."

"What does it do?" Once Dennis was finished looking it over he grabbed the center of the trinket where the shackle's hinge was and snapped his wrist forward. As the metal pieces clanged together they latched in place and several small spikes exposed themselves on the inside of the band. Kyden jumped back when he saw the spikes come free. Dennis then showed them a key he had placed on his belt loop and unlocked the shackle.

"You get them with this, it'll inject preserved garlic oil right into their veins."

"Wait, wait, wait. You want us to do that to a person? Isn't that dangerous?" Dennis glared at Kyden from the corner of his eye as he pocketed the holy water and buckled the stringed bulbils to his belt.

"These aren't people, Kyden. You'll learn that soon enough. Here they come!" Dennis motioned for Asher and Kyden to follow him up a small ladder on the opposite side of the boat they came around. Once all three were on the rear of the second platform, Asher could see Feeder and the others going towards the same table they had just left moments ago. The only light they had on the posse was the single red paper lantern that sat in the center of the small round table. "Lay down. Listen." The three got as close to the ground as they could and watched over the edge as Feeder and the others looked around the platform.

"Are you certain you saw them?"

"Yes. I know that odor."

"So you didn't see them, you could smell them?"

"Well, y-yes. I thought I saw the-"

"Did they see you?" Feeder was clearly annoyed with James for giving him what he thought to be a false alarm, but he didn't express this clearly as there were still a few other party goers around.

"I-I-"

"Enough. Go find them." James didn't try to speak again and simply nodded weakly as he made his way back around to the populated end of the ship. Asher and the others kept themselves close to the ground and as quiet as possible.

"Idiots." Feeder mumbled. "Less than a week of their time left and they spend it following me? Do they think I'm a joke?"

"I doubt anyone thinks you're a joke."

"You *doubt*, Blaine?" Blaine got choked up and didn't reply. "How has Mabel been doing there?"

"She's been alright, still has the Heart."

"Of course she does. The girl doesn't know what's best for

her yet. She'll learn in time. I'm the only option she'll have, whether she likes it or not, and she WILL like it." Blaine and the second vampire, Marcus, remained quiet. "Asher doesn't understand his full potential yet." The three on the balcony shared confused looks before continuing to listen in. "He has no understanding of his role in this world and it's best that way. If he found out the truth-"

"I found them!" Feeder's gaze shot up towards the platform, where James was now standing directly behind the three on the ground. "Up here, they're up-" James was silenced by Dennis, who made quick use of the strung bulbils by coiling them around his throat. Asher could see now why Dennis was so cautious with this tool, as the bulbils cut into James's flesh and exposed the blades hid beneath their surfaces.

"Take him down!" Asher and Kyden didn't hesitate when given the command, getting up quickly and driving James to the ground. His balance had already been compromised by his efforts to free himself of the serrated vegetations and he made no efforts to get back up once he was down. As Asher and Kyden held him down, Dennis slammed the shackle against one of his panicked wrists. James squealed in agony as the shackle drew blood. "Run!"

"Tear them apart!" Feeders order sent the others into a full sprint towards the balcony, which they scaled with ease. Kyden was stunned at their speed and what they had just done to James and stood motionless as the others took off.

"Kyden, run! Now!" Blaine and Marcus hissed at Kyden as they rushed him, but shrieked as their skin started smoking. Kyden turned to see that Dennis had emptied the holy water on them and took that time to book it towards the front of the yacht. Once they were at the front of the platform they stopped at the railing and looked down at the rest of the crowd.

"Where do you think you're going, Cor?" Asher turned to see Feeder sprinting down the same path they had come from and closing in at incomprehensible speeds for a man.

"Jump!" Asher took the lead and leapt from the balcony, slamming hard into the glass dance floor below and sending a wave of panic over the crowd. Dennis and Kyden followed, but as their conjoined weight hit the glass, it shattered. Students screamed as they were submerged in pool water and Asher fought to breathe as he moved towards the edge of it, followed closely by Dennis and Kyden. "Ditch your jackets!"

"What?" Kyden seemed offended by this gesture as they got out and caught their breaths.

"Just do it! We'll lose them if they don't recognize us!" Just as Asher had finished suggesting this, the sounds of fear and confusion started to fade. From the direction of the balcony, people seemed to be turning docile and calm and this was progressively reaching their location at a steady rate.

"What's going on?" Kyden stammered as he removed the velvet jacket.

"Feeder." Dennis's eyes grew wide as he looked across the platform to see Feeder walking through the crowd, steadily passing each individual and brushing their shoulders and foreheads with his hands as he skimmed over them, hunting for the three that stood furthest away. Asher noticed that the sounds were also seizing from the opposite side of the yacht and spotted Blaine and Marcus making their way through the crowd in the same manner.

"We have to get out of here!"

"Mass hypnosis." Kyden watched in awe as the screams stopped instantly on contact with the individuals.

"Come on, Kyden." Dennis grabbed Kyden by the back of his shirt and pulled him to the edge of the ship. "The docks aren't far. Let's get down this ladder and into the sea quietly." Dennis started down the ladder first and was being sure that neither his feet nor his hands slid off the bars. Asher had Kyden go next to keep him from freezing up again and then followed close behind, as Feeder and the others had made their way through the crowd and were approaching like a pack of wolves stalking their prey.

Once the three were in the water, the silence that fell over the yacht became increasingly terrifying. Asher kept calm as he turned to face the ship, swimming towards land on his back. He could see Feeder, Blaine, Marcus, and a severely disturbed James all looking over them from the yellow and white lantern light that hung high above the water and yet still danced on the surface. Even from where they were at in that inky black ocean he could see the same grin on

Feeder's face as he leaned against the metal railing and held out five fingers. It sent a chill down Asher's spine knowing that Feeder wouldn't struggle in the least to pull him under and end everything, yet didn't for the sake of playing his own games.

Chapter Twelve: Stars in Pentad

Clouds above hung low in the void, disturbed only by the moon's light as they coasted in from the east before crossing the great giant, which filled them with a white glow before each continued on its way over dark treetops and into the night. Between the passing clouds were speckled areas of small bulbs, illuminating nothing but themselves and remaining almost perfectly still as their multicolored neighbors did the same. Below, amongst large pines, sat the cabin. The front door opened wide and the screen door creaked along with it, clattering shut as a figure made it's way out on the porch. A second figure sat at the edge of the front steps and ran his eyes across the hemisphere.

"You alright out here?" Dennis walked to the end of the porch and leaned against one of several wooden beams as he spoke to Asher, who seemed lost in thought. Asher didn't answer for a few moments as he proceeded to study his surroundings.

"What do you think he meant?"

"Who?" Asher's silence filled the space between them once more but was short-lived in comparison to the previous quiet.

"Feeder. What do you think he meant by my role and my potential?" Dennis folded his arms and looked up at the moon as Asher did the same.

"I don't know, but it can't be good." Dennis pushed himself away from the beam with his shoulder and made it down to the same step Asher was sitting on, then sat alongside him. "If Feeder wants you dead, whatever he's trying to do must involve getting you out of the way first, but I've never even heard him speak your name before school started this year."

Asher didn't respond to this. He simply sat and continued to look about the stars for an answer, unsure of where he was in this world anymore. His best friends and the father he couldn't return to were the only ones who knew he existed now and he had no place to truly call home. He then turned to face Dennis, who seemed to be thinking about similar things, which Asher assumed by taking in Dennis's twisted frown and pleading eyes as he flicked them across the constellations.

"When this is all over, I promise, I'll help you find out as much as you can about what he said if it's that important. Asking him ourselves doesn't seem like the best option." Dennis didn't look away from the stars as he spoke, but Asher continued to face him and nodded with a broken smile.

A faint howl became audible through the trees and both boys turned in the direction they thought it came from. It was soon followed by a second and third howl. Dennis sighed and pulled himself up to his feet. Asher got up as well and examined the wood line, knowing he wouldn't catch a glimpse of anything as the howls were too far to see a source through the forest.

"Were those wolves?"

"Mhm." Dennis nodded as his expression grew cold and stern. "They know where we are."

"The wolves?" Asher's question was answered by Dennis shaking his head from side to side.

"Feeder, and the others." He then turned away from the front yard area and held both doors open for Asher. "Come on, it's best none of us be out at night anymore."

Asher headed inside and went straight to the shared room upstairs to lay down. After a few minutes of listening to the wolves' howls in the distance, his eyes grew heavy and a deep sleep ensued. As his eyes adjusted to the darkness behind their lids, a faint blurry light started to emerge. Without opening his eyes, Asher watched the orange glow come into focus. The image in his mind was that of his Amber Heart, still placed within the cage of Mabel's amulet necklace. He could make out each curving metallic vine and the leaves that branched off them. However, some parts of the amulet and the illumination of the heart were covered by something else. He studied the dark areas until he could tell what their form was. Mabel's fingers were locked around the amulet and the chipped paint on her nails became clear.

"Asher, I hope you can hear me." Mabel's hands shook as they held the Amber Heart tightly, which Asher could now see was starting to crack in several places. Fine lines were scattered about the surface and a few sank deep into its' core. *"Feeder is up to something. His plans changed and I don't know what's going on. Please, be careful. Don't trust anyone you might come across and keep the others close. Whatever Dennis did to James, it angered all of them."* The sound of rustling footsteps in a nearby room became known and Asher could see through Mabel's eyes that she was watching the open entrance to the area of the den she was in, being sure that nobody saw what she was doing. "I have to go, I don't want to make you any worse off. This is the last time I'm going to use your Heart. Feeder plans to keep me fed in other ways so I don't have to drain your life force anymore. I don't know what's going on, just be careful. I have to go now.... I'm sorry."

Asher tried desperately to speak back to her, but none of his words were vocal. All sound he tried to make failed except a strange gurgling he couldn't seem to stop. His efforts to shout to her proved useless and catching his breath after each attempt was exhausting. As the glow of his Heart faded back into a blurry image, he could feel an outside force shaking his body. Just as the Heart vanished entirely, his eyes snapped opened and the force rolled him onto his stomach with his face hanging off the edge of the bed. Asher choked and coughed as he heaved into the propped bucket that had been resting there.

"You alright?" Asher used what strength he could find to turn his head over his shoulder. Kyden was standing beside him with a hand on the same shoulder he was looking over. "You started choking on it in your sleep." Asher convulsed once again and felt Kyden's hand shiver with disgust. "Alright, well it seems like you've got this under control. I was going to get breakfast, but I think a shower will do." As Kyden's footsteps went into the next room, Asher wiped his mouth and caught his breath before sitting up. He was quivering and covered in cold sweats but sniffled and placed his feet on the floor, brushing it off the best he could.

"Hey..., Kyden?" He managed through exhausted breaths.

"Yeah?" Kyden came back to the bathroom doorway but stayed within it. Asher finished catching his breath before trying to speak again or stand.

"How are you doing?"

"You mean after everything last night?" Kyden snapped. He then tsked and shook his head viciously. "Dennis assaulted a guy and I watched the most impressive hypnotic act I've ever seen. Nothing about last night was right." Kyden looked over Asher and then turned back into the bathroom. "It also wasn't exactly supernatural."

"You still don't believe us?"

"What's to believe?" Kyden shouted as he started running water in the stand-alone shower. "Dennis gave a guy several lacerations and puncture wounds. That would do plenty of damage to anybody. Next, to that, professional hypnotism is done everywhere, what do you expect to happen when a bunch of teenagers get their hands on that kind of knowledge?" Asher was annoyed that Kyden still showed such strong disbelief, but could also see where he was coming from. Nothing from the previous night could only be marked as supernatural and logical arguments were still a possibility. What irritated Asher the most was that it was a C-average student telling him about the logical side of things and Asher being the one to accept only the supernatural answers.

"We aren't lying to you."

"I never said you were, I just don't know if you know what the truth is yourselves." Asher began to get angry but let it slide and took several deep breaths to avoid throwing up again. "So does that mean you're going to call law enforcement on us?"

"Why would I do that?" Kyden returned to the door one last time and looked out with his eyebrows furrowed.

"You watched several crimes take place and you clearly don't believe what we're telling you, so are you going to call them?"

"The only crime that was committed was assault. There's no law against hypnotism that I know of."

"So no?" Kyden smiled and relaxed his brow.

"No, man. You guys are my best friends. Whatever this whole thing is, it won't get solved in a jail cell." With that, Kyden made his way back into the bathroom and closed the door behind him.

Asher chuckled and made his way out of the room and down the stairs on wobbly legs, guiding himself the entire way with one hand following each wall and the other on the handrail. Once he was in the living room he took a look around and noticed that Dennis was nowhere to be seen. He then twisted his lips and continued to check each downstairs room. After a few minutes of searching, Asher took to resting on the sofa and waited for Kyden to make his way down as well. After what felt like hours of watching basic cable, Asher could hear heavy footsteps marching towards the living room from atop the stairway. He turned to see Kyden drying his hair with a white towel as he trudged down the steps.

"Aren't you supposed to be going to school to keep a low profile?"

"Does it matter?" Kyden tossed the towel over the newel cap as he reached the bottom of the staircase and leaped over the back of the sofa, plopping down next to Asher and raising one foot to rest on the coffee table. "They already know where we are. Didn't Dennis tell you that?"

"Where is Dennis?" Kyden shrugged uncertainly.

"He said we needed a few things for the house and took off first thing in the morning." Kyden leaned over and grabbed the remote, proceeding to flip through channels and getting further from the show Asher had been boredly staring at. "He's only been gone a couple of hours. I'm sure he's alright.

"Aren't your parents worried about you?"

"You trying to get rid of me?" Kyden grinned jokingly and glanced over at Asher before returning to the television.

"No, just seems odd that you spend all of your time here." The grin faded from Kyden's face gradually as he replied.

"They aren't that concerned with where I am, long as I check in with them occasionally." Asher decided not to ask any further questions, remembering why he always avoided the subject of Kyden's parents. He'd never gotten to meet them, but their reputation in Bristlewood was notorious. They were known for being neglectful and greedy, which Asher found to be strange coming from a less fortunate family where the family is all that they have. "Anyways, got any plans for the day?"

"Not really." Asher shrugged and stared blankly at the shopping channel.

"Well, Dennis and I were supposed to put up a few more of those UV lights today as an added precaution or whatever, but it doesn't seem like we'll have the time if we wait for him to show. Care to lend a hand?"

Asher agreed and the two made their way outside, where Kyden pulled a large box from the backseat of his car. The contents were that of stringed UV bulbs. Asher counted at least 200 bulbs on the wired string and they began lining the outside of the cabin with them. The project took several hours, even with the simplicity of it, as Kyden informed him that Dennis had a specific way he wanted the bulbs to hang. This left Asher holding up each bulb and splitting paths in the wires so that Kyden could nail them to the mid-height of the exterior walls and every other bulb at the highest point of the walls.

"I guess the ones about mid-height are supposed to keep them from getting too close and the higher ones are supposed to stop them from passing the tree line" Kyden showed Asher a sequencing switch that made it so either the top row or the bottom row was lit up at a single time and a third option that lit up every bulb simultaneously. Once the project was complete, Asher could hear his own truck rumbling down the path. A small wave of relief rushed over him, as the sound meant that Dennis was safe. The two waited on the porch for the truck to show and waved at Dennis as he came into view. Asher could see that there were several small plants in the bed of the truck and the side panels were covered in dirt smudges and loose leaves. Just as he started to grow annoyed he heard the driver side window rolling down.

"No worries, I'll get it cleaned up first thing in the morning." Asher pretended he wasn't irritable and helped unload the many grown garlic plants Dennis recollected from his old hideout.

Once the plants were laid out carefully on the ground, the three went back inside for the night, being sure that they were hidden away before dusk. Asher spent that night thinking about Mabel and informing the others of what information he was given the night before. After everyone was caught up and he answered what little questions were offered, they all went to sleep and Asher was the first to wake up the following morning. *"Four more,"* was his first thought as his eyes cracked open, *"then this all ends."* He sat up in his bed and listened to the birds chirp outside as the morning sun slowly crawled across the floorboards. *"How can the world act like nothing bad is happening out there?"* He quietly got to his feet and made his way out of the room, being sure not to disturb the others. The amount of energy he had was strange to him, as it was the best he had felt in several weeks. The only thing he could think this meant was that Feeder had found something else to give Mabel. *"What could possibly make him want me alive, after all this time of wanting me dead?"* Asher pushed the thought aside, trying to keep his focus on getting everyone else away from the situation over figuring out how to get more involved just because of his own curiosity. Making his way down the stairs, he removed the towel that

Kyden had thrown the previous day and tossed it into a hamper located in a closet to the left of the front door. He then turned back towards the stairs and went into the living room, where the smell of coffee beans permeated the air.

"Morning." Asher jumped and spun to his right. Dennis was sitting at the dining table with a newspaper and a large white mug. "Want one?" He asked as he lifted the mug above his head.

"Yeah, might as well. I thought you were still in bed." Dennis folded up the newspaper and set it down on the table as he got up and made his way over to the cupboards and counters.

"Nope, I got up about an hour ago to get an early start."

"Early start on what?" Dennis turned around with a second mug filled with coffee and outstretched his arm for Asher to accept it. As Asher collected the cup he could see that Dennis's shirt had several small dirt stains on it. He then noticed that the dirt was also under Dennis's nails and on some parts of his face. "Oh." Dennis chuckled.

"Yeah, figured it was the best option for me to handle the herbs seeing as I've been the one who's worked with them the most." Dennis sat back down at the table and grabbed his mug, raised his hand and pointed with one finger out the front window, keeping the others under the handle. "Brought that, too." Asher peered out the window and caught a glimpse of Dennis's heavy birdbath sitting in the front yard, just beyond the pitfall traps. "Figured we could use it to keep making holy water."

"What's so special about that birdbath?"

"Think of it as a holy chalice." Dennis smiled as he examined the structure proudly from afar. "Built it myself with this exact intention in mind. The interior is lined with consecrated salts so that the process of making holy water goes smoother." Dennis held the same expression as he returned to his newspaper, flicking it open and continuing to read where he left off. Asher sat across from him and Dennis noticed that his expression became that of confusion. "What's on your mind?"

"I was just thinking, how did the crossbow burn Mabel's hands?"

"Ah, common error based on folklore." Dennis set the paper back down and took a large swig from his mug. Asher did the same. "Some people believe that all vampires have the same weaknesses, but that isn't true. A Sagina has all the weaknesses an ordinary vampire has and then some. Most people believe that only the werewolf has a weakness to pure silver, but this same belief is true in the Sagina." Dennis got up from the table and made his way into the living area where he grabbed his duffel bag and returned to the kitchen. Once he was back in his seat he threw the bag up and let it crash against the tabletop, unzipping it as he did so. He then pulled free one of the crossbows and handed it over for Asher to look at. Asher took it from Dennis's hands and gazed across the table at his friend, waiting for an explanation. Dennis pulled out a second crossbow and tapped the flat metallic left side of the handle. Asher looked at the weapon in his hands and turned it so that he could view the same side as Dennis. He then realized for the first time that the plating on the handle was made of silver and was bolted down to the wooden frame. "Make a crossbow like that and nothing as dark as the creature you use it on can use it against you."

"What about James and the others? Could they use it on us?"

"If you're not careful, yes. Odds are they'll resort to more primitive means, such as physical attacks, seeing as that's their strength. None of them have any use in a weapon like this, but it's best to be sure that they have to get close to you to cause harm because that'll give *you* the advantage in a fight." Asher nodded, completely understanding Dennis's points on the matter.

"So what makes a Sagina different from vampires, other than the obvious?"

"That, I'm still unsure of." Dennis shrugged and raised his brow. Asher turned to face the kitchen counter and spotted the ancient book Kyden left there about a week ago.

"Still a chance we can find out." Asher got up and opened the book, resting his back against the kitchen wall as he shuffled through the beaten pages. In the midst of his search, he could hear the same heavy steps as the day before and saw Kyden coming down the stairway with his hair a wreck.

"Wow, look at that!" Kyden stopped as Dennis spoke and

turned to look behind himself as if there were something else Dennis could be talking about. "Looks like you got crowned prom king last night." Asher and Dennis both chuckled as Kyden remained confused in a dazed half-asleep state, with spikes of hair circling the entire center of his scalp.

"Just give me coffee and stop talking so loud."

"Of course, your majesty!" Dennis got up once again and poured another mug, handing it off to Kyden as he trudged into the kitchen and sat in one of the vacant chairs, rubbing the sleep from his eyes. Asher continued to rummage through the pages until he noticed a small patch of torn sheets near the binding.

"Hmm...."

"What is it?" Dennis looked up at Asher as he sounded his concerns and Asher turned the book to face Dennis.

"I don't remember all of these missing pages." Asher turned the book back towards himself and looked over each page still contained in the book nearest to the missing clump of sheets. "It's like somebody got their hands on it at some point between the times I've had it and-." Asher immediately looked up at Kyden, who looked cranky and continued to rub at his eyes while sipping from his mug. Kyden noticed this and stared back.

"What?"

"You didn't do this, did you?"

"Why would I tear pages from a book?" Asher reminded Kyden that that was how he'd seen him *studying* for the past 6 years and Kyden's face remained unchanged but with an added shrug. "It wasn't me. Why is all this stuff out on the table?" Kyden pushed Asher's crossbow back towards the duffel bag and Dennis picked it up to return it to its containment.

"You going to help us when things start happening?" Dennis faced Kyden, who was blinking a lot as if trying to clear blurred vision.

"Yeah, yeah, I'll be there. With my potato launcher." Kyden then reached into the duffel bag and pulled free a large clear plastic tube with a black base. At the end near his shoulder was an area of the pipe that was thinner than the rest and had a cap that was pressed against Kyden's shoulder. Asher assumed this was the part that built pressure when pushed in. "It's definitely not the best model one could use."

"Well, it's homemade and does the job."

"What are you supposed to do with that?"

"You know what it's for." Dennis looked back at Asher and crossed his arms, waiting for Asher to prove him right.

"Garlic powder?" Dennis then nodded and looked back at Kyden, who was acting as if it had sights that he was aiming down.

"It'll coat a pretty large area in a cloud of the stuff."

"Do you really want to use that, Kyden?"

"Uh, yeah," Kyden smirked at Asher before speaking again, "I don't know exactly what's coming, but I know it isn't illegal to gas someone with garlic powder if I have to."

Asher shrugged and returned to the book, running his fingers along the missing pages. The page on the left of the missing bundle was that of the Amber Heart and the page on the right was that of a dog-like creature posed in several human stances. Asher examined the page on the right further and though most of it was destroyed by several areas of water damage, including the sketches, one word was still clear: Polymorphism.

Chapter Thirteen: Lone Barrier

Time grew more and more sluggish with each passing hour as those that separated Asher and the others from the inevitable drug on. The cabin sat seemingly desolate with the lack of attention it was given and the bleak silence that fell over its inhabitants so early in the morning. All but one, that is. Kyden continued to move about as the final sun rose above the pines, warming the exterior walls of their home. He proceeded to make the others breakfast and mimic the words that came from his headphones. The wires dangled loosely in front of him and he continuously pushed them away from the crackling grease on the stove that he had been working with. Minutes into this session, Asher appeared in the kitchen entrance and rested his right side against a wall, crossed his arms, and rubbed his inner biceps with his hands to warm up. He didn't speak and simply watched as Kyden remained unaware and upbeat. With eggs in a pan at the front left of the stove and bacon sizzling at the back on a tabletop grill, Kyden knocked his head side to side and did the same with his hips. Asher cleared his throat harshly and turned away from the awkward scene. Kyden jumped at the abruption and whipped around, slinging grease and a single shredded egg yolk off the spatula he was using and across the kitchen floor.

"How much of that did you see?" Kyden hollered out over his music. Asher shook his head and raised a palm in Kyden's direction before moving further into the kitchen and sitting at the table. "Not even a grin from that, huh?" Asher twisted towards the living area and watched the television screen over the open bar separating the two rooms. Kyden sighed and removed his headphones before turning back to what remained of the eggs.

"Where's-"

"Dennis?" Kyden interrupted, seemingly proud of how well he knew his friend. Asher nodded to confirm the assumption was correct. "Left as soon as the sun came up to do a perimeter check."

"What does that mean?"

"I don't know." Kyden slid two eggs on a plate and used a pair of black plastic tongs to pick up a few strips of bacon, which he then put alongside the eggs and handed off to Asher. "All he said was that he had to make sure they'd know where to go."

"They?"

"Feeder and the others." The stove made beeping sounds as Kyden flipped several switches, turning off the burners. He then made his way over to the table and sat across from Asher.

"Wait, so he's *trying* to lead them here?" Kyden raised his shoulders and nodded simultaneously as he tore a piece of bacon in half with his teeth. "I thought we were trying to save all the time we could get?"

"Hey, I'm just telling you what he told me. I have no clue what's going on."

"How's he leading them here?"

"If I had to guess," Kyden gulped hard and moved what food he had in his mouth around before speaking again, "he's probably using his 'scent'." Kyden seemed to be using the term jokingly, but Asher assumed it was true.

"That makes sense."

"If you say so." Kyden stuck a fork into the center of a badly damaged egg white with almost no yoke and stuffed it in his mouth before swallowing what he was already chewing. Asher sighed and stared at his own breakfast as he became anxious about Dennis's choice to go alone. "So tonight's the night, huh?"

"What do you mean?" Asher stopped trying to hook a slightly gooey egg with his fork and shot a glare up at Kyden.

"I'm gonna get to see what you guys have been talking about- the truth." Kyden took a swig from a mug he had already had set out on the table and gulped hard before pointing in Asher's direction with one loose finger. "It might even surprise you guys."

"I doubt that." Asher snapped. He then got up from the table and rinsed his plate, which was covered in grease and yellowish goop from the eggs. Once he was finished he made his way outside and sat at the base step of the porch with his feet planted on the ground. His irritation with Kyden was one he didn't quite understand himself. He knew that what was happening was as he himself had told it, but the rationality that Kyden gave with most every detail still made him question things. His annoyance was met with understanding on almost every level, which bugged him even more. However, the things Kyden never seemed to justify in any way, were that Mabel had been kidnapped and nobody remembered who she, or Dennis, or Asher was. *"At least he knows something isn't right, I guess."* Asher sat in place for nearly an hour as he watched the sun lift itself from the horizon and begin trailing the skies. His nerves were on edge as he thought about how long it had been since he'd last seen Mabel and wondered if the coming night would be the next time he got the chance. *Crack!* Asher turned his head over his left shoulder and his heart skipped a beat before resting again. At the edge of the clearing was Dennis, who was trudging through knee-high brush and making his way back to the cabin.

"Morning." The greeting flowed through the empty space that separated the two, but a reply didn't follow. "Was just out making some markings."

"Spot anything?"

"No." Dennis lifted a large fabric container he had slung over his shoulder as high as he could and dropped it back to his side again after clearing the brush. Asher recognized it as the duffel bag and became curious.

"Why did you need that?" Dennis looked down at the bag and then up at his friend as he came closer to the porch.

"Figured I'd bring it with me to get some more supplies." Asher nodded in understanding but noticed a small rectangular area at the bottom of the bag that he hadn't seen before. His attention related to the object had been broken when a firm hand came to rest on his shoulder. "How are you feeling today?"

"I'm better..., cold." Dennis raised one side of his lips but also showed a pity that Asher had grown accustomed to.

"Well, tonight we'll get that cleared up."

"Maybe... but, what if me living kills her? I can't be the reason she dies." The weak expression on Dennis's lips didn't change, but his eyes showed true pain, which was something Asher had never seen on his friend's face before.

"I'm sure Mabel feels the same way about you." Muffled clattering rang out from inside the cabin followed by cursing.

"Do you think we're doing the right thing, bringing him into all of this?" The expression had now slid off Dennis's face and the pain became even more obvious as he stared through the walls at Kyden. Another, more filled out smile then made itself known.

"He'll be fine. You'll want to thank me after all of this is over. Remember that." Dennis used the hand he had on Asher's shoulder to pull him into a tight hug.

As a little more time passed the sun floated overhead, making it the warmest day of the year at the time. All three boys were back inside and had been laughing, playing games, and finding any other ways that they could to occupy their time and remain positive. For Kyden, this was an easy task. However, for Asher and Dennis, constant mental reminders of what was to come kept nudging their way in throughout the evening. Both were handling it as best they could, but Asher saw that Dennis was struggling even more than himself. They could tell that Kyden was aware of their emotional flip-flops and did their best to play it off. Asher pressed on with the games and shows that the three partook in, but his internal irritability and eagerness to get the agonizing wait over with was almost unbearable.

After what felt like a lifetime, the sky began to slip off into a multitude of colors and the clouds did the same. Asher watched as the purple atmosphere reflected off the clouds, which gave them a pink, cotton candy appearance that turned a dark blue as it reached their bottoms. The tops of each pine became a dull green, much more gloomy than their former afternoon selves. The ground was shrouded in gray darkness that reminded Asher of a photo that would have been taken in the '60s.

"Hey, you going to join us, or are you just going to stare out that window all night?" Asher turned to face the others who were sitting around the coffee table and readjusted himself to participate in a card game they were about to start. Collecting the hand he had been dealt he noticed that all of Dennis's cards were exposed to him. He looked up to see Dennis staring at a wall clock behind the TV and snapped his fingers. As the *click* became audible between his digits Dennis shot a look at him and then down at his own hand of cards. He then lifted the cards and readjusted himself in his seat, clearing his throat as he did so.

"Who's first?"

"Well, I handed off the cards so you should go first, Dennis." Dennis grunted at Kyden and threw down a card. Just as the ace touched the polished tabletop, Asher's vision shifted elsewhere. He could see the same sky he had just been admiring a few moments ago and the trees that touched it.

"Asher?" His vision snapped back to his own and Dennis was waving a hand in front of his face. Beads of cold sweat began to form on his skin as a migraine set in. His vision sparked between those of his own and those outside, separated by rapid frames of bright whites. Eventually, the flashing stopped and his sights were focused again. He was looking at the front of the cabin. His breathing intensified when he noticed that the eyes he was looking through were making their way across the front of the building horizontally, remaining behind the tree line as they migrated. Thin fingers then reached out from where the figure stood and grabbed hold of a tree branch, seemingly trying to sneak away from something or towards something. Once the embodiment was aligned with the front door of the cabin, Asher could see the back of his own head and Dennis frantically shaking him.

"Asher!?" Mabel's voice rang through his head like a siren and he quickly regained control of himself.

"M-Mabel!" Asher shoved at Dennis the best he could and stood up, but the drainage he felt was immense and left him little strength. "She's here! She's-" Asher stomped on shaky legs to the front door and twisted the knob ferociously.

"Asher? Wh- Mabel? Asher. Asher, wait!" Dennis made ground on him fast, but not fast enough to block the door. Asher swung the large solid barricade open and pinged the lock mechanism against the wall as he did so.

"Mabel!"

"Asher, don't!" At the tree line, he could make out the familiar dark long hair and handmade jacket as Mabel rushed from the forest towards the front door that he held open.

"What are you doing!?" Dennis moved to the opposite side of Asher that he was on and grabbed hold of the door. As he pried at the door, Asher kept all of his strength focused on keeping it open. "Let it go!"

"No, she can make it!" Dennis continued to fight against him for a few more moments before Asher let go, springing Dennis forward with the door and back into the living room on his hands and knees. Asher then pulled it open again and caught Mabel as she flung herself inside at him. The two sobbed as he clutched her in his arms, rocking back and forth and still shaking from the use of his Amber Heart.

"A-Asher...." Kyden stuttered. Asher ignored his words at first but could sense the concern. "Asher!" The sobbing between the two seemed to grow distant as Asher pieced together what was happening and remembered what Mabel had last told him. He then pulled his eyes open a little and took in a deep nasally breath.

"No rosebuds."

"That's not Mabel!" The sobbing from the girl became low sadistic laughter as Asher went to pull his face away from her. Looking towards his shoulder he noticed fresh red nail polish on an unfamiliar hand. Just as he had confirmed what was going on, a sharp pain shot across his exposed neck. Warm liquid began to run beneath the collar of his shirt as he turned towards his friends. *POP!* A large white cloud filled the room and the girl began shrieking in what Asher could only comprehend as agony similar to his own, but he couldn't react to the pain he felt himself. As the cloud fell heavily to the floor, so did the girl. Through the searing pain of the powder filling his eyes, Asher could see Kyden holding the potato launcher and Dennis pulling a crossbow and several stakes from the duffel bag.

"Set him down!" Dennis commanded Kyden, who remained frozen in fear and disbelief. "Kyden, now!" Kyden dropped the launcher and rushed towards Asher to keep him from falling over as the blood loss set in. "Use the powder to keep him from bleeding out! Don't touch the girl!" Kyden frantically grabbed at the garlic powder that covered the floor and stuffed it in and around Asher's open wound, while avoiding the shrieking, incapacitated vampire. As shock had already set in, all Asher could do was take Kyden's treatments and stare at the girl on the floor. He recognized her as the same girl that was with James, even through her contorted powder covered expressions.

"What now?" Kyden got back to his feet once Asher's head was elevated against the wall and he was seated two steps up towards the second floor.

"Get a crossbow and take aim out that window!" Dennis pointed towards a window on the opposite side of the door that he was on.

"No way, I'm not killing anybody!"

"These aren't people Kyden! Look what they did to your friend!" Kyden examined Asher from where he stood in complete horror as the realization that everything he had been told was true. "Now!" He then rushed over to the duffel bag and grabbed a second crossbow in unsteady hands, arming it with a stake and slamming the front door shut on his way over to the window he was told to guard.

"Don't worry Asher, we'll get you treated! Just stay still!"

"Come out, Feeder! We know you're there!" Dennis kept his eyes lined up with his weapon and ran the crossbow every direction out the window that he could, slowly. The forest was dead silent. All that Asher could hear was his own raspy breathing and the panicked breaths of Kyden. However, it wasn't long before more laughter could be heard circling the cabin, followed by a voice that couldn't be any more than ten feet in front of Asher.

"What's the matter, boy?" The voice chuckled as knuckles tapped threateningly against the exterior side of the door. "You didn't think I'd be so merciful after all we've been through, did you?" Asher watched as Dennis fired a stake in Feeder's direction, but didn't hear a connection when he'd hoped to. Instead, Feeder laughed and his voice became more distant as the voices of the others drew nearer. "Tear down the walls! You don't need permission to enter if it isn't a home." The laughter grew more maniacal as boards could be heard splintering and snapping like twigs.

Dennis was quick to pull a small remote from his pocket and engage the UV lights outside. Intense beams blasted through the windows and screams could be heard as the vampires fled to the safety of the trees.

"Come on, then!" Dennis continued to launch stakes through the opening, seemingly without concern for what they hit. Asher feared Mabel could still be in the line of fire and tried desperately to find his feet.

"Asher, stay down!" Kyden begged, but remained stationed to assist Dennis. "You'll bleed out if you don't stay low and calm!" Asher ignored the request and got up, keeping his hand pressed tight against his neck. The world spun as he straightened out his back and his own grip on the guardrail was flawed, but he kept his vision as steady as possible. He then watched as Blaine got hold of Kyden's crossbow just outside the framework and fashioned a vicious, fanged grin in the eyes of terror.

"What's the matter, Kyden? We're friends, remember?" Blaine started to outstretch an arm towards the frightened boy but made sure he didn't pass the barrier. "Come on, let an old pal in, huh?" Kyden's muscles started to relax and one of his hands began slowly moving towards that of Blaine's. The grin remained strong as he could sense Kyden's resistance weakening. Asher, more concerned than he had been throughout the entire event, tried desperately to call out for Dennis's help, but no sound could be made from his shredded vocals. Kyden's hand was nearly out the window as a whistling sound emitted from somewhere beneath his shoulders. Blaine's grin vanished immediately and bewilderment filled his eyes. He then looked down at where the sound had come from and found Asher's finger on the crossbow's trigger. Kyden blinked incredibly fast for a few seconds as what was going on hit him. He then wrenched the crossbow from Blaine's grasp and loaded a second stake, quickly sending it through the vampire's center torso. With two stakes in his chest, Blaine stumbled a few steps before falling on his back and gasping for air. With his lips quivering, he fought to turn his eyes towards the boys in the window, meeting theirs' with his own. "Th-thank yo-" Blaine sputtered up some dark, heavy blood before his neck began to twitch and dropped his head against the porch. Kyden looked at Asher with wide eyes before shaking off the trauma and loading yet another stake, continuing his firing frenzy.

"Back away from the window!" Asher turned to face Dennis, who was crouched beneath the glass as small rocks bolted through the opening and smashed several UV lights in quick succession. "Don't let them grab you, again!" Shattering glass and splintering wood was all that Asher could hear and even those sounds were growing dull. His head swam more than it ever had before and he could feel his skin getting colder. Just as he had thought he couldn't stand any longer, the front half of the cabin collapsed, exposing the contents inside and all three boys. Dennis and Kyden had both been knocked back by the crumbling structures and were recollecting themselves as the remaining two vampires moved in on their disheveled group. Asher was laying against the steps with several boards pinning down his exhausted legs when he felt the weight on them grow even heavier. Looking up, he saw the furious face of James, who was standing over him triumphantly whilst pointing at a white heap to his right that was also partially buried.

"What did you do to her?" Asher could see the girl still

buried under the powder and now knocked unconscious by the pain it caused her. "You'll pay for this!" In less than a second, Asher was airborne and the destroyed pieces of the cabin that covered him were soaring in every direction. Moments after James had lifted him by his neck with a single hand, Asher was crashing against the steps yet again. Dazed and nearly incapable of moving at all, he forced his eyelids open and saw James standing with his arm outstretched as if to still be choking Asher. He then heard a sick creaking, and deep, heavy cracking that was followed by James limply dropping his arms and head. The vampire was patiently lifted off the ground and Asher could see the lower half of someone else behind him.

"This one is mine." Feeder moved the corpse off to his side and dropped it as one would with a filthy garbage bag. Asher could see from the way James was laying that Feeder had plunged a hand into his back and crushed his spine. "You know, things could have gone so much smoother if you simply hadn't interfered." Feeder took a step forward and leaned over Asher's feeble form. "You could have stayed in Bristlewood and made Mabel happy for what time you had with her. Given, you'd have forgotten about her when I was ready anyhow." Feeder examined the dark blood covering his hand and aligned all of his fingers tightly together. "No matter. There's still a chance I can make her give you up." Feeder then turned his fingers in an upward direction before angling them down towards Asher's heart. "I just need you as close to dead as possible." He then pulled his arm back to its full length and swung it forward with immense force. Just as his fingertips were about to connect with Asher's chest, whistling sounded out again and Feeder pulled away, straightening out his back and gritting his teeth as he threw his head up. "You damned child!" Feeder stood and turned towards Dennis, who was several feet away and in what remained of the living room. Asher could see an empty crossbow and heard another whistle come from the opposite direction. This one didn't connect, as Feeder spun and caught the stake midair, but his success didn't last. As he pulled the stake Dennis hit him with from his ribs he was sent flying further into the cabin by another girl.

"Asher, I'm here!" Mabel rushed in from where the door had been and hastily made her way over to Asher, hugging him tightly and crying as she examined him. "You're going to be fine. Just, hang on!" She then bolted from the girl on the ground back to Asher in the blink of an eye. He hadn't noticed that the girl was wearing the amulet during the attack. Mabel yipped and dropped the necklace, which was still covered in powder. She then raised a fist and slammed it against the article, smashing the metal encasement that surrounded the Amber Heart.

"You ungrateful girl! I am giving you eternity and still you want this putrid waste?" Feeder took a step towards the two once he was back on his feet but stopped to catch yet another stake from Dennis. Rage was filling Feeder's eyes as Dennis removed a silver dagger from his pocket. "I've toyed with you long enough. Let's end this." Dennis's expression became stern and he gripped the dagger as he approached Feeder.

"D-Den-" Asher tried to raise an arm in Dennis's direction but Mabel pushed it down delicately and held out the Amber Heart.

"Asher, take back your Heart. Please!" Mabel pressed the Heart against Asher's chest, but he resisted the urge to end his suffering and wrapped his fingers around hers. Mabel began to cry harder and Asher could see it in her eyes that she was begging him to accept the Heart. "Please don't make me do this."

"Dennis, look out!" Kyden launched a stake at Feeder and sank it deep in his back, which Asher saw from the corner of his eye.

He could also see that Feeder had Dennis lifted in the air by the collar of his shirt and was crushing the hand that Dennis was holding the dagger in. The expression on Dennis's face had changed to that of pain and Asher could see he was trying desperately not to be overwhelmed by it. Dennis's eyes then met Asher's and they begged for forgiveness.

"Take... the Heart!" Dennis fought hard against the urge to scream and spoke through gritted teeth. "Please!"

"Asher, take the Heart from me!" With what strength he could summon, Asher looked back at Mabel and with an apology written across his face, he pressed the Heart into her chest. "No!" The Heart began to glow a mixed tone of gold and white as it started sinking beneath her skin.

"Don't!" Kyden sprinted passed the two on the stairs with a stake in hand and rushed towards Feeder, who had turned the dagger towards Dennis and was forcing the blade against him. With one swing, Feeder knocked Kyden to the ground and slammed his palm against the hilt of the dagger, sending it deep into Dennis's chest. "No!" Asher, with his last breath, watched Dennis's struggles seize and lost the will to fight against Mabel.

A flash of white and gold light filled the room as Mabel and Asher both collapsed. Feeder shielded his eyes, dropping Dennis as he did so. Kyden then crawled on sore hands and knees over to his faintly breathing friend.

"Dennis, don't do this to me! I can't lose both of you!" Kyden clutched one of Dennis's hands, avoiding the hand that Dennis was still holding the impaling dagger with. "Please, don't do this!" He rested his head against Dennis's chest and began sobbing uncontrollably, filling the cabin with muffled cries. The clopping of new shoes was the only other sound as Feeder walked around examining his work. Near the front of the cabin lay a lifeless Asher, an unconscious Mabel, and behind him was a lifelong enemy who was about to be put to rest.

"Come out, Marcus." Feeder turned to face the rear of the cabin and watched towards the kitchen area, where the remaining vampire had been tucked away. As Marcus made himself known, Feeder took in a deep, long breath and smiled as he looked over the events that unfolded, yet again.

"Yes, Feeder?"

"Collect the girl. It's time for us to move on."

"What about the book?" Marcus held up the large ancient book and Feeder outstretched an arm for it.

"We'll need it too. I suppose I was wrong about the boy, but we have an eternity to find someone worthy enough." As Marcus moved his hands out and placed the book in Feeder's, wooden shrapnel began rapidly scraping together. *Whoosh!* With one quick blow, Feeder dropped the book and was sent through the television set and the wall behind it. As he rolled across the grass outside, he could hear Marcus struggling to get free of something. Stopping himself from continuing to tumble, Feeder looked back at the cabin just in time to see a black smoky cloud rush out through the same hole he had made and vanish into the shroud of darkness that was the midnight sky. With what light poured out and over him, Feeder watched as the silhouette of a man made itself known. Surprise and awe briefly took hold of him but were outweighed by his satisfaction and a toothy, crooked grin flooded over his face. In a similar cloud of smoke, Feeder shot up into the air and left only the sounds of a squeaking bat in his wake.

Heavier footsteps thumped against the living room carpet as the figure made his way over to Kyden and Dennis. Once there, he placed a knee against the floor and reached out to remove the dagger. As the figure's fingers moved over Dennis's heart, a faint golden glow emerged from his chest. As this happened, Dennis lifted a shaky hand to avoid being helped. Kyden, noticing the glow, raised his head and watched it fade as the figure was pushed away.

"No." Dennis said, with a twitching smile across his face. He then used the same hand to point towards Mabel. "Go to her, Asher." Kyden looked at Dennis's eyes and then followed them to the face of the figure. For a moment his crying let up but didn't stop as he watched Asher obey Dennis's request and walk back over to the stairway. Once by Mabel, he lifted her up and carried her over to the couch, closer to where Kyden and Dennis were. Just as her head hit the pillow, her eyes started to open. Seeing that Asher was alive, she immediately clutched at him and tears of joy and relief washed over both of them. As Asher cradled her, he pressed his head against her shoulder and opened his eyes to see Kyden laying Dennis's pale white hand against his still chest and continuing to sob, quietly.

Chapter Fourteen: Ravaged Remedies

Asher remained awake for the rest of the night, keeping certain that Feeder didn't return. Aside from this, he was far too distressed to sleep. With grieving and severe stomach pains, resting wasn't an option. Laying on the floor only a couple feet away was a heavy, dull white blanket. It was placed with respect and no one in the cabin dared disturb it that night. Asher could still see his friend beneath the covers, where the bridge of the nose and base of the jaw created small mounds around a hidden face. He kept his eyes away as best he could, for looking too long would send memory after memory soaring through his mind.

"How are you feeling?" Carrying a large glass filled with reddish liquid, Mabel took soft steps towards Asher from the nearly untouched kitchen, being careful not to make any noise as she maneuvered around debris. Asher didn't reply and kept watch through a large opening that was made near the front of the cabin. He clenched at his stomach occasionally and winced at the pain. "It'll pass." Mabel spoke in sympathetic whispers and passed off the glass to Asher.

"Why does it hurt?"

"Your body is adjusting. Being a creature that drinks blood your stomach has to become stronger and more acidic." Asher stirred the drink he was given with a finger and gave Mabel a look of confusion. "It'll make digesting iron and things safer for you. Drink the tea. The pain will pass a little easier." Asher took a few swigs of the warm fluid and shivered as it sloshed about within him. "You'll get used to that, too. Lighter drinks will make you queasy for a while." Mabel took Asher's free hand as he sat the drink on a nearby end stand. "How are you holding up?" Asher brought his second hand over hers and rubbed his palm against the back of it as he looked over the blanket with sorrowful eyes.

"I'll be alright." Mabel smiled softly and moved forward to hug Asher. After a few moments of embracing each other, she stood up and slipped away into the dark, second-floor hall.

"I'll be right back."

Once she was out of sight, Asher took a couple of deep breaths to calm his nerves and settle his stomach. Then, he examined the dark room. Kyden had turned all the lights off earlier on after shielding Dennis's body. Asher was okay with this, as he didn't want to see the sight before him in any better lighting than he was currently in. Rubbing a hand over the bandages that covered his neck he could feel that the wounds were already closing up, as Mabel said they would. Feeling secure enough to move around, he got on his feet and carefully made his way across the room, collecting Dennis's duffel bag and heading back to the sofa. He felt off going through the contents, but his previous curiosity could now only be answered one way. Stuffing a hand into the bag and rummaging about at the bottom, he made out the pointed corner of a hardback book. Asher pulled it free and studied the front surface. The cover was black and blank of any text to say what it was, but Asher recognized it as a common journal. Opening the fairly new book made the spine creak and each sturdy page he turned ruffled about. With every blank page he came across, he began to think the journal was empty and his heart sank a bit. In an effort to find any entries, Asher turned the journal with the spine facing the ceiling and let the pages flutter downward. After about half the pages had slapped against the interior part of the back cover something fell out and landed in his lap. Asher pinched the pages that remained to keep the journal open and put it down next to himself. He then grabbed what had fallen out and recognized it immediately as the folded up parchment he'd found in the library's book earlier on. Wrapped around the parchment, which was no longer bundled in twine as it had previously been, was the necklace Dennis used to bring Kyden out of the hypnotic fog. Returning to the journal, even more intrigued with his findings, Asher found an entry where the parchment had fallen out. In the middle of the book were several cut up pages that made a small square pocket for the parchment and stone to fit in. One page before this pocket was the entry:

"Asher,

If you're reading this, that means Feeder didn't get the map. I took the liberty of storing it here in hopes that you'd find it after what's to come does. I want you to know that I'm sorry, even though I can't tell you in person. I'm sorry that I let you follow me to my hideout that day knowing the damage it would cause and I'm sorry for it costing you Mabel as long as it did. I'm sure by now you have her back, as I'd hoped you would, but that doesn't make up for my recklessness. Mostly, I'm sorry I won't be there to help you finish this and get your family back, but I want you to know that all my faith rests on you. Feeder won't stand a chance against you, so long as you have a clear conscience. With that said, there's something I need you to do. I need you to-"

"What's that?" Asher looked up from the entry to see Mabel standing at the base of the stairs to his right. She was now wearing the same gray hoodie the other girl had been wearing earlier on and stood with her arms crossed as if to keep warm. Asher held the journal out with more grief in his eyes than before. Concerned, Mabel walked over to the couch and took a seat next to him, reading the entry for herself. As she finished reading, she turned back towards Asher and hugged him apologetically.

"Here." He then passed her the parchment and she began unwinding the necklace from it. "It's the map from the entry, but I'm not sure what to do with it yet." Mabel unfolded the parchment as carefully as she could, not wanting to damage the ancient contents. Her brow then furrowed as she skimmed over the drawings with Asher hovering over her shoulder.

"Wait, I think I know what this is." Mabel turned the map 90° to the right and pointed at a single black square drawn over the brownish background. Asher looked at where her finger landed and took in the surroundings as well.

"What do you think it is?"

"I believe it's the witch's abode."

"You mean from the book?"

"Yeah. The rest of these buildings over here must be Prosper." Mabel moved the map onto the coffee table and grabbed a marker from a drawer that sat under the surface of the end table Asher had his drink on. She then started drawing lines over parts of the map, which made Asher uncomfortable.

"What are you doing?" Mabel didn't reply, seemingly trying to focus all her mental willpower into this one task. "Mabel, you're damaging it!" Asher hissed.

"Shh!" Mabel responded as she continued to draw squiggly lines and large circles. "There." Asher looked at the sketches she made over the original piece, partially making out what she had drawn and partially trying to be sure the map was still understandable. "Do you recognize it now?" Realizing that Mabel had drawn what the area on the map looked like in the modern day over what it used to, Asher sighed with relief and nodded his head.

"It's the base of Prominent Peak."

"Exactly, and her house was right here!" Mabel pointed at the square again, which was now surrounded by a large black and curvy circle.

"In the middle of the lake?"

"Yes!" Mabel placed the marker next to the map and flattened it out with her hands. "I think Dennis wanted us to get to the Amber Cellar before Feeder finds it. There must be something there he needs." Asher agreed and folded the map back up, being sure to put the necklace around it again before placing it in his pocket.

"We'll have to come back to this. We've got some things to take care of here before we go anywhere." Mabel tipped her head towards the covers but avoided looking right at them as she agreed.

Deciding that they weren't in danger, for the time being, Asher and Mabel headed out the back door towards the old shed. Once there, Asher removed a large wooden plank that held it shut and sat the plank against the exterior as he opened the door, allowing Mabel to go in first. As he followed, he could see the sky starting to glow a dim blue in the distance and shut the door behind himself. Once inside, he pulled a small chain on the ceiling and the musty building was instantly lit up by a single clear glass bulb. Mabel walked around the room's edge, making her way behind a chair that had an exhausted individual bound tightly to it. Asher remained near the door. The thin figure didn't budge when they came inside as it was still too weak from the night before. Asher could see his own blood, staining the front of the girl's shirt.

"What... do you want?" The girl spoke but hardly moved with her words.

"We need your help."

"You know more about Feeder than either of us." Mabel took a step towards the girl, which seemed to make her stir.

"I don't know anything about Feeder." The girl lifted her head and opened her eyes, staring into the single swaying bulb. "All I know is what he did to me."

"That isn't true." Asher snapped. He then took another step towards her and leaned down as she dropped her head. "Why don't you look at me?" Asher cocked his head to one side, trying to look her in the eye, but the girl immediately jerked her head up again.

"You're one of them now."

"One of what?" Asher asked genuinely. The girl knocked her head back as if to point at Mabel.

"Them."

"A Sagina?" The girl nodded. "I'm not a Sagina." Asher looked across the room at Mabel. "Am I?" Mabel exhaled through her nose and walked around the chair to be next to Asher. Noticing she was coming towards him, he stood back up. Once she was only a foot or so away, Mabel stopped and nodded slowly as she lifted a hand to Asher's chest.

"I didn't bite you to make you what you are." As Mabel's fingers hover less than an inch away from his skin, Asher pulled the corner of his shirt down to get a better look at what was happening. Beneath his ribcage was a wavy blend of white and gold light that seemed to react strongly to Mabel's touch.

"But, you can't be alive if you gave me back my Amber Heart."

"She didn't give you the exact same Heart." Asher turned

toward the girl in the chair, who was now flicking her eyes up at him and back at the floor each time she spoke. "I saw it." Asher then faced Mabel, who was still resting her hand on his chest and staring back at him. "You surrendered your Heart and pressed it into hers, but she didn't want it either."

"What does that mean?" Mabel took her hand away from Asher's chest and slid her fingers down his left arm, intertwining them with his. She then moved his hand over her chest, keeping her eyes on him. Asher watched as his fingers connected with the soft tissue but remained confused as nothing else happened.

"We share the same Heart." Asher's eyes widened a little as he stared back into Mabel's.

"Touching, isn't it?" The vampire made a low scoff and dropped her head again. "I'll help you." The duo turned to face the girl, intrigued, but remained skeptical. "I have nothing else to lose. Feeder killed James. Why not go for revenge, maybe break this curse?"

"You won't live long enough to get the chance." The group

turned to face the door, where Kyden had just made his entrance.

"Kyden, are you-" Kyden thrust a shoulder into Asher's as he passed and lifted a stake he had tucked behind his back above his head. The girl squeezed her palms together and hid her face as the expected blow failed to make contact. Opening her eyes, she looked up at Kyden. His arm was drawn back but was struggling to move forward.

"We need her." Asher let go of his wrist and Kyden dropped the stake.

"For what? Two Sagina against one and you still need help?" Kyden stomped passed Asher and Mabel again and ripped the door open, exposing a sliver of morning sun on the horizon. The light was blinding to Asher and forced him to shield his eyes.

"Kyden, I know you're going through a lot right now. We both are, but what's gotten into you?"

"What's gotten into me? Ha!" Kyden slammed the flimsy door as he left the shed, causing it to shake and remain open a hair.

"You could have saved him!" Stunned, Asher kept his eyes locked on the opening.

"Hey, just give him time. He'll come around."

"He blames me for it? I didn't know I could save him."

"It isn't your fault. Dennis was ready to go. He accepted his fate long before it came, you know that." Asher let his eyes drift to the floor and turned back to the vampire, trying to find any way to clear his mind.

"What's your name?"

"Does it matter?" The girl looked over her peers and acknowledged the lack of a reply by rolling her eyes. "Jessi." She said with defeat in her voice.

"What can we do for you if you help us?" Mabel let her hand rest on Asher's upper bicep as she spoke with Jessi, trying to comfort him whilst progressing with their work.

"There's nothing I want from you. All I want is to break this curse and maybe getting rid of its source will do that for me." Asher, leaving Mabel where she was, walked behind the chair and began undoing the chain bindings. "You know, these were a little overkill. A tight enough rope would have held me in."

"Better safe than sorry." Jessi shrugged in agreement and rubbed her shins after her hands were freed.

"Now, where do we start?"

"We've still got some things to take care of here." Asher looked back at Mabel as he stood from the crouching position he was in behind the chair.

"Like what?"

"Are you any good at hypnosis?" Jessi seemed taken aback by the question as she got up, too.

"I mean, I've done a little bit, but nothing to the extent of what Feeder and the others have done."

"A little should do fine." Mabel gave Jessi a cautious but faithful smile. Jessi didn't return the expression and simply looked over the two with complete loss written on her face.

"I should probably apologize for trying to kill you guys before we go any further with this." Jessi turned to face Asher specifically as she spoke. "I'd have never done any of those things if it weren't for Feeder and these new... urges."

"I don't blame you." Asher gave her a weak smile himself and started towards the shed door. "I've been told otherwise, but I believe there is still some humanity in there."

The three made their way back to the cabin with shovels Asher gathered from the shed. Under the shade of several trees, three graves were dug out and soon after covered in soil and stone. Two graves had jerseys numbered 13 and 62 slung over the large, obscure boulders that had been placed at the tops of them. The third grave, which was furthest to the left, had leafy green stocks planted all around the headstone and a handmade crossbow resting on top of it with a necklace wrapped around the handle. Asher, Mabel, and Jessi all stood before the graves in silence for a few minutes before Kyden was seen coming from the cabin with a potato launcher held out in both hands. Asher smiled and walked over to his teary-eyed friend, resting a hand on his back and guiding him to the graves. Kyden then placed the launcher against Dennis's headstone and put both hands on it as tears trickled down his face. Mabel comforted Asher as the same was happening to him, and Jessi sat at the foot of number 13 with glossy eyes. Once Jessi got back up, she walked over to Kyden and rested both hands on his shoulders, rubbing them soothingly as the tears that fell became less and less. Asher watched this as it happened, but ignored it the best he could and held tightly to Mabel's hand as he ran over the words from Dennis's journal one last time in his mind.

"I need you to forget about me. No matter the outcome, no matter what you think you'll lose, let me go."

Asher watched as the last tear fell and Kyden took a step away from the stone.

"I'll always remember you and Kyden and if it's possible for me, I'll be watching over the two of you till the end."

Kyden then turned and walked inside the cabin without a word, headed upstairs, and went straight to bed. As he disappeared inside, Jessi moved over to Asher, who was still sobbing and held his eyes closed as she placed her fingers on his forehead.

"To the only family I have left, I'll miss you."

As Jessi returned her hand to her side, no more tears fell. Asher then did as Kyden had and turned away from the graves, headed inside, and went straight to sleep. The girls stayed behind and Mabel comforted Jessi as she fell to her knees and continued to quietly weep over her loss and ill-doings.

Chapter Fifteen: Blind Amygdalas

Wind flushed between open fingers as Asher let them dangle freely out the driver's side window. His dark hair fluttered about as the breeze passed through the opening and out another in the rear. He kept his other hand on the steering wheel and smiled as Mabel and Jessi kept up with each song on the radio. Behind him sat Kyden, who was holding out a large piece of paper and fighting against the winds to keep a grip on it. Asher watched him and Jessi through the rear view mirror, acknowledging the distance Kyden tried to keep from her, whilst Jessi nudged and prodded, attempting to get him to join her lyrically. Asher then rolled his neck to the right, giving Mabel his full attention. In return, she flicked her eyes in his direction and smiled, proceeding to keep up with the verbal rhythm. Both looked back at the road as the truck rolled off the pavement and onto a gravel entrance. Pebbles crunched about as he pressed the brakes and everyone who was along for the ride got out once the vehicle had completely stopped.

"Any luck with that thing?" Asher closed his own door and watched as Kyden did the same, distractedly.

"Sort of." Kyden then leaned against the door he had shut and everyone else gathered around him. "As long as the map was drawn with this being north," Kyden pointed at the top portion of the lake Mabel had added before continuing, "then all we need to do is get around Prominent Peak Trail."

"It's north." Mabel stuffed her hands in the pockets of her jacket and smiled proudly. "I memorized maps of this place long before I came to the area. Drawing this one out was simple."

"Good work, Abel." Kyden remarked jokingly. He then skimmed over the drawing once again before noticing the lack of laughter or response around him and looking up at the others. A wave of confusion covered every face. "You know, Abel Buell?" Again, no response. Kyden sighed. "The first citizen to make a map of-" he shook his head and cut himself off. "It doesn't matter. I finally have a wise joke to crack and you guys ruin it."

"Well, just tell us who it is." Asher pulled his hood over his head to keep the sun off his face as he made his request.

"No, it isn't funny if I have to explain it." Kyden whipped the map at the corners as if to straighten out any creases and continued to look it over. "Now, how are we going to get around this thing?"

"We could fly over it." The rest of the group faced Jessi as she chipped away at the paint on her nails.

"I, uh... can't fly. Remember?"

"Is there any real reason for you to come?" Jessi muttered with her earthly gaze set on Kyden's blank expression.

"He's safer with us." Asher let his eyes express the

importance of what he'd said and stepped away from the group, examining the poorly repaired trail entrance sign he'd previously hit. The snapped wooden peg that kept up one side of the sign was being held together with blue duct tape, which was extremely obvious against the painted green surface. "You're right though." He stated as he turned back toward the others. "We'll go over it. Kyden can use the trail up top that leads down the other end." Kyden dropped the map to his side and slouched forward.

"We seriously have to walk up that thing, again?" Asher chuckled as he started towards the front of the trail with Mabel. The two that remained next to the truck stared at each other for a few moments before Jessi shrugged and took a couple of steps towards the trail herself.

"See you on the other side." She then darted forward in a cloud of blurry black smoke, staying low to avoid the sunlight that split through the treetops and bolting up the mile-long pathway. Mabel pressed her hair against her shoulders, keeping as much of it down as possible as Jessi shot by and Kyden rushed to the entrance after them, partially to regroup and partially to catch the map he'd lost to Jessi's antics.

"So, what exactly happens if you stay in the sun too long?" Kyden snatched the map as it touched the ground and studied it for any damages once he found his balance.

"I have no clue." Mabel looked at Asher as he spoke and then back at Kyden, being sure that Asher hadn't seen what happened with the map. "It stings a bit."

"That's it?" Kyden scoffed as he folded up the parchment and stuffed it in his back pocket.

"Feeder told me to avoid it at all costs, so I'm guessing it can get pretty bad if you're in it for too long." Mabel shared another brief moment with Asher before turning back to what remained of the trail ahead. "My best guess is that we'd wilt."

"Wilt?" Asher knocked his head back curiously but kept his eyes forward.

"Yes. We drink the blood of the living because ours is tainted and it's the only thing that gives us every nutrient that we need to regenerate our own. So, if we were to get burned by the sun, our blood would cook too fast to be replenished and we'd dry up, like a flower with no roots."

"That has to be one of the worst ways to go." Kyden stared at Mabel with horror-struck eyes.

"I imagine it's far worse if you're using an Amber Heart to feed instead."

After nearly 40 minutes of walking the three crested the hill and quietly moved towards the peak. Upon reaching it, Asher looked out over the tops of redwoods below and admired the shimmering surface of a distant body of water. The sun's beams seemed to bounce off the rippling face in every direction, making the trees that surrounded it appear more vibrant than those most anywhere else. Asher even saw the swirling rays dancing in Mabel's eyes as she took in the view. It amazed him that she could still see the beauty in a place where something so tragic had happened to her.

"Alright," Mabel and Asher turned to face Kyden, who was standing with both arms outstretched, "I'm ready."

"Ready for what?"

"You didn't *really* think I was walking back down this thing, did you? Just to walk the rest of the way and eventually reach the lake?" Kyden shook his arms and lifted his brow. "Let's go."

"I've never flown before. You know that."

"Good time to practice." Kyden continued to stare at Asher, ready to accept whatever was to come.

"You'd rather risk dying instead of just walking?"

"Yes." Asher looked back at the edge and studied the distance between himself and the ground below. He then gulped and looked over at Mabel, who seemed to be choking back a laugh.

"Think you'll go two for two?"

"Shut up!" Mabel giggled hysterically as Asher glanced back at Kyden, whose arms were now trembling under their own weight.

"How do I do this?" Mabel didn't answer and simply walked to the edge with her arms folded over her chest. "You've never flown either?" Mabel smiled and pushed off with her toes. "No, wait!" Asher clutched at the air as his hand missed hers and saw as she plummeted downward. Moments before she'd surely hit the ground, a dark flowing cloud of smoke spewed out from her feet and quickly engulfed her. He then watched as the mass changed directions and darted off into the shaded trunks below.

"Ahem!" Asher sighed and turned back to a growingly impatient Kyden.

"I don't know if I can do this."

"Come on, man. If your girl can do it, so can you." Kyden continued to stare as he fought the urge to drop his throbbing arms. "She did do it, right?" Asher rolled his eyes and motioned for Kyden to move closer to him. "I think it's best if you start back here with me."

"Why?"

"It'll give you a little more leeway to practice with." Asher agreed, walked over to Kyden, and picked him up on his back. "Don't drop me." He chuckled nervously as Kyden's grip tightened around his neck and waist. Then, took a single step back and went down into a sprinting position, with both hands and feet planted on the ground.

"Ready?" Kyden didn't reply. Instead, he took in a long, deep breath and kept his eyes on the cliff's edge. "Me neither." Asher then kicked off, hard, and dashed towards the peak. He tried focusing on flight as nothingness approached but found it difficult to remain focused when his feet left the ground for the last time. With Asher's legs swinging wildly beneath himself, Kyden's weight began gaining on him and the pair started tipping on their backs. Asher fought this by thrusting both legs at the same time but was having no luck with the efforts.

"Any time now!" Kyden's grip was like that of a hungry cobra around Asher's neck and breathing had become uncomfortable, between the pressure Kyden was creating and the disturbed air around them. As the two tipped upside down, Asher caught a glimpse of the grassy landing zone and clenched his eyes shut, bracing for impact. Kyden began letting out a restrained scream through gritted teeth but regained himself as gravity stopped pulling them to their deaths. Asher opened his eyes just in time to dodge a tree that they had been approaching and frantically navigated his way around others as they came into view. Flying made him feel weightless and he was amazed by how easy it was to control without wings. "Woah! Woo!" Kyden's relief was obvious, but his grip didn't let up. Asher could see the smoke flowing off himself as he turned his head and felt the true potential of what he was for the first time. After only a few seconds of flight, the two breached a clearing and startled a large flock of birds, which had been resting on the rocky shore of the lake. "There they are!" Asher looked where Kyden was pointing and spotted two figures standing at the edge of the water on the opposite end of the lake. Mabel was the most obvious, as she had her arms lifted above her head and was trying to flag them down. Pulling a hard right, Asher directed himself towards the girls and was becoming increasingly aware that he didn't know how to stop. "We're getting a little close, don't you think?" Asher watched as the shallows grew nearer but didn't want to startle Kyden and continued to fly straight.

"Jump!" Kyden's grip remained, making it difficult for Asher to speak.

"What?"

"Jump, now!" Kyden seemingly got the hint through the raspy words, as the shore was no more than a football field away at this point. With that in mind, he let loose of Asher's neck and almost immediately shot off and into the water. Asher could see him briefly skip across the surface before sinking into the dark depths and shot up into the air himself to avoid the trees. Once he was at about the same height as Prominent Peak, which he could see from where he was hovering, he'd lost the speed he was traveling at and sat in place for a moment before gravity took control again. The gorgeous view of wavy pines was short-lived and he was rapidly approaching the water below. *Splash!* The smoke that trailed behind him mixed with the water and dispersed into the air, quickly. Within a couple of seconds, all the smoke had dissipated and Asher was breaching the surface.

"That was awesome!" Asher spotted Kyden only a couple of dozen feet out from himself, where he was raising a fist in the air and smiling wildly. Asher then faced the girls, who were far less impressed. Jessi was shaking her head with her arms crossed and Mabel had covered her mouth with both hands.

"Are you alright?" Mabel approached Asher as the two came up on shore and was followed closely by Jessi, who stopped off where Kyden was.

"We're fine," Kyden started, pressing a finger in his ear to get the water out, "just a rough landing."

"You rode on the water with your face." Jessi shielded herself as Kyden shook himself off like a wet dog and then glared at Asher. "I can't believe that fall didn't kill you."

"Thanks?"

"Don't worry about getting dry." Mabel undid the buttons on her jacket and slid it off. She then removed her socks and shoes along with it.

"What are you doing?"

"The Amber Cellar is at the bottom of the lake." Mabel walked to the edge of the water and let it lap over her feet. "So, we've got to swim to it."

"Without any gear? We'll drown." Asher then noticed Jessi removing her own footwear and proceeding to pass them, going even further into the water than Mabel.

"Are you two coming?"

"What about me?" The group turned to face Kyden, who was still dripping wet from head to toe and standing with his hands on his hips. "Should I just wait here?"

"No, please, follow." Jessi smiled and motioned for Kyden to go ahead of her, already being at waist height.

"I-I think I'll wait." He then sat at the edge of the lake and wicked water away from his eyes.

"Don't worry, Asher. You can hold your breath far longer than you've ever been able to before.

"How does that work?"

"Tainted blood, remember?" Asher looked over at Kyden, who was watching the small waves come up on shore before returning to their turf.

"He's right. We don't need as much oxygen as someone who's truly living, so we can go without certain things longer than they can." Mabel offered her hand to Asher and he took it reluctantly.

"Don't worry about drowning either. There's enough oxygen in the water to keep you breathing. It's transferring between breathing air and breathing water that hurts like hell." With that note, Jessi sank her head beneath the surface, leaving a plethora of emerging bubbles behind. Mabel was next in going under, followed by Asher, who held his breath on the way.

Once the three of them were a few feet below, Asher opened his eyes. After a few seconds of cloudy vision, they began to adjust to his new surroundings. He could see Mabel ahead of him, kicking her legs but keeping her arms free at her sides. Ahead of her was

Jessi, who was doing the breaststroke as she searched the bottom of the lake on her way down. Asher was amazed at how well he could now see in the dark. Without his new abilities, even goggles wouldn't have allowed him to look about the things hidden in such a place, as the lake's water was far too murky. After swimming for a few minutes, he noticed a large object in one of the deepest valleys. It sat so far away at the time that it was still a bit blurry to him and making out what it was exactly seemed impossible. Tapping Mabel on the heel and pointing to his left, the three turned course. As they got closer, Asher could see that it was an old cobblestone building. What he assumed to have once been the entrance was in shambles. The entire building was covered in algae, snails, and several other plants and creatures. Asher was the first to approach the would-be doorway and pulled himself inside using the walls. The interior of the abode was heavily damaged by the water. Frames were warped, plants were growing up the walls, and smaller creatures had dug holes into the wooden floors and ceilings to hide away from bigger animals. The ecosystem that had made itself at home also made it easy to spot a large hole in the floor, as the dark opening was clear against the swaying greens. Asher wasted no time sinking deeper into their search and threw himself through the opening. To his surprise, the room had almost nothing in it. The one he had come from still had old fashioned, handmade furnishing, along with pottery, crates, and fabrics of all sorts. The room he had found seemed barren in comparison. In one corner was a set of stone stairs, leading up to angled, wooden double doors. In the other, a single pantry rack. Though Asher was certain the double doors led outside, he saw nowhere else to go. Swimming over to the doors, he spotted a small amount of light pouring in through the worn planks that made them up, which confirmed to him that they wouldn't give him a lead. Annoyed, he knocked a fist against one of them. As the door swung open about a foot, Asher could feel the water around him being pulled towards it and once it returned, two dull thuds sounded out. One from the door as it hit the frame and the other from somewhere behind him. Curious, he lifted a leg and kicked hard at the same wooden remnants. As lake muck broke off into brownish clouds, the door flung open and slammed against the exterior of the house. As before, the water around him rushed out through the door, which meant that more was coming from elsewhere. As he turned to face where the second knock had previously come from, he was slammed against the stairs by the pantry rack. Startled, he examined the rack and found that it was anchored to a stone slab. Tossing it off to one side and letting it clunk against the floor as he floated back up, Asher looked to where the rack had been sitting originally. Another opening appeared where the stone slab made a false wall. Certain he'd found what they were looking for, he thumped his palms against the ceiling before swimming towards it.

"This is it!" After a few moments of waiting, Mabel and Jessi appeared through the hole in the first floor and followed Asher into the hidden passageway. The path was still free of life due to its hidden entrance, which gave the group the advantage. As Asher reached the bottom of the stairwell, he confirmed to himself that they were where they needed to be. Using his hands to spin and face the others, he pointed at the contents that were strewn about the floor. Innumerable heart-shaped crystals. He had guessed there to be at least three hundred of them and headed on his way to inspect some. Jessi made her way ahead of him and picked one up. The crystal was clear and seemingly insignificant as she turned it about in her fingers for a moment before losing interest. Mabel then held out a hand to take it for her own examination. As the crystal came within inches of Mabel's hand, a golden glow appeared at its core. Jessi stopped just before the crystal landed in Mabel's palm and stared at it. Both girls looked at Asher who was just as surprised as they were. He then spun about to get closer to the floor and put out a hand. As with Mabel, every crystal his hand passed over let off a faint glow and the

closer he got to them, the brighter they became. Awestruck, he ran it against several gems and filled the room with vibrant, dazzling light. The group was stunned at their findings, but something had caught Mabel's eye and broke the enchantment that was put over her by the blissful sight. A single Heart sat amongst the glowing heap, flaunting a grand difference. Mabel lifted the Heart to expose a brilliant white core. Asher shared a moment of fear and achievement with her as the realization of what they'd found hit them. *"Adelram!"*

Kyden watched as the trio emerged from the water and made their way onto shore. The air grew chilly with how much time had passed and the sun was resting on the opposite end of the sky that it had been over before they started their excavation.

"Finally! What took you guys so long?" Nobody spoke immediately, though Jessi appeared to have something on her mind. "Well, anybody?" Kyden remained in place as the others sat at the edge of the water to rest. "I was starting to think something had happened and clearly couldn't investigate my concerns. So-" Kyden was interrupted by Jessi hacking up water and breathing heavily as her lungs readjusted to the thinner atmosphere. "Are you alright?"

"I'm fine, just takes a minute to get back to normal."

"How many times have you done something like this?" Kyden cleared what space was separating himself from Jessi, got on one knee, and placed a hand on her back to help get the water out.

"Because I had to? None."

"Then why did you before now?"

"To try ending this! Okay?" Kyden stopped patting her back and stared into her distant emerald eyes as the others grew silent. "Just leave me alone." Sighing, he got back on his feet. Moments later, Jessi was sniffling under his hoodie and Kyden had stepped away to speak with Asher and Mabel.

"Did you guys find anything while you were down there?" Asher nodded and held out his hand for Kyden to accept the contents. Kyden cupped his own beneath Asher's and grew wide-eyed as the crystal fell into his palm. The glow slowly faded as Asher moved away, but what short life it had was still enough for Kyden to recognize it. "Is... is this an Archaic?" Mabel shot Kyden a look as she dried off with her own jacket.

"You know about these?"

"Yeah, Asher was reading from that big book one day at the cabin and he'd mentioned this type of Heart." Kyden examined the crystal by placing it between his index finger and thumb and turning it about in the remaining sunlight. Each face of the crystal shimmered as the beams passed through it. Creating pinks, purples, and even faint blues as he twisted it about. After a few moments of admiring the Heart with this method, he stopped dead as the realization set in. Then, as if his neck were a spring, he extended it towards Asher with a look of disbelief on his face. "Is it-"

"Yes, it's Adelram's." Kyden shifted his arm from the sun's direction to Asher's and gave back the Archaic, which Asher swiftly tucked away in his back pocket. The cloth was luckily thick enough to conceal the glow that was emitting from it yet again.

"You did some studying in my absence then, did you?" Mabel giggled at Asher and leaned against him to rest her back as they sat by the water.

"Do you think this is what Feeder was after?"

"Not a doubt in my mind."

"What are we supposed to do with it?" Kyden looked back at Jessi, who was still clearly upset and sighed before speaking again. "Feeder will undoubtedly come looking for it and he'll know we have it."

"We use it as leverage." Both boys looked at Mabel, waiting for an explanation. "When Feeder realizes that we have the Archaic, he'll do just about anything he can to get it from us. So, we use it to trap him and kill him."

"What do you think he even wants with the thing?"

"Isn't it obvious?" Mabel looked up at the setting sun, watching as what few strands that remained faded into a dark red before hiding behind distant silhouettes. "His father's resurrection."

Chapter Sixteen: The Calm

Oranges, reds, and yellows flickered about the unsprung traps making up the lawn. Each complimented the next as they danced over the remnants of a once cozy home. Around these crackling embers sat a party of four, which mostly spoke with celebration and enthusiasm about their accomplishments, but also sorrow and eagerness. One of the smaller framed individuals kept her head low, less entertained by the gathering that took place. Sitting on a stump opposite of her was the second largest of the bunch, who kept his lengthy hair swept off to one side and away from the hot fireflies coming out of the campfire. Sitting to the left of this one was the second smallest, who had her palms facing the flames to keep warm.

Opposite of her was the largest, standing nearest to the burn pile and holding out a stick with a darkening marshmallow on the end.

"You're about to burn that, you know?" The largest figure shrugged and rummaged about in a bag that sat next to him, pulling another marshmallow free from it and popping the treat in his mouth.

"It's better that way." Kyden stated through a mouth full of the sticky goop. "Want one?"

"I'll pass." Asher smiled and shook his head as he admired the base of the flames.

"Suit yourself." Kyden pulled the stick from the blaze and started blowing on the black puffy ball at the end.

"I'm good, too." Jessi put up a hand to block one Kyden was offering her and shivered. "I could use something to eat though if you know what I mean." She shot a look at Mabel and Asher, who both gave the same look back. Then, all three looked towards Kyden, who distractedly lowered the marshmallow back into the fire.

"What are you guys looking at?" The marshmallow lit up, slid off the stick, and clung to a piece of charred wood in the pit. "I-I think I can find something for everyone." Nervously, Kyden tossed his marshmallow prod in the fire and gathered up his crossbow and a couple of stakes. The rest of the group chuckled as he walked off down the gravel trail and away from the cabin.

"You think he'll be alright out there on his own?"

"I don't think it's in his best interest. Would you mind-" Before Asher could finish his sentence, Jessi nodded and was on her feet, leaving Asher and Mabel at the camp. Asher watched the others walk off into the dark side-by-side and turned back to the pit when he heard something disturb the logs. Sitting in the middle of the fire was a small black book, already singed in the corners. "What's that?"

"Bad memories is all." Mabel smiled lightly and watched the contents of the book ignite and curl up as they turned black and gray before the heat started launching them into the air. Within seconds, small pieces of paper were floating back towards the ground, and others drifted further and further away.

"So, what are we going to do after all of this is over?"

"I don't know," Mabel seemed lost in a state of regret as she watched what remained of the book turn to ashes, "what do you think?"

"I think we should all get a clean start." Asher picked up a small bundle of sticks and tossed it over the fire, watching as the flames licked between each branch before swallowing them up. "All of us should just go somewhere and set down roots." Mabel smiled, seemingly liking the idea.

"Where would we go?" Asher looked up at the cloudy sky, admiring what little bit of it he could make out as he thought it over.

"Somewhere on the coast." Mabel nodded in agreement and joined Asher's admiration. "Do you think Jessi will get what she wants? You know, break the curse?" Mabel didn't answer and simply watched the moon occasionally peek between clouds. Asher could tell something was on her mind and as if she could read his, she spoke.

"It's still a full moon." Asher looked up and verified for himself that this was true.

"How is that possible?" Neither had an answer and simply kept their eyes glued to it as an orange hue started gradually shading the bottom left. Just as their curiosity was peaked, the moon became fully exposed.

"Look out!" Startled, Asher and Mabel shot up from their seats and looked to their rights. A streaking black mass launched itself in their direction and from the mass fell Kyden, who seemed more frightened than Asher had ever seen him. His eyes were greatly enlarged and he was staring directly at Asher as he lay flat on his belly. Jessi then emerged from the smoke as well and helped Kyden to his feet.

"What's going on?" Asher and Mabel rushed to the others' aid as Asher questioned them.

"Wolves!" Jessi moved in front of Kyden and faced the area they'd come from. Asher and Mabel watched with her as a large gray wolf exposed its face and forelegs.

The wolf didn't growl or rush towards the group. Instead, it remained still and calm. The eyes told Asher that the creature was in some sort of trance. A couple of seconds into the staring match and a few more wolves made themselves known. These wolves appeared normal, baring their teeth and snarling as they looked over what must have seemed to be a decent meal. Remembering where he stood against other living things, Asher let down his guard and took a step forward, but was stopped by Mabel, who placed an arm across his chest.

"You don't want to do that." Asher looked down at her and watched as the fear filled her eyes.

"A wolf bite will kill any of us." Jessi nudged Kyden back a couple more steps, trying not to startle the beasts as they made their way alongside Asher and Mabel. Realizing his underestimation of the pack, Asher straightened up and kept count of them. Then, as suddenly as they'd appeared, the wolves turned tail and sprinted off into the forest, howling as they went. The last wolf to leave was the first that they saw and led the howling before backing away and following the others.

"What was that about?" Asher faced Mabel as he spoke, but her expression never changed.

"Feeder." Cautiously, Mabel moved towards where the wolves had gone.

"What are you doing?" Asher took her wrist to keep her from walking any further.

"She's right, we have to follow them."

"What?" Asher was stunned by Jessi's words and gave her a look to show it.

"If we're to end this, Feeder is going to make sure we do so his way. Games are all he knows. So, we follow." Collecting herself better than anyone else, Jessi walked ahead of Mabel and grabbed her other wrist, pulling her free of Asher and pressing on through the trees. Asher looked over at Kyden, who held the same frightened expression as he tried to form words before giving up and tailing the girls. Asher shook off what he could and copied, listening to the wolves' continuous howls as he did so.

Before long, the wolves had the group sprinting to keep up and their cries became more distressed. Jessi and Mabel held the lead, with Asher and Kyden close behind. Asher could see that Kyden was struggling to hold the pace and with this distraction, he could feel that the wolves weren't their only company. Occasional squeaking and chirping filled his ears as he shot his head to each side, waiting for something, or someone, to try ambushing them. The group hurtled fallen trees and small streams as they kept sight of the closest wolf, which seemed to be doing its best at shaking them. Asher lost all sense of direction as the pack continued to twist and turn through bushes and low hanging branches, making it too difficult for him to pinpoint the third creature he had yet to identify. *Sploosh!*

"Agh!" Asher stopped to see where the cry had come from and spotted Kyden, breathing heavily as he tried crawling out of a puddle.

"Hey," Asher called out, "wait up!" Seeming to not hear him, the girls continued on their way. Anxious about losing them, he rushed back to Kyden with an arm outstretched to pull him up. "Here, take my hand!" Kyden groaned as he held an injured leg and reached out for Asher. *Whoosh!* With no time to react, Kyden was swept into the air by a large winged creature, which knocked Asher to the ground before fleeing. "Kyden!" Asher could hear the squeaking of the beast as it soared high into the air, but didn't give chase. He followed the sound of Kyden's cries and listened for the howls. Both were headed in the same direction.

Panicked, he kicked off the ground and burst through the air staying low enough to spot the girls as he tore through tree limbs and small trunks. The beast's squalling and the howling had stopped. All Asher could hear was the snapping and cracking of wood and the violent thrashing about of pine needles as he continued to pummel through anything that stood in his way. He gritted his teeth as the pain became increasingly unbearable and was relieved when it finally stopped. Exhausted, he collapsed to the ground to catch his breath.

"Asher?" Opening only one eye, he could see Mabel rushing over to him. "What happened? Where's Kyden?"

"Something... got him." Mabel helped him to his feet and searched frantically behind him, as if Kyden would appear at any moment.

"Are you sure?" Asher nodded. "What was it?"

"You mean *who* was it, darling." The pair turned to face where the voice had come from and for the first time since his arrival, Asher took in his surroundings. The trio, with Jessi not far off, was in a rather large clearing. He could see several disheveled buildings that sat in rows, with others sitting completely alone. None had been treated kindly by time and proved vacant, as many had collapsed roofs and rubble where their stone walls once stood. To his far left and his far right were the wolves that led them to the strange place and above their heads hung a blood red moon. Asher looked down from the heavens to see a single man standing a short distance from the ruins. He was wearing a familiar suit and had something else laying before him. "It seemed appropriate to wear something so formal to such an event, don't you think?" The man lifted his arms and did a slow turn to show off the attire, but kept his eyes locked on the group as he did so with a deathly smile across his face. Asher broke eye contact with the man to recognize the heap before him.

"Kyden!" Asher took a step forward but stopped as the man lifted a finger and placed a foot on Kyden's neck.

"One more move from you and I break it. You wouldn't want to lose both of them, would you?"

"Both of them?"

"He's immune to your mind tricks, Feeder." Jessi scowled at the crooked form, which had turned its attention on her.

"Ah, practicing without your master, are you?"

"You are not my master." Feeder held his expression, but let his eyes drift off towards Asher again.

"No, I suppose I'm not. For now."

"Look, I have what you want." Asher pulled the Archaic from his pocket and displayed it up high for Feeder to see. The white light seemed to capture his interest as he let off some pressure he had already applied to Kyden's throat. "Let him go and it's yours!"

"I'm afraid that's not how things are meant to go." Feeder lifted his foot and stepped over Kyden. Asher clutched the Heart in his fist, turning his knuckles white. Feeder stopped in his tracks and lost his mood completely. "What are you doing, boy?"

"One more move from *you* and I crush it." Feeder raised his nose high into the air and stabbed through Asher with his eyes.

"So be it." He then turned away from the trio and looked up at the moon himself. "Do you like it? It's a gift from a rather vengeful old hag." Asher thought over one of the articles he had read from the book and scrunched up his brow. "Yes, you know the one." Feeder then turned towards to the others and looked over them, as well as the snarling wolves at each corner.

"Wait, does that-"

"Indeed it does, my precious girl." Feeder motioned with a single hand for them to gaze upon the structures behind him. "Welcome, to Prosper. Though, I wouldn't say the name does it justice anymore, would you?" He chuckled and placed both hands behind his back.

"What is it you want with us?"

"Wh- all of you? Nothing. You alone, however," Feeder pointed at Asher and narrowed his eyes, "you have something very important to me." Asher shot a look at his closed fist and then back at Feeder, who twisted the left side of his lips. "Not just the Archaic, boy. You've passed every test I've thrown at you, though a few times, I must say, I was sure you'd let me down an-"

"What is it then? Tell me!" Feeder's offense towards being cutoff was apparent as he scowled at Asher.

"Why must I tell you of something you live?" The unimpressed expression on Asher's face caused Feeder's to contort even more. "You are it. The one who will undoubtedly fulfill what must be done. A pure heart, even in death. You started off rather rough around the edges, still are in some ways. However, with a little bit of refinement, I've guided you down the necessary path." Feeder motioned towards Mabel. "With the girl, I rewrote your life.

You took that and persevered, kept hold of the truth, and brought it to light." Feeder then directed his gaze towards Jessi. "With this one, I was sure she'd killed you, but being that she hadn't you've proven persuasive, to some degree. My abandoned specimen has become your unlikely ally." He then shifted around to face Kyden, who was still cradling his injured leg. "Another of your tests. Perhaps, the coldest of them all from your end. You allowed an innocent to join your efforts at self-gain, with nothing to offer. A truly cold feat." Feeder spun on his heel and raised his right brow, with the left side of his lips still curled. "Your fourth test seems to have been erased, but nonetheless, you passed. The loss of another didn't stop you. A true warrior." With one hand, Feeder lifted the left side of his suit's vest and slid his right hand beneath it. "Now that you're caught up, it's time for that one last test." Asher shook his head vigorously before speaking.

"Stop toying with me so we can end this!" Feeder removed his hand from beneath the vest and held out several, large pieces of parchment. Asher's hardened expression relented.

"Recognize these?" Feeder tossed the parchments forward, allowing them to scatter across the ground. As Asher was distractedly looking them over from afar, Mabel noticed the first wolf walking away from its pack.

"Jessi, what's going on?" Jessi shook her head, unsure, and watched the wolf as well. The beast remained calm as it approached Feeder, with Asher still staring at the pages as he pieced together what they meant.

"You know what they are, boy." Feeder put out a hand as the wolf got closer to him and brushed it up the creature's snout. "You know what your final test is."

"If I can do whatever it is you want me to do, then you can too!"

"This is quite true." Feeder lowered his other hand beneath the wolf's chin and scratched at it, with the first hand rubbing behind its ears.

"Then why don't you!?" Feeder looked away from the wolf, stopped both hands from petting it and stared Asher in the eye. The wolf appeared to be waking up from its trance at that moment and let out a low growl as it dropped its ears.

"What would be the fun in that?" The wolf yipped in pain as Feeder lifted it off the ground by the neck and lunged at it with his fangs exposed. The creature kicked frantically at its assailant but the efforts proved futile.

"Leave it alone!" Mabel cried out as she stepped forward. The rest of the wolf pack growled and whined as this happened and gathered as one to protect their own. Eight wolves sprinted into the clearing, but all stopped as the one Feeder had fell limp.

"Let's see if you're truly the worthy Sagina." Feeder's body twitched violently as he spoke before he tossed the wolf aside and fell on his back. The remaining wolves whined and paced around Feeder as he shook and groaned. "What's going on, Asher?" Asher remembered the last word he'd read from the book but found it difficult to speak at that moment.

"Asher, what is this? Tell us what it is!" Jessi stomped back toward Asher but froze in place as a deeper, darker growl sent a chill down her spine. The hairs on Asher's neck stood up and the same happened with Mabel. All three watched as Feeder thrashed about and the wolves became even more distressed, yipping and howling as they tucked back their ears. The back of Feeder's vest began tearing, with each fiber straining to hold in what was emerging from them. Feeder arched back and left only his knees on the ground as he gazed up at the moon, howling.

"Polymorphism." The wolves darted back, creating much larger circles around their target, but as Feeder stood on two hind legs, they all stood still. Silence fell over the pack as Feeder looked over each one, grunting and slobbering as he called out to them. The wolves were terrified as the beast they circled communicated with them, not wanting to show weakness. Asher could see that Jessi was trembling at the sight. Feeder stood two feet taller than he had before and was covered in thick, gray fur. His limbs had buckled and broke many times over to become elongated and more animalistic. His hands and feet had been extended as well, fashioning large black claws. The creature that was once Feeder had no tail, but was in every manner, a werewolf.

"The group watched in horror as Feeder's grunting and growling started to set the wolves at ease. Their tails were no longer tucked between their legs and had begun to furrow near their ends. Their ears were perking back up and the fear in their eyes was no more. Their yips had all but stopped when Feeder arched back and let out another low, guttural howl. His form, even more menacing in the carmine moonlight. As his howl was near its end, the wolves joined in. Mabel stepped back and gripped Asher's wrist. All three were badly shaken and their morale had diminished to almost nothing. The wolves then turned on them, remaining by their new alpha's side as they did so.

"Prove to me, Asher Coyle, that you are who I made you." The voice Feeder spoke with was heavy and phlegmy, but didn't seem to be coming from his lips. Instead, it was as if the voice was embedded in the minds of everyone who heard them.

"I won't play your games anymore, Feeder!" The wolves growled at Asher's resentment and stalked towards the trio in an unnatural manner. It was as if Feeder had given them specific instructions on what to do and they were following them as best they could.

"The way I see it, you have no choice." The werewolf got on

all fours and lifted Kyden by his wounded leg.

"Please, don't let it kill me!" Asher chocked up on what he had to say and watched helplessly as Feeder stood back up and brought up an open paw, ready to slash through Kyden's abdomen. "Help me!"

"It's either you, or your friends."

"No!" As Feeder started his forward swing, Jessi slammed into his exposed chest, knocking Kyden from his grip and tumbling with the beast.

"Foolish girl!" Jessi made haste by soaring away from Feeder and grabbing Kyden on her way back over to Asher and Mabel.

"What do we do?"

"We have to stall him!"

"No! Both of you get out of here and take Kyden with you!" The girls looked at Asher, as if in disbelief with what he had said, but didn't move. "Go!" The wolves were closing in fast, growling and salivating as they did so. Helplessness filled Mabel's eyes as she stared back at Asher.

"B-But-"

"Mabel, he's right. Feeder isn't after us. We have to go, now!" Jessi helped Kyden sit up against a tree as Mabel rushed back to Asher, hugging him tighter than ever before and planting her lips on his. The wolves snapped their teeth together as the fur on their backs stood up.

"I love you." Mabel's eyes welled up with tears as her trembling lips spoke these words. Before Asher could respond both girls had Kyden up by his arms and were soaring through the air. He could feel the hot breath of a wolf on his heels and turned to face the creatures. Each one had claimed a spot near him, forming a crescent line that separated him from Feeder, who was walking in his direction on all fours.

"Come, prove yourself to me, Cor."

Chapter Seventeen: The Storm

Asher lunged towards the wolves before veering left, swerving passed their gnashing teeth as he made his way towards Feeder. The werewolf remained low to the ground, watching as Asher caused several members of the pack to slew about in his efforts to escape the endless barrage of razor-sharp teeth. To his own surprise, none had managed to latch onto him during the attack. Though several segments of clothing around his abdomen and lower legs had been punched and torn away. Once he had gotten to safety, having leapt away from the enraged pack and landed on a stone roof, he watched as the wolves remained in place, seemingly unsure of what to do next. Their snarls and growls remained audible, but their moral had faltered. Asher took count of the wolves in what time there was, but just as he had confirmed they were all where he left them he was knocked further into Prosper by a much larger mass of fur. Chunks of stone walls and brown clay shingles followed him to the ground on the opposite side of the building, with several needing pushed aside as they attempted to pin him down. A ghastly howl from overhead caught Asher's attention, leading him to collect a large hunk of debris in either hand.

    Several feet above the remains he had been ripped away from was the werewolf, descending with its upper limbs extended and every claw exposed, and the hind legs angled inward with the polished black tips ready to pierce Asher's stomach. In one quick motion, he flung the debris towards the beast. *Whoosh!* Feeder let out a wheezing breath as the first chunk collided with his ribs. Once the second connected, Asher could hear the meaty knock of teeth slamming together as it smashed into Feeder's chin. He swiftly rolled to his left as the werewolf plunged all four claws into the dirt he was laying over. He then got to his hands and knees and listened as the other wolves thumped their paws against the ground and made their way into Prosper- towards him and Feeder. The wolves snarled and barked as Asher came into their line of sight. Thirty-two paws pushed themselves off in his direction, slinging blades of grass and clumps of soil into the air behind them. Even with the heavy red moon being his only source of light, Asher could make out each individual canine as they pressed on, chasing him towards the town square whilst Feeder was pulling himself out of a blunt forced daze.

As Asher rounded a street corner, being sure he held the wolves' attention when doing so, he searched for an opening. Ahead of him, beyond a large wooden platform, was what he assumed to be the town hall. All that stood in his way was a ligneous door, which he tore through with his own speed and weight. Making his way inside, he turned to survey the group, which continued to pursue him throughout the building. Asher searched every corner as he rushed down the central aisle, looking for anything that he could use to fend them off. As he reached the wall opposite of where he had entered, it became clear that there was nowhere else for him to go. He pressed his spine against the cold surface and faced the entrance, preparing to kick himself off and soar over the wolves towards it, but quickly dropped the thought. As he took his back away and leaned in to spring forward, Feeder blocked his escape. Even in his current form, Asher could see the same smile across his face.

"It's me, or them, Cor." Asher shifted his gaze between the different creatures, looking for any way to free himself from his enclosure.

"No, it's not!" Feeder's ears perked up as he turned away from Asher. Just as he'd exposed his back, Asher could see a large wooden beam come down on top of his head and split on contact. Feeder collapsed several feet from where he was standing and Asher took advantage, darting over the wolves and through the door as Jessi kicked out one corner of the remaining archway. Large portions of stone split off from the exterior wall and crashed against the flooring, grinding together as they formed a blockade that trapped the wolves inside.

"What are you doing?"

"I couldn't let you do this alone." Jessi kept her eyes locked on Feeder, who was dragging his claws against the cobblestone as he got back up. "Besides, you're not the only one with a score to settle." Jessi then leapt into the air and landed on Feeder with her knees digging into his ribs, locking her arms around his neck and squeezing as she pulled back on it. "Help me!" Asher was astounded by her bravery but didn't let it distract him from what had to be done.

Feeder lashed at his own neck as he tried getting her off, but the grip was so tight that her arms were buried beneath his fur. He made almost no sound as he fought against her, occasionally trying to bark, but gaining nothing from it. With each attempt he made, Jessi tightened her grip a little more, using his cries as a way to tell if he could still breathe. The amount of force she was applying caused her eyes and teeth to clench shut and her arms to shake. Asher navigated his way around the wildly swinging daggers as Feeder kept himself on two legs and continued to turn every which way in his efforts to get free. Asher ducked to avoid any lacerations and saw his chance as he neared Feeder's lower body. The werewolf fell forward and tried picking himself back up, but found that his hind legs were locked together. Asher held them as Jessi did his neck and tightened his grip each time one started to break loose. Jessi didn't waste a moment with getting off Feeder's back but kept her arms in place as she stood up and looked across at Asher. He motioned with his eyes towards a few large columns that still remained from those which once circled the town square. Jessi understood his plan clearly and nodded. They then sprinted towards the pillars, effortlessly keeping the same speed as one another and using Feeder's body as a battering ram. Within seconds, they had looped around the entire square, severed the remaining columns, and used the bases of those that were already broken to slam Feeder against in a downward fashion. As the structures tipped and crumbled around them, Asher pulled at his end and Jessi did the same on hers in the opposite direction. Feeder's body was softened by the work they had done and his efforts to break away grew weak. Asher could hear several bones creaking under the tension they were creating, encouraging him to not let up.

"Asher, I can't do this!" Jessi's hands began trembling as Asher's strength and stamina outweighed hers.

"Just hold it a little longer!" Feeder's whines could be heard again as he tossed his head about, continuing to gash open his own neck with each attempt made to break away.

"I... can't!" Jessi continued to pull as hard as she could, but her efforts proved futile against those of a Sagina and her grip let up.

Not wanting to off himself and not expecting Jessi's release, Asher whipped Feeder's body around his own and demolished another building when he finally let go. Dust and debris particles clouded the area as Feeder remained still under the heap. Asher then turned away and helped Jessi to her feet as she panted and clutched at her arms.

"Are you alright?" He could see the pain written on her face as she removed her shaky hands from the forearms they were shielding. Dark blood oozed from several deep wounds that covered the both of them and Asher returned her hands to apply pressure.

"Don't worry. Without sunlight, the bleeding won't kill me."

"It will if you lose enough. You're not immortal." Asher tore the sleeves from his jacket and started wrapping both arms as best he could. He quickened his pace as the sound of rubble rolling and knocking about filled his ears.

"Is she alright?" Asher looked up to see Mabel and Kyden rushing towards them. Kyden was limping and Asher could see that his leg had been bandaged and smelled of fresh blood. The scent distracted him from what he was doing before Jessi placed her free hand on his shoulder and shook it.

"Ignore it. We need you to focus!" Jessi stared into his eyes for a brief moment before Asher nodded and finished the remaining wrap he was making.

"She's fine, why are you two back?"

"We had to make sure you were alright." Kyden looked up at the destroyed ruins as a massive chiseled brick slid off the pile. "Looks like you handled things quite well."

"No," Asher shook his head as he spoke and gave Kyden a very stern look, "we're not finished yet." As he finished these words, a sound like that of a large explosion filled the air and the entire group faced where Feeder's body was laying. Two incredibly large, bat-like wings had emerged and shot detritus in all directions. The wolves that had been trapped were producing long, meaningful howls as the wings' thumbs touched the ground around the pile.

"Th-That's the thing that grabbed me!"

"No," Jessi's knees had begun to tremble as she continued to craddle her wounds, "it's worse." Mabel, Kyden, and Jessi all remained where they were as Asher took cautious steps towards the monstrosity.

"Feeder, it's over! We've beaten you at your own game! Just give up!" Shingles and woodworks tossed and turned as the resources seemed to expand, filling more and more area with each breath Feeder took.

"No, child. We're not finished just yet." Bewilderment filled Asher's head as he watched the wings continue to grow more and more, and he could only assume that whatever was hidden away was doing the same. "Your ability to overcome obstacles you've never faced before is quite... impressive." The air grew colder in Prosper, as Feeder seemed to be pulling energy from any source he could find. "However, it isn't enough."

"What is this? What's he doing?" Kyden took a step back, ignoring that his own hair was blowing in his face as he watched the rubble swell near the top.

"He's switching forms."

"The thing that snatched me up wasn't *that* big!"

"That's because he wasn't polymorphed last time." Jessi didn't break eye contact with the tufts of dark fur that had exposed themselves and continued to watch the rest be revealed as she spoke. "Sagina don't lose a collected form when they switch between those they already have." Two wide, pointed, bald ears had started to show through and stopped moving only when they were facing the group. "The forms just... join together."

BOOM! Rubble and dust filled the air, knocking everyone to the ground as a violent screech echoed off the walls of Prosper. Asher shielded his eyes long enough for most of the new dust to settle and wreckage to stop falling from the sky. Once it was clear, he opened them to see the werewolf high in the air, beating its diabolical wings to stay elevated and gazing down at its prey. The ears had morphed more into those of a bat and the fur around its chest and back had grown much longer. The lengthy fur was black and faded into the gray that made up the wolf parts. A large, webbed tail had also grown and hung freely, nearly twice the length of the hind legs it was connected to, which remained like those of a wolf.

The eyes had also grown in size, being nearly twice that of which they were previously and showing as polished onyx without any whites to be seen. The hybrid screeched into the night as it faced the moon, flaunting much more primitive and elongated fangs.

"We have to get out of here!" Jessi started to turn away from the beast but stopped when she noticed that nobody else had moved. "What are you all doing?"

"He's not going to stop just because we run. He'll follow until he gets what he wants." Asher continued to walk towards the horrific sight but was caught by Mabel, who had grabbed his wrist. He could see the fear in her eyes and rested a hand beneath her chin and another against her cheek in an effort to soothe her, all the while being sure that she knew what needed to be done. "I'll be fine. Get these two to safety." Mabel nodded rapidly in little motions and kissed Asher before breaking away and leaving behind a dark cloud in her wake. He could see two streaks leading off into the woods as the emissions around him dissipated. He was alone once more.

"A truly heartfelt way to end things." Feeder's voice was even more enhanced by the second transformation and bellowed out over the entire town. "The *hero* saves everyone but himself."

"Enough talking!" Asher leaned forward and picked up another large chunk of debris before setting his sights on Feeder. "Let's finish this!"

Feeder chuckled demoniacally before beating his wings in an extremely aggressive manner. A shock wave washed over Asher, knocking him off his feet as Feeder shrieked and dove towards him. Asher scurried across the ground and nearly missed being gathered up in Feeder's talons, but his ankle had gotten caught and he was soon being lifted high into the air. He thrashed about vigorously as he tried to pull himself up, but the speed and wind that was working against him proved too much. As they passed a layer of clouds, Feeder rang the airspace and threw Asher higher up. Asher spun wildly as he tried to control his direction but was caught in one of Feeder's front paws before he could manage it. The grip tightened around his lungs, with a large thumb pressing into his chest as his rival basked in the full moon light.

"As I feared. You stand no chance against the events yet to come." Asher struggled to pull himself free, unable to even shift around in his restraints.

"If I'm not what you want, kill me! I'm tired of your contradictions!" Asher continued prying at the only claw he could reach as he spoke, with his arms being trapped too high up to loosen the others that were also constricting him. His efforts were soon crushed by a vicious amount of whiplash as Feeder changed their upward direction to a downward motion. Feeder's wings were buckled against his spine and Asher was being held out towards the earth below. Asher struggled more than ever to free himself as they plummeted to his death and still managed to achieve nothing.

"Goodbye, Cor!" The wind whistled in Asher's ears as the back of his head and legs started warming up. He could sense the ground growing nearer as Feeder stretched out to lob him the rest of the way. As Asher passed by Feeder's body, an idea came to him. Feeder drew back his wings, preparing to extend them and catch himself as he held Asher out at the fullest distance behind him that he could. As Feeder slung the mighty limb forward, Asher plunged his fist through the soft tissue of the wing behind it and wrapped his arm around the radius, just beneath the thumb. With no time to react, Feeder continued with his forward swing and cried out in pain as

Asher shredded the soft tissue from the bone and dislocated the femur on his way down. He knew he had done this by watching Feeder attempt to flap the wing, but not being able to do so. Asher continued to hold onto the pinion- no longer being in Feeder's grasp- and watched as the behemoth helplessly dropped from the sky. The beast continued to screech and writhe about as Asher kicked off, canceling some of the speed he'd gained. Several more buildings collapsed as Feeder's broken form was silenced by the fall. Asher took that moment of safety to fly himself to the ground unharmed.

He could still hear the deathly breathing as he drew nearer, but no longer felt threatened by what he saw. The wolves that had been trapped were almost silent, only letting out occasional whines as they sniffed at the blocked exit. Asher stopped walking towards the beast as it started to move. Feeder found enough strength to roll himself over and began morphing once again as he limped away from Asher, back towards the clearing they met at earlier on. Asher walked behind the injured creature as its wings and tail withdrew and its size began to diminish. He took a moment to look up at the moon but found it hard to see through the clouds that had filled the atmosphere during their conflict. The restored werewolf whimpered as it held its front right paw up against its body and continued to flee the battlefield.

"Feeder, stop!" Asher planted his feet in the grass and clenched his fists as he watched the beast proceed to move forward. "STOP!" The werewolf hesitated, then huffed and heeded his word. Asher watched as Feeder sat and licked at the injured paw, continuing to whine as he did so. "What more could you possibly want from me?" Asher remained where he was, almost certain that Feeder had nothing else up his sleeve.

"There... is only one more thing... you *must* do." Asher scowled as he too caught his breath.

"I don't have to do anything you tell me to." Feeder attempted to chuckle, but all that came out was a winded breath. He then offered Asher an open palm.

"Give me... the Archaic." Asher scoffed.

"You think, after all of this, I'm going to just *give* you what I'm keeping from you?"

"No." Feeder pulled himself up and weakly prepared to charge. "Once I fuse it with my own, it won't matter what you do. You can't stop him."

"You mean your father?" Feeder's lower legs shook beneath their own weight as he grinned at Asher one last time before rushing forward. His physical capabilities had been taken from him, as his clumsy and frail efforts shown through. His legs dangled beneath him as he ran and his head swayed too much for him to focus as he opened his jaw and prepared to snap at Asher, but never closed it. Feeder stood on his hind legs, having been stopped in the middle of a pounce. Beneath him was Asher, who had sunk a fist deep into his chest cavity and held him up as a pike would. Briefly, after planting the fist where it was, Asher removed it. Feeder fell to the ground and continued to breathe heavily in his weary state. Asher then bent down next to him and opened his fist, feeling a small amount of remorse for what he had done. Sitting in the middle of his palm was Feeder's Archaic.

"Take it, Cor." Asher's focus had been broken away from the glowing crystal when he recognized the voice as that of Feeder's human form. He turned to see the limp human body watching over the light. "Do what you see fit with it." Asher closed his fist around the Archaic and straightened out his legs and back.

"Don't call me, Cor." Feeder's breathing started to sound phlegmy as he struggled with each wheezing breath he took, but Asher knew it to be that he was internally bleeding and would soon drown in it. As he listened to the restricted breaths, Asher heard Feeder's heartbeat skip and after a short while, stop altogether.

"Is he gone?" Asher turned to see Mabel and Kyden approaching him from the direction of Prosper. He nodded and looked back at the body, which lay lifeless and with no hate to be directed towards it from him.

"Good." Kyden limped over to Feeder's corpse himself and kneeled next to it as if to verify there were no signs of life.

"Where's Jessi?" Asher asked, directing the question towards anyone who would reply. Kyden sighed and got up before pointing towards where they had come from. Asher could see the form of a girl sitting on a large rock with her head hanging low. "Is it the curse?" Kyden nodded and started off in her direction.

"I'll give you two a moment." He then split off from the group and Mabel moved in to hug Asher, being sure to keep a distance between herself and the corpse.

"Are you alright?" Asher nodded and looked off towards the others. Kyden had made his way over to Jessi and was sitting next to her. Jessi wasted no time resting her head on his shoulder and locking both hands together with his.

"Do you think she is?"

"I think she's finding new reasons to be." Asher looked back at Mabel, who was smiling in the direction of the others as Kyden's flushed cheeks became obvious. He then looked down at his hand, where Feeder's Archaic had been collected. He was startled to see that patches of dark fur had started growing up his arm and his nails had become jet black.

"What the-"

"Don't worry," Mabel took one hand and placed it behind her

back, "it's in the parchments Feeder dropped." She then returned the hand with a bundle of rolled pages she had been keeping in her waistband. "See?" Mabel pulled the innermost sheet free and showed it to Asher. In the center of the page was a drawing of an Archaic and around it were several creature sketches. *"When a Sagina finds a form that suits their needs, they can use their Archaic to trap the soul of whatever it is they seek and take on the look (in a humanoid fashion) and the attributes of that being."*

"So, that means-" Asher left the Archaic held out and turned to face the body of the wolf Feeder had killed. He then moved towards it, pitying the creature for what it went through and running his fingers through its coat.

"You can do it." Mabel smiled widely as she watched Asher rest the Archaic against the creature's wounds. Her eyes then filled with glistening speckles as the Archaic sent slow-moving streams of white light through the wolf's veins. Lengthy howls sounded out behind them as the wolf took its first breath and gradually opened its eyes. Mabel gasped and quickly dashed into Prosper. Asher stood alongside the wolf and helped it up as eight others sprinted through the broken down fencing that surrounded Prosper and out into the clearing, with Mabel not far behind. The wolf looked up at Asher and allowed him to pet it for a while as it rubbed up against him. Asher could see Kyden looking nervously over the pack and laughed at him just before the wolf let out a howl of its own. The rest of its kind followed suit before all nine sprinted around Mabel and Asher and then off into the woods, with the one Asher revived being the last to leave. As its pack shuffled between the trees, their redeemed leader gave Asher a small forward bow before doing so as well.

"So," Asher and Mabel looked back towards the others to see that they'd made their way over, "what's next?" Kyden was still holding one of Jessi's hands as he spoke but was clearly trying to hide it between himself and her. Asher looked down at the Archaic and removed Adelram's from his pocket, setting the two side-by-side.

"I know what we need to do."

Chapter Eighteen: Ripples on the Loch

Pinks and yellows splattered themselves across the blue canvas above, taking hold on what areas were already filled by fluffy white cotton. Beneath them, sweet melodies permeated the air as morning birds and woodland creatures opened their eyes to the new dawn. As several types of these birds, big and small, stretched out their wings and took flight over the lake below, trails of mist flowed peacefully and upward, disturbed only by the rapid beating of tiny wings as the birds passed through each vapor deposit. With many searching for breakfast to feed their young and themselves, the surface of the water began to stir, disturbed by each beak that sought out the scaley fruits below. The tiny frantic waves soon joined together and rushed towards shore as a breeze guided them. Wave after wave, the water lapped over the toes of an octad of pale feet.

Asher admired Mabel's smile as the sunrise filled her eyes and a gust of wind kissed her face, blowing strands of long dark hair over her shoulders. A smile spread itself across her lush lips as her gaze wandered over the sight above. He then turned his attention to Jessi and Kyden. Kyden was vigorously drying his hair with a large white towel as Jessi wrapped herself in another and did as Mabel was doing. Once Kyden had finished drying off, he pulled away from the towel and exposed a hairdo, not unlike a sea urchin. Asher chuckled under his breath and shook his head as he joined the others in their admiration of the high heavens.

"Are you two ready?" Asher and Mabel broke away from the marvel and faced Jessi. "If anyone is to do it," Jessi stopped in the middle of her sentence and grabbed at something to her left before dragging it through the sand in front of herself for everyone else to see, "it should be the both of you." Asher and Mabel looked down at the large, brown, fabric sack that sat at Jessi's feet before coming to a nonverbal agreement and getting up to brush the wet sand off themselves.

"What are you guys going to do with them?" Kyden used an open palm to flatten out his hair and watched as small amounts of water dripped off the base of the pouch as Asher lifted it and slung it over his shoulder. Asher could tell that the question was directed to him specifically, but didn't answer immediately. Instead, he looked over his shoulder at the still soaked bag and listened as several of the contents clinked and slid across one another, trying to settle in the bottom of their containment.

"We're setting them free." With that, Asher smiled at Kyden and turned away, with his available hand held out for Mabel to accept. Once she did so, the couple walked towards a small, white rowing boat that they'd found along the coast earlier on and boarded it. As Asher sat at the stern, he placed the sack between his feet on the sole and collected both oars, with one in each hand. Mabel sat at the bow with her legs facing Asher but twisted herself in her seat to watch where they were headed. The sun was on a slow approach towards the zenith and Asher knew they only had so much time to do what they must before getting back to shore.

Once the pair of them had made it near the center of the lake, directly over the witch's abode, Asher let the oars rest and leaned over the pouch. Mabel straightened out her back and watched as he untied the thin roping that held the sack shut. The surrounding waters continued to knock and stir against the boat as Asher exposed the contents to her.

"Do you think we missed any?"

"No," Asher stated, "we checked several times before coming back to the surface." He examined the crystals within, watching as those that sat against his legs continued to glow, whilst those near the middle of the pouch and the far corners remained clear and seemingly lifeless. He then stuffed a hand into the cold crystals, causing them to let off a much more energetic bloom. It seemed to him that the souls within understood what was happening and were using the light produced by their Amber Hearts to show appreciation. "Here, you take the first one." Mabel nervously collected the Heart between her fingers and stared into Asher's eyes as he smiled at her.

"Are you sure this will work?"

"If I can return a soul to its body with someone else's Archaic, you can set a soul free with its own Amber Heart." Asher continued to smile as he used his own hand to roll Mabel's fingers over the Heart. Mabel nodded and took in a deep breath as she started building up the courage for the task at hand.

Getting off the bench she was sitting on and resting against her knees, she moved her clutched hand over the edge of the boat. Then, she adjusted her grip around the Heart and slowly let out the breath she'd been holding as she tightened her fist. As Mabel closed her eyes, still concerned with what she was doing, Asher watched in awe. The Heart began to let out audible cracking sounds as fine lines became visible. Soon after, small grains of crystal started breaking away and falling into the water. As each grain hit the surface, it would seemingly dissolve on contact and fill the area with a golden glow that would quickly fade. As the pressure became too much for the Heart to handle, it began letting out a low ring before bursting into millions of particles and flooding the surface around where they had landed in the water with light. Mabel's eyes shot open as her fist clenched shut on itself. She then opened it and tipped her hand to let the rest of the Heart's powder freefall into the lake. Once the light had dispersed entirely, she caught a glimpse of both Asher's hands out over the water as hers was from the corner of her eye. She watched as he clutched two Hearts, with one in each hand, and let her bottom jaw hang a little as the grains enchanted the water. The two of them continued to do this until all the lost souls of Prosper had been freed from their imprisonments. Still, with what good they were doing, Asher pitied those who could never be saved. All the souls that had been completely consumed by Adelram in their own time were forever lost. Asher turned back towards the pouch and studied the contents as he thought about this. The majority of Amber Hearts that sat far beneath the waters were empty. All that could be saved, of several hundred, fit in a single potato sack.

"Are you alright?" Asher felt one of Mabel's hands rest against his shoulder before he instinctively placed his own over it.

"I'm fine. It's just- what about everyone else from the book? What about B.A.? What about his daughter?" Mabel frowned as she thought about the lost settlers herself and rubbed her hand back and forth over Asher's shirt.

"Well, there's nothing we can do for them now. So, if you ask me, it's best to just move on." She then shifted her hand through the pouch and pulled out one of the remaining two objects before freezing over entirely. Asher looked up at the object and then stuffed his hand in the pouch after her to remove the one that remained. Mabel, certain that these were all that remained, turned back to the water and clutched the Archaic she had gotten, tightly. Asher could see her forearm and wrist shaking as she tried to destroy it. "The least we can do...," Mabel continued to struggle with the Archaic's durability as she spoke, "is be sure that... these two... never... come... back." As she finished her sentence, she squeezed the Archaic as hard as she could between both hands. Asher heard the Archaic let out an increasingly loud ring as one large crack almost immediately appeared under the intense added pressure. Moments after the crack appeared and the ringing grew almost unbearable, the Archaic shattered and a wave of energy knocked Mabel back into the boat. As a large circular ripple emerged from where the Archaic was destroyed and flowed out over the lake, a strong breeze and the sound of thunder rumbled off from where Mabel had crushed it. Asher caught her on her way back and thumped his back against the boat. The two laughed as the boat rocked back and forth before getting up and bracing themselves for the obliteration of the remaining Archaic.

Asher gripped the crystal as he had seen Mabel do, with it being placed between both hands, and started applying force to it. As before, the Archaic began to ring loudly as a deep fracture spread out across it. He could tell by the size and shape of the stone that it once belonged to Feeder. The ringing made him feel that he was somehow hurting Feeder by destroying his lifeforce, even with him no longer having any connection to the physical realm. Still, Asher eased off the amount of force he was applying. He kept it tight enough that he could still hear it creaking and whining under his strength, but not tight enough to grind it to dust too easily. Once he felt that he had given Feeder the proper amount of punishment, he told Mabel to brace herself and did the same. Buckling his knees against one side of the boat and his feet under each bench, Asher pulled back both hands, keeping the glowing, heavily damaged Archaic exposed. He then turned to be sure that Mabel was prepared. After seeing that she was holding onto one of the benches herself, he looked back at his hands and drove them together. His arms whistled like branches in heavy winds before his fingertips slammed together. Another crack of thunder sounded out. The boat bucked up on the port side, where Asher was and shoveled through several feet of water as it skimmed across the reflective surface. In the direction the boat had come from to where it sat after was a wide trail of white light that continued to sink and fade away as time passed. Asher used his own weight to straighten out the rowboat before he caught sight of the trail and felt a wave of relief wash over him.

"Is it done?" He nodded as Mabel looked out at the trail as well, just before the light had completely vanished.

"It's done."

The two then made their way back to shore, covering up with their hoodies as the sun poked through the highest leafy needles. Asher could feel the boat run against the sandy shallows as he came within a few feet of the beach and continued to push forward until it was in no more than a foot of water and dug itself a trench to rest in. Jessi and Kyden were already waiting nearby as they hopped out of the rowboat and placed their bare feet against the damp, brown shore. Kyden didn't speak as he made his way over to Asher. Instead, Asher got a firm hug from him and Kyden rocked himself and his friend side-to-side. Jessi made her way over to Mabel and gave her an awkward hug, seemingly unsure of whether or not it was her place to do so. She was stunned when Mabel pulled her in but accepted it with little hesitation. Kyden pulled Asher over a foot or so to get closer to the girls and wrapped an arm around them, getting everyone into a group hug before breaking it up.

"So that's it then? No more vampires? No more Sagina?" Asher, Mabel, and Jessi all faced each other before giving Kyden a conjoined look of confusion. "You all know what I meant."

"You're right, it's just us now." Asher patted Kyden on the back before walking passed to get to his own truck.

"So, where are we going next?" Jessi caught up to Kyden as everyone followed Asher towards the vehicles, with Kyden's car sitting next to Asher's truck. Mabel had already made her way over to the passenger side of Asher's truck by the time he was at the driver's side and was only waiting for him to unlock the door.

"I've heard that New Haven can be pretty cloudy. That should be a good place for you all to go." Jessi stopped walking as Kyden reached the driver's side of his own car and looked back at her. "What's wrong?"

"You're not coming with us?" Asher and Mabel stopped what they were doing and looked over the situation as it unfolded.

"Well, I-I thought about it, but I just don't know if it's what's best for me." Kyden made his way back over to Jessi, leaving his door ajar. "I'll still be in Bristlewood if you ever decide you want to-" Jessi didn't let him finish as she turned courses and walked towards the back seat door of Asher's truck, opened the door with a *pop*, sat down inside and shut it again. Asher looked towards Jessi, then back at Kyden with his key still only halfway in the lock of his own door. Kyden scrunched his brow and pointed at Asher's keychain. "You-uh... never unlocked that, did you?" Asher shook his head. Kyden bit his lip and nodded. "Huh."

"Are you sure you want to stay here?" Mabel opened her door as Asher unlocked the truck and stood just outside of it as she spoke with Kyden. Kyden placed both thumbs in a belt buckle loop on his jeans and nodded as he let his head sit low.

"This town is all I've really known. It doesn't feel right uprooting myself when I don't need to." Kyden looked up and let his eyes shift from Mabel to Asher. "You think you guys will be able to visit sometime?" Asher and Mabel locked sights briefly as they were clueless on what to say. Kyden shrugged. "I thought so." Asher stepped away from the truck and gave Kyden one long, hard hug before hopping inside and shutting his own door. Mabel remained outside a few moments longer than everyone else and gave Kyden a look of pity and remorse before pulling herself inside. Kyden watched as the headlights lit up and listened as the engine roared. The truck backed away as he stood a few feet in front of it and eventually made a U-turn to leave the beach. Asher watched his friend watch them leave through the rearview mirror for as long as he could, but there wasn't much time before all that remained was a dirt trail with deep tire tracks and the forest on either side of the road. Once Kyden was out of sight, Asher turned the mirror towards Jessi and watched her eyes well up as she hid her face behind her hair and hood. He then turned the mirror away from her so that he didn't have to watch any longer.

"So," Mabel started, trying not to show that she was hurting too, "where *are* we headed next?" Asher looked at the sky above and pulled his sleeves down his arms, trying to cover up as much as possible. He then sighed and listened to Jessi's sniffles from the backseat. He could see it on Mabel's face that she was pleading him to come up with some sort of distraction.

"I'm not sure just yet. The only thing we have left to run from doesn't move, so anywhere is better. Any opinions?"

"New Haven." The group fell silent, leaving only the engine and tires to fill the space with sound. Jessi wiped her cheeks and looked up at the black ceiling as her head rocked about from the rough road below. "I hear it's cloudy there." She then let a weak smile show. Asher and Mabel noticed this and did the same.

Before long, the dirt road came to a fork and Asher stopped the truck to examine each direction and think about where they led to. He knew that the road furthest to the left would lead back to Bristlewood, which still hurt for him to think about. Straight ahead was their freedom. At the end of the road, too far to see or hear, sat the interstate. To the right, Asher could picture the cabin he and Kyden had spent so much time in and the condition it was currently in. The memories he could come up with were nearly as sad as those in Bristlewood, but something further down made him feel that the cabin was where he wanted to be least.

"Asher?" Mabel placed a hand on his forearm, which brought him out of the cloud he was floating in. "Are you okay?"

"Yeah, it's just-." Asher sighed and showed his sorrows by letting his grip on the wheel grow limp. He continued to contemplate until Mabel sat her other hand near the first and stared up at him longingly.

"Go where you feel you need to go." Asher bobbed his head and pressed the gas as he made a left turn. Jessi shot up in her seat and watched the straight stretch disappear behind them.

"Wait, where are we going? I thought we agreed that we had to get out of here?" Jessi was growing more and more annoyed with each passing moment that she didn't get an answer and was soon breathing heavily. "I can't live in Bristlewood. I've lost too much there and I'm not about to be hurt by watching everyone I know not know me."

"Calm down, we won't be staying long." Asher continued to watch the road ahead as he thought about an undertaking that he had just given himself.

"What are we doing then?"

"There's something I have to take care of before I turn my back on this place."

Asher continued to drive down the dirt road, which soon ran into a paved road that split to the left or right. Without hesitation, he turned right and watched as the neatly trimmed hedges and grand, fenced in homes became visible without the interruption of trees. The town seemed strange to him since he had been in the woods for so long and he was certain his truck no longer looked up to par. The dirt covered vehicle rolled down the smooth street as Mabel and Jessi examined each passing home, still unsure of what had to be done. Minutes into their drive through Bristlewood, Asher pulled the truck into an alleyway and parked it. Mabel finally recognized the street and took in a sharp, nervous breath.

"Asher, what are we doing here?"

"Don't worry," Asher said as he unbuckled his seatbelt and opened his door, "I'll only be gone a few minutes."

"Wait, do you think this is a good idea?"

"What's going on? Where are we?" Jessi questioned Mabel as Mabel questioned Asher. Asher stood next to the truck and looked between the road they had come from and the open window Mabel was watching him through.

"Everything is going to be O.K., just wait-"

"Asher, please, think about this for a second," Mabel spoke rapidly to avoid being interrupted, "most of these people don't remember who we are. You know that in the same way that we do." Mabel pointed back at Jessi as she spoke but continued to face Asher. "We've lost our closest friends, our favorite teachers, our parents-." A look of shock covered Mabel's face as she spoke these last couple of words. "B-But-"

"Just wait here." Asher smiled and pulled his hood over his face as far as he could before walking away from the truck and back out to the roadside, where the morning sun was already crawling over the concrete.

Passing a couple of blocks, Asher walked into the same front yard he had grown up playing on and swiftly made his way to the front door. As he unlocked it and pushed, sunlight poured onto the carpeted flooring inside. All the lights were out, which is what he had hoped for. He proceeded to tiptoe into the living room, making sure to close the door behind him. Once in the living room, he took in the surroundings for what he was sure would be the last time. The white walls were littered with photos of his family, all of which excluded him. The fireplace that sat just beneath the television, where he would roast marshmallows when his parents were away, and the lines that had been drawn on the inside of the closet door next to the piano, where his mother kept track of his height. Asher smiled as he looked over the lines before freezing in place when he heard a thump on the second floor. Trying to remain stealthy, he crept back towards the door to turn up the stairs and stopped at the base, remembering how loud the wooden boards could be. Another thump sounded out. Asher was certain the sounds were coming from his parents' room and paced his steps on his way up. Each time he heard the sound, he moved up one platform. With his patience intact, he eventually made it to the top of the stairway and cuffed the knob to his parents' room on his right. He then gradually turned the mechanism and popped the door open.

The room was dark, as a thick black curtain blocked the only window. Asher remembered the day his father put the curtains up as a way to get better sleep after spending all night in his study. Asher could see the rays creating a rim around the curtains as he stepped inside, but paid them no mind as he prepared himself for what was next. He could see his father laying on his back, breathing heavily in his sleep and occasionally kicking hard at the air as he mumbled nonsense. Next to his father was his mother, who remained still and regularly slept so peacefully. Asher was walking on eggshells as he got closer to the bed, letting the thick carpeting absorb almost all the sound he produced. Once he was next to the bed, he held his breath entirely and continued to soak in all that he saw until he was caught off guard by his father's mumbling.

"Asher... I'm looking." Asher started listening closely to the mumbling as he examined his father's bedside stand. "You... real." Near the front of the stand, Asher could see a small note and immediately recognized it as the one he had left for his father. "I'll find you." Asher turned back to his father and saw the sweat around his brow as he kicked at the air again. Asher sniffled, pressed a hand against his father's head, and looked about the room. On the opposite end was a bookcase, where Asher searched for ideas without moving. He read the names of several books and small phrases on paperweights but saw nothing of use. Having no luck he looked along the side of the wooden case instead. Attached with a thumbtack to the outer frame was an open calendar that possessed a photo of a tropical beach. It reminded Asher of a time when his parents told him about their honeymoon and how they longed to visit the island again. Then, it clicked.

"Bali." He turned back to his father, who was breathing even heavier than before and continued to move about under his hand. Asher took advantage of his own memories and started focusing on thoughts about the island as he kept his palm firmly in place. As time passed, his father became more at ease and the memories of Bali were no longer just his own. Asher soon realized he had tapped into his father's memories and was watching small portions of his parents' honeymoon. He could see his mother walking along the edge of the water as small white and blue waves came in. Then, he was at a restaurant and watched as his father dropped a drink in his own lap and his mother laugh about it. He could hear the laughter echo from his mother and his father both before the image continued to change.

With each new image that crossed his mind, Asher replaced one of his father's memories of him with it, filling his head with a love for the island. With each memory he replaced, his father grew more and more at ease and the cold sweats subsided. After a few minutes of this treatment, Asher started to tear up but knew he had to finish what he had already begun. He found himself in a honeymoon suite, laying on a large white bedspread with a glass of wine in hand. His mother was at the window, holding one of her own as she watched the moon's reflection on the water. Next, he was out on a boat in the late afternoon, holding a small swordfish that was still on the hook and cheering with the captain. Asher replaced as much as he could before the memories seemed to subside. His father was now still in his bed, breathing normally and even smiling occasionally. Asher was sure the treatment had worked and wicked at his eyes with his bicep before looking back at the note on the bedstand. A sudden knock at the door woke his father, who shot up in bed and turned to face the door.

"What's going on?" Asher's mother asked, still groggy from being asleep. His father looked around the room, searching for anything out of the ordinary before he heard the knock once again.

"It's nothing, honey. Someone's at the door." He wiped the sweat from his forehead and reached for the only other object on his bedstand that wasn't his alarm clock or lamp. Once he had collected his glasses, he got up and headed down the stairs.

Asher watched from around a row of hedges across the street as the same neighbor from before knocked at the door. Once his father answered, the neighbor asked if he knew that somebody was sneaking about. Asher could see that his father was puzzled and shook his head before stating to the neighbor that he had not seen anyone. Asher took his father's lack of assumption as assurance that his treatment worked. He then raised his hand from his side and opened it. In it sat a crumpled piece of paper, which he then balled up even more and tossed to the ground before making his way back to the girls.

"There he is." Jessi stated, turning in her seat to watch Asher walk over.

"How did it go?" Mabel questioned as Asher got in on the driver's side. "Did you-" Mabel was cut off by Asher swiftly pulling her into a hug. "O-Oh!" He then pulled away and kissed before smiling and sitting back in his own seat.

"Everything worked out." Asher started the truck and backed it onto the road. As the last tire hit the pavement a loud screeching sound abrupted through the air in front of the vehicle. The entire group spun to face the sound and saw a dilapidated white car with its rear end swerving all over the road as it braked, hard. The car stopped less than a foot away from the grill of Asher's truck.

"Kyden!?" Jessi popped her door open and jogged to the other vehicle as Kyden emerged from it. She then leaped into the air, giving him no other choice but to catch her.

"Hey- oof!" He buckled his arms around her waist to hold her up and planted one of his feet a few inches behind the other to keep his balance.

"What are you doing!? You could've gotten yourself killed, man!" Asher stepped outside of the truck as well and held his arms out to his sides to show his annoyance and concern.

"Well, it's not like I expected you to be right there!"

"What were you even doing in this part of town?"

"I was on my way to try catching up with you guys." Jessi pulled herself down and cleared her throat as she crossed her arms over her chest, trying to take on a serious demeanor.

"What made you change your mind?" Jessi raised her chin a little as she spoke and kept buckling and unbuckling one of her knees.

"I grew up in this town. Everything I've ever known is here and I didn't see a small group of friends as enough reason to leave behind my future. I mean, hundreds of people versus three? I- I know I'm not making this any more rational or less offensive but, like- I'm pretty sure all three of you are dead at that-" Jessi cleared her throat more harshly and glared deep into Kyden's eyes. "What I'm trying to say is that I was looking at it all wrong. I'll never get from this place what I got from you guys. Well, I guess technically this place gave me you guys so-"

"Just. Shut. Up." Jessi wrapped her arms around Kyden's

neck and planted her lips on his. His eyes immediately grew wide and he looked passed her at Asher, as if unsure of what to do. Asher could see this in his stunned gaze and smiled as he raised his hands to his own face and pinched his index fingers and thumbs together as he closed his own eyes. Kyden got the hint and closed his eyes, wrapping his arms around Jessi's waist as he did so. Once the two had separated from one another, Kyden and Jessi got in the car and Asher climbed back into the truck with Mabel. Kyden then followed behind Asher as they headed back between the pines, seeking out their new lives somewhere along the interstate and laying ruined memories to rest.

Far from where they found themselves going, under the lake of Prominent Peak, the witch's abode remained in its state of preservation. Murky waters and aquatic life stirred about, unaware of the threats that lurked below, through a hole in the floor. Through that hole was a dark passageway, no longer a secret as it once was. Bubbles flowed up from the depths beneath it, ran along with the ceiling above it and escaped through an open basement door. They grew in size and quantity as they burst against the surface, letting off steam with each that emerged. The black waters boiled and sent flocks of birds cawing and soaring in all directions to escape as a muffled, harrowing cry sounded out from deep below.

Made in the USA
Columbia, SC
18 June 2020